MURDER MOST PERSUASIVE

MURDER MOST
PERSUASIVE

A Mystery

TRACY KIELY

MINOTAUR BOOKS

A THOMAS DUNNE BOOK

NEW YORK

This is a work of fiction. All of the characters, organizations, and events portrayed in this novel are either products of the author's imagination or are used fictitiously.

A THOMAS DUNNE BOOK FOR MINOTAUR BOOKS.
An imprint of St. Martin's Publishing Group.

MURDER MOST PERSUASIVE. Copyright © 2011 by Tracy Kiely. All rights reserved. Printed in the United States of America. For information, address St. Martin's Press, 175 Fifth Avenue, New York, N.Y. 10010.

www.thomasdunnebooks.com
www.minotaurbooks.com

Library of Congress Cataloging-in-Publication Data

Kiely, Tracy.
    Murder most persuasive : a mystery / Tracy Kiely.
        p.   cm.
    ISBN 978-0-312-69941-3 (hardback)
    1. Murder—Investigation—Fiction.   2. Police—Maryland—Fiction.
3. Saint Michaels (Md.)—Fiction.   4. Domestic fiction.   I. Title.
    PS3611.I4453M88 2011
    813'.6—dc22

                                                              2011018780

First Edition: September 2011

10 9 8 7 6 5 4 3 2 1

For Jack, Elizabeth, and Pat—much love, Mom

ACKNOWLEDGMENTS

I'd like to thank Barbara Kiely, Ann Mahoney, Sophie Little-field, MaryAnn Kingsley, and the BUNCO ladies for their con-tinued friendship and support. A big thank-you to Terry Mullen-Sweeney for her early read and edits (we'll always have Paris and Gavi di Gavi!). Bridget Kiely was once again an in-valuable source for Janeite inspiration and snarky humor. Barbara Poelle made the whole dream happen (again) and talked me down from the ledge of fear several times. Toni Plummer's suggestions were wonderful, and Cynthia Merman deserves the editing gold star (plus an all-inclusive two-week vacation). My husband, Matt, should win the award for Most Cheerful View-ings of Austen, and my children, Jack, Elizabeth, and Pat, were once again lovely and supportive throughout it all.

MURDER MOST PERSUASIVE

CHAPTER 1

*Unfortunately . . . there are so many who forget to think
seriously till it is almost too late.*

—PERSUASION

ARTIN REYNOLDS'S DEATH came as a surprise to no
one. No one, that is, except his wife, Bonnie. It was
the final and most telling example of the total lack of commu-
nication that existed in their marriage. The fact that the cancer
he'd battled for years proved more than his weakened seventy-
seven-year-old body could handle somehow managed to escape
Bonnie entirely. But to be fair, most things escaped Bonnie entirely.

"My poor, poor Marty!" Bonnie now murmured with a
mournful shake of her blond head. "How could this have happened?" No one responded. The funeral services had been held
at ten in the morning, after which the family had escorted Martin's remains to Arlington Cemetery where, as a former naval
officer, he was granted a burial spot. It was now one in the afternoon. By my modest count, Bonnie had uttered this same question some eighty-seven times since the day began. After about the
sixty-fifth utterance, most of the family had stopped trying to
console her, as our words of sympathy fell on deaf ears. By the

seventy-second time, even the nicest among us had fallen silent. Now, unfortunately, her rhetorical murmurings were prompting unabashed eye rolling from the more callous attendees.

"Stop that!" I hissed at my aunt Winnie, whose orbs now seemed in danger of disappearing completely into her skull.

"Oh, please," she retorted with a toss of her head. The small movement sent her bright red curls quivering. "This is nothing more than standard Bonnie drama."

She was right, of course, and as Martin's younger sister, Aunt Winnie had had a front-row seat for several of Bonnie's performances over the years. "Besides," Aunt Winnie continued, "you know how I hate artifice of any kind."

I rolled my own eyes at this and glanced meaningfully at Aunt Winnie's trademark curls, which, if anything, had only grown redder during her seventy-odd years. Curving her equally red lips into a warning smile, Aunt Winnie murmured, "Don't be a smartass, Elizabeth."

"Me? Perish the thought. I didn't say a word."

"No. But you were thinking it."

"True."

"Careful," she said meaningfully, "or I'll tell your mother."

"Tell her what?" I inquired after a moment's pause.

Aunt Winnie opened her green eyes very wide and leaned in close. "Do you really need me to catalog all the dirt I have on you?" she asked good-naturedly.

Aunt Winnie is my great-aunt on my mother's side. More important, she has been my confidante ever since I was twelve years old and she bagged me trying to stuff my pathetically empty bra with toilet paper. I'm now twenty-eight. While I no longer stuff my bra—more due to a resignation to certain facts than because of any major developments in that area—Aunt Winnie still has enough dirt on me to start a landfill. I sat back in my chair, an exaggeratedly polite expression on my face. "Blackmailer," I hissed.

She gave a firm nod of her head. "Damn skippy."

Seated opposite me, my mother kicked my leg under the table while sending me a reproachful look across it. Next to her, my older sister, Kit, eyed me with the slightly superior expression she generally adopts whenever she perceives that I have stepped out of line. While I've never actually caught her, I suspect she practices it in the mirror. Not that she needs much practicing. Kit has those angelic features that lend themselves perfectly to holier-than-thou looks. She inherited my mom's straight blond hair. I had ended up with my dad's curly brown hair, which looks just fine cut short and close to the head; grow it shoulder length and that's a whole other story. Add to that large blue eyes, perpetually clear skin, and a smirking mouth, and Kit looks like a smug Botticelli angel. I, on the other hand, have green eyes and freckles. Throw in the aforementioned chest issue and I'm more likely to be compared to Botticelli's *Portrait of a Young Man.*

While I restrained myself from sneering at Kit, Aunt Winnie sent me a sly wink before demurely ducking her bright red head into a position of quiet respect.

Forcing myself not to roll my own eyes, I focused my attention on Bonnie just in time to hear her murmur again, "Poor, poor Marty! I just don't see how this could have happened!"

Bonnie was Martin's second wife. His first wife, Rose, died

some twenty-five years earlier, leaving Martin in the unenviable position of sole parent to three young daughters. Although a savvy businessman who had built a family construction company into a national business, Martin was no match for the demands of parenthood and he knew it. Using the same cool determination he employed to build his multimillion-dollar business, he set out to remedy the situation the only way he knew how—by remarrying. Of course it helped that he was both very rich and very handsome. Within two years, Bonnie McClay, a naïve thirty-five-year-old secretary employed in the head office, was tapped for the role. It was one of only a handful of times where Martin's legendary acumen failed him, as Bonnie was even more helpless about children than Martin. Within three months, the children had dubbed their stepmother "McClueless" and commenced an unspoken war of resistance against her. Looking around me now, it appeared that the war still raged today.

We were sitting at a long table in the Hotel Washington's elegant Sky Terrace restaurant. Located on the hotel's rooftop, it afforded a spectacular view of Washington, D.C. The first strokes of autumn's vibrant hand were apparent in the nation's capital and the city was awash in color. A mosaic of purple, yellow, and red foliage reflected in the rippling waters of the Tidal Basin. Flora in riotous golden hues bloomed along the perfectly groomed grounds of the monuments. The monuments themselves stood tall and proud, the timeless lines of their crisp, white façades majestic against the clear indigo sky.

As glorious as the view was, it couldn't hold a candle to the scene that was playing out around me. Clutching a lacy black handkerchief and gently dabbing it to her teary sapphire eyes,

Bonnie sat like a Victorian queen in mourning. Swathed from head to toe in black, her outfit was faintly reminiscent of Scarlett O'Hara's garb in *Gone with the Wind,* the one she wears after her first husband, Charles, dies. In fact, I thought, as I peered closer at the dark, flowing dress, I wouldn't be at all surprised if it *were* an updated copy. Given Bonnie's flair for the dramatic, as well as her love of Margaret Mitchell's epic classic, it would be entirely within her dingbat character. (Bonnie was not only named for Scarlett's daughter, Bonnie Blue, but also had an annoying tendency to quote Scarlett's lines from both the book and the movie. A lot.)

Now, while I've been known to quote my fair share of Jane Austen, I maintain that it is an entirely different habit. Muttering "Capital! Capital!" is one thing. Randomly calling out "Fiddle-dee-dee!" is quite another.

At Bonnie's insistence, Uncle Marty's burial flag had accompanied us to the restaurant. Tightly clutching the flag to her chest, Bonnie had advanced on the poor hostess and mournfully (and rather loudly) announced, "My husband is dead. May I have some lunch?" Hostesses in D.C., especially those in such close proximity to the Capitol, have seen their fair share of the odd and have as such developed a certain immunity to it. However, based on the way ours took a sudden step back and seemed incapable of speech, I think Bonnie managed to penetrate that professional façade.

The flag now sat propped up in a chair next to hers. Not just any chair, mind you, but the chair at the head of the table. From time to time, Bonnie would glance at the flag and then quickly press the hankie to her quivering mouth. Like now.

Next to her, Frances, who at age thirty-five is the second eldest of Bonnie's stepchildren, gave a loud sigh of exasperation. Frances is something of the family expert on sighs of exasperation. Over the years, she's cultivated it into its present deep, melancholy, breathy sound. Hearing it, a stranger might legitimately expect to find that it originated from a kind of modern-day Marilyn Monroe rather than a dowdy plump woman with a penchant for tweed.

"Bonnie," Frances said, running her fingers through her short nut-brown hair, "Father had been ill for years. His passing is a blessing, really. He's in a better place now."

Bonnie lowered her black hankie and peered in astonishment at Frances. "A better place?" she echoed, her chin wobbling. "A better place? How can you say that?" With an accusatory gesture at the flag, she added, "He's in a coffin!"

Frances blanched at this blunt, although apt, description of her father's whereabouts. Pursing her lips and studiously not looking at the flag, she tried again. "What I meant is that he's no longer in pain. He's at peace." Frances's voice held the steely intonation that adults often use with petulant children, not that I ever heard Frances use it on her own kids. Steely intonations have no effect on Frances's twin boys. Referred to by the rest of the family as Thing One and Thing Two, they respond only to threats and bribes. It is only a matter of time before stun guns are employed.

Bonnie gave a loud sniff and raised the hankie back up to her eyes. "Well, *he* may be at peace, but *I'm* certainly not," she moaned from behind the black veil.

Frances threw up her hands in defeat and looked beseechingly around the table at the rest of us. Her gaze settled on her younger sister, Ann. Catching her sister's eye, she jerked her head toward Bonnie's slumped form and hissed, "Do something!"

"Like what?" came Ann's frustrated reply.

Hearing the exchange, Bonnie peeked up again from her soggy hankie. "Annabel, were you saying something?"

Ann (aka Annabel) is the youngest of the Reynolds siblings. In my opinion, she couldn't look more unlike her name. To me, the name Annabel conjures up an image of a curvy figure with masses of wavy, golden hair and a coy smile. Ann is none of those things. She's trim, with short auburn hair and a direct, intelligent gaze. Ann obviously felt the same about her given name and long ago opted to shorten it to Ann. It was far more suitable, and in fact, no one ever called her anything but that.

No one, that is, except Bonnie. At the sound of her given name, Ann winced slightly, the faint lines of exhaustion around her large hazel eyes making her look older than her thirty years.

"Bonnie," Ann said, shifting her body to face her stepmother, "I know this is a hard time for you. It's hard for all of us. But we need to be strong. Father would want us to celebrate his life rather than cry at his passing."

A watery blue eye peered over the hankie. "Celebrate?" Bonnie asked.

"Yes." Ann nodded. "We should concentrate on all the good times."

I applauded Ann's efforts, but the sad fact was that Martin Reynolds had been a dyed-in-the-wool workaholic. If we were to celebrate all his good times, we would either have to hold the party in his opulent board room or down at the bank. However, the idea appealed to Bonnie and she cautiously lowered the hankie.

"Do you really think Martin would want that?" she asked dubiously, glancing at the flag as if for confirmation.

No doubt glad that the hankie had finally been cast aside, Ann nodded her head. Across the table, Frances added, "I'm *sure* of it."

"What do you think, Reggie?" Bonnie asked, turning to her oldest stepdaughter.

Regina "Reggie" Ames, née Marshall, née Stewart, née Reynolds, lowered her martini glass and studied her stepmother with undisguised scorn. At thirty-seven, Reggie ran one of D.C.'s more popular wedding planner services, services that she herself has used quite frequently. She's now, as she puts it, unaffiliated with a husband—hers or anyone else's. But by no means is she through with the institution. Reggie attracts men the way butter pecan ice cream attracts me. She's one of those women who are better-looking today than they were at twenty-one—and at twenty-one she was gorgeous. She's slim, toned, and still has all the right curves. Some of my closest friends still refuse to believe we're related. In fact, if we weren't related, I'd probably hate her. If I'm completely honest with myself, there likely would be a voodoo doll involved.

"What do I think about what?" Reggie asked.

"About having a party for your father," Bonnie replied.

"Bit late for that, isn't it?" Reggie murmured, before raising her glass to take a sip.

"Reggie!" hissed Frances.

"What did you say?" asked Bonnie, leaning closer. "I didn't hear."

"I said I think it's a wonderful idea," Reggie said, setting down her glass. Pushing a lock of her glossy black hair behind one ear, she said, "Let me know what I can do. I'd love to help."

Bonnie leaned back in her chair, a faint line forming between her brows. "I don't know. I'd hate to appear insensitive." Reaching out to the flag, she lightly stroked its stars and stripes, before continuing. "Annabel, you're always so sensible. Do you really think we should have a party?"

From the way Ann blinked several times before answering, it was clear that she was a bit perplexed that her suggestion that her father's life be celebrated had been taken seriously. Nevertheless she said, "I think a party honoring Dad would be lovely."

Bonnie considered this before announcing with a teary smile, "Then it's settled. I'll start planning it as soon as I get back."

"Get back?" asked Frances, an edge in her voice. "Get back from where?"

"Oh, didn't I tell you?" asked Bonnie, her blue eyes round. "I was sure that I did. I'm going on a spa retreat, out to a place in Arizona. The horrible suddenness of poor Martin's death has been so stressful for me. I need to find my center. I need to unwind."

"What exactly does she call what she does now?" Aunt Winnie muttered to me.

It might not be the most diplomatic question, but it was a fair one. Much of Bonnie's day was spent either shopping or lunching. It was hard to see how such a schedule would require unwinding.

Frances shot her husband, Scott, an anxious look. His round face mirrored his wife's concern. Rubbing his large hand across his chin, he leaned across the table, his posture reminiscent of an arm wrestler—an arm wrestler wearing an expensively tailored gray suit. However, despite its obvious excellent quality and fit, it still looked all wrong on him. Scott Phillips was one of those men who are more at ease in jeans and a T-shirt. Although he'd been tapped to take over Uncle Marty's business years ago and had shown great promise in continuing the company's success, he'd never gotten used to having to wear the suit.

"When are you leaving, Bonnie?" he asked.

"Tomorrow. I'll be gone just a week."

Scott coughed. It was not the cough of someone with a cold. It was the cough of someone with a problem. "Bonnie, I know this isn't the best time," he said, with an uneasy glance at the rest of us, "but there's that matter I discussed with you earlier."

Seeing the perplexed expression on Bonnie's face, he continued, "The property in St. Michaels? We need to discuss the proceeds of the sale of the house."

"Oh, fiddle-dee-dee, not that again," said Bonnie, with a dismissive wave of her hand.

"Yes, *that* again," said Scott through gritted teeth. "I realize this is a difficult time, but it's best we get this sorted out as soon as possible."

"I understand that," she replied. "And I fully intend to do just that. When I get back."

"But—"

Bonnie interrupted. "But nothing! I need to get away. I realize that everything's in a jumble right now, but it's not as if we can't sort it out when I get back. I know you think the proceeds are to be split among the three of you, but I don't agree that that was what Martin wanted. I'm sure he meant for me to have a fourth. However, we can discuss it when I get back."

"But—" Scott continued.

Again, Bonnie interrupted him. "But nothing!" she said, her voice becoming petulant. Over the years, I've seen only two sides to Bonnie's personality—flaky and petulant. She was a spoiled child in a woman's body. "We'll deal with it when I get back," she said. "But I have to say, I don't think the proceeds on the house are the problem."

"What do you mean?" asked Scott.

Bonnie placed both of her hands on the table and leaned forward. Lowering her voice, she glanced furtively at the flag before continuing. "What I mean is that I can't shake this feeling that poor Martin's death was . . . well, as God as my witness, it was *wrong*."

"What do you mean, 'wrong'?" Reggie asked, hastily setting down her empty martini glass.

"I mean *murder*," came the breathless response. Pressing her hand to her chest, she moaned, "Oh, my poor, poor Marty!"

Bonnie's oft-repeated sentiment of the day was again met with silence. But this time, we weren't ignoring her. Based on the horrified expressions around me, I suspected that for the first time today, Bonnie held everyone's complete attention.

CHAPTER 2

My sore-throats, you know, are always
worse than anybody's.
—PERSUASION

URDER!" REGGIE SHRIEKED. She sat upright in her chair as if someone had just dumped several ice cubes down the back of her dress and glared at Bonnie. "Just what the hell are you talking about?" Reggie's temper was almost as legendary as her beauty. Even though her anger wasn't directed at me, I still squirmed uncomfortably in my chair.

Bonnie's pale hands fluttered before her face as she tried to explain. "Well, the *suddenness* of it, of course! I mean, didn't anyone else think it was . . . well, *strange?*" Her large blue eyes stared questioninly at us.

"Strange in what way?" asked Ann, her voice struggling for composure.

"Well, that nurse, for one." With a cautious glance around her, Bonnie lowered her voice an octave. "I think she was *foreign.*"

Bonnie was forever suspicious of "foreigners." Last year, a series of prank phone calls in which the caller said nothing and hung up after a moment were also blamed on this demographic. When asked how she could possibly know the identity of the caller, as he or she did not speak, Bonnie calmly replied, "The breathing; it was *foreign* breathing."

"For Christ's sake, Bonnie," Aunt Winnie snapped now, her patience gone. "There are so many levels of wrong with what you just said, it truly boggles the mind. But for starters, of *course* she was foreign! The girl's name was Rona Bjornstad and she spoke with a heavy Dutch accent. You're just figuring out *now* that she wasn't born here?"

Someone snickered. However, Bonnie, unaffected by Aunt Winnie's tirade, merely sniffed. "I read the papers," came her enigmatic reply. "I know things."

"My dear Bonnie, skimming the headlines on the gossip rags doesn't count as papers," Aunt Winnie shot back. "You make Sarah Palin look well-read."

"Oh, I love her!" Bonnie gushed.

Aunt Winnie grimaced and muttered something. I leaned in to her. "Did you say what I think you just said?" I asked, aghast.

"Of course not," she retorted primly. "That's just your vulgar imagination."

Across the table, Frances brushed an errant strand of brown hair off her face and leaned forward. "Bonnie," she said, her tone full of exasperation, "Nurse Rona was wonderful with Dad."

"That's my point," Bonnie countered with a tip of her blond head. "Maybe she was a little *too* wonderful."

Frances's brow furrowed. "Meaning?"

Bonnie pursed her lips. "Meaning, I think she liked him. You should have seen the way she was always hanging over him and trying to hold his hand."

"She tried to hold his hand?" asked Ann.

Bonnie gave an emphatic nod that caused the lace on her black ensemble to shudder. "Of course, when I called her on it, she *claimed* that she was just trying to take his pulse, but *I* knew better. Oh, if I wasn't a lady, *what* I wouldn't tell that woman."

There was an awkward pause as everyone around the table tried very hard not to laugh.

With monumental effort, Ann finally said, "Bonnie, I don't think Rona had any designs on Dad and I don't think he was . . . murdered." She briefly closed her eyes, as if the sound of her voice calmly uttering this statement in the dining room of the Hotel Washington was too much to bear. "I think you're very tired. We all are. Go on your spa retreat and get some rest. You'll feel better when you get back, and all these thoughts about murder will be gone."

Bonnie sniffed again. "All right. If you say so, Annabel."

The muscles in Ann's jaw bunched, and I made a private bet that while Bonnie's thoughts about murder might disappear, others' would only grow stronger.

"Good God, but Bonnie is a piece of work," Aunt Winnie said to me after we left the restaurant. We were in my mother's car on the way to the airport. Aunt Winnie had to catch a flight back to Cape Cod, where she and her boyfriend, Randy, own and manage a bed-and-breakfast. Randy had stayed behind to keep things running.

"Marty could be a cold son of a bitch at times," Aunt Winnie continued, "and he certainly bamboozled Bonnie into marrying him all those years ago, but there are times when I think that her utter craziness helped somewhat to redress that balance. Life with her could not have been easy."

"Where on earth do you think she got the idea that Uncle Marty was murdered? The man had been hanging on by a thread for years. I can't believe she was surprised by his death," my mother asked.

"Yes, well, that's Bonnie for you. Never met a fact she couldn't ignore," Aunt Winnie replied, her mouth twisted into a small red smirk.

"So you don't think there could be any truth to what she said?" I asked.

From the front seat, Kit let out a whoop of laughter and swung around to face me. "I knew it! I knew it!" she crowed. "As soon as Bonnie began all that nonsense about Uncle Marty being murdered, I knew you were going to get all *weird*. Just because you were around when a murder happened doesn't make you Nancy Drew!"

"I never said I was Nancy Drew!" I shot back. "And for your information, I was involved in *two* murder investigations, not just one, and I helped solve them both!"

"Oh, please," said Kit, with a lofty air of superiority. "Not this again."

The thing that drove me crazy was that I *had* been involved in two murder investigations and I'd helped solve them *both*. Hell, in one case I'd been in a full-on fight with the murderer, resulting in a bash to the head (mine, of course) and a temporary imprisonment in a dark basement (again, that would be me). Yet Kit still treated the whole thing as a giant joke.

"Kit!" said Aunt Winnie, coming to my defense. "I don't know how many times I have to tell you this, but Elizabeth was invaluable in helping solve the murder that happened at my inn. If it weren't for her help in finding the real killer, the police probably would have arrested me!"

"Yeah, well, that may be so," Kit said in a tone that indicated she thought anything but that, "but I don't think that Uncle Marty was murdered and neither do you."

"Well, no . . ." began Aunt Winnie.

"And that's my only point," said Kit blandly. "But what was all that business with Scott about the property in St. Michaels?"

Aunt Winnie leaned forward. "Before Marty died, he arranged for the sale of the St. Michaels house. I'm not sure what Bonnie is talking about, but *my* understanding was that the proceeds were to be split three ways among the girls. They could do what they wanted with it. They were all happy with the arrangement. Well, that's not completely true," she amended. "I don't think Reggie wanted to sell the house, but she was outvoted."

"Sounds like Scott really wants his share of the money. I gather it's a lot?" asked Kit.

"Probably," said Aunt Winnie. "I imagine the house sold for quite a bit."

"It was a beautiful place," I said. "At least, from what I can remember."

Kit sniffed indignantly. "I wouldn't know. I never saw it."

I held my tongue, sorry I'd mentioned that particular bone of contention. Although Kit is nearer in age to Ann, Ann and I had always been closer. As a result, I'd been invited to the house in St. Michaels a few times for summertime overnights. I was sorry to hear that they had sold it; it was a magnificent house with a spectacular view of Maryland's Miles River.

A few minutes later, we pulled into the crowded passenger dropoff lane at Ronald Reagan Washington National Airport. As she got out, Aunt Winnie turned to me. "Now, are we still on for October? I need you and Peter to help me with the new place."

Peter is my boyfriend. I've known him since I was little, but that's not to say that it was love at first sight. Far from it, in fact. Back then I lumped him in the same category as clowns, flu shots, and other nightmares of youth. But a bizarre occurrence two years ago at Aunt Winnie's inn had changed all that. A man had been murdered during Aunt Winnie's New Year's Eve party, and the police stupidly suspected her of the crime. While trying to clear her name and discover the real murderer, I also discovered that Peter had improved with age.

"Absolutely," I replied, giving her a hug. Aunt Winnie, like me, is a die-hard Jane Austen fan. Her current inn is the Inn at Longbourn; however, she and Randy recently purchased a second property on Nantucket. They are in the process of converting it into another inn. Like Longbourn, this one too is going to have an Austen theme. Each of the six rooms is going to be named and decorated for one of Austen's novels. Aunt Winnie had named the inn Aust-Inn-tatious. Peter and I were going to spend two weeks later in October helping her and Randy get the place ready. As Peter had recently joined his parents' national hotel company, he was going to help with the business aspects while I was to help with the Austen touches.

"I'd love to come and help you with the inn, too, Aunt Winnie," Kit said now, a faint note of melancholy in her voice. "I have a fabulous sense of design. All my friends say so."

Aunt Winnie smiled at Kit. "And I'd love to have you, but I think you'll be rather busy," she said, with a meaningful look at Kit's belly. Kit is eight months pregnant with her second child. When Kit was well and feeling fine, she could be fun, but to steal a phrase from Austen, any indisposition sunk her completely and it was easy for her to fancy herself neglected and ill-used. These days her pregnancy left her feeling exceedingly neglected and ill-used, and so she was pretty well completely sunk most of the time. If Mary Musgrove's sore throats were worse than anybody's, well, then the same could be said of Kit's pregnancies.

Kit's crabbiness had only further strained our relationship, which was rocky at best. Kit was the "responsible" one in our family—happily settled with a nice house and a nice family. I was the "irresponsible" one who still hadn't decided on a career and only recently entered into a stable adult relationship. Kit's sheets smelled of lavender; the only thing that smelled in my place was the kitchen sponge. As a result, she tried to advise me on how to run my life and I tried to refrain from openly scowling.

Kit glanced down at her rounded belly now, patting it fondly. "True," she said. "I *will* be busy. But if Elizabeth is going to be there, she can help *me*, while I help *you*. I know she'll be wonderful with the baby. She's been just amazing with little Pauly these past few weeks; she's much more patient than I am—but that's probably because he's not hers."

To steal another line from Austen, Kit always thought a

great deal of her own complaints, and was always in the habit of claiming me when anything was the matter.

Aunt Winnie grinned at me. "Yes, I could see how you would think that Elizabeth is the properest person to watch the baby."

I nodded in mock agreement. "Quite. For I have not a mother's feelings."

Kit stamped her foot in annoyance while Aunt Winnie and I giggled. "I hate it when you two do that!" she said. "It's like hanging out with people who insist on speaking in some juvenile code!"

It drives Kit crazy when I quote Jane Austen at her, mainly because she never gets the references. "Jane Austen is not juvenile!" I said with a laugh. "She's a classic!"

"Sorry, I guess that makes *you* the juvenile," Kit retorted.

"Kit, if you read the books, you'd get the references."

"Sorry, but unlike some people, I don't have the luxury to spend time reading. I have a house to run and a child to raise."

I bit my tongue and said nothing. Restraint was a skill I'd been forced to perfect over the last few weeks ever since my apartment had been deemed "unfit" to live in due to a rampant mold issue. Armed with my landlord's promise that the problem would be rectified in two weeks, I moved into Kit's guest bedroom in her house in Silver Spring. I would have preferred to have stayed with Peter, but his place was in Annapolis, too far a commute to my newspaper job in D.C. Don't get me wrong. I was extremely grateful to Kit for taking me in, it's just that Kit has the ability to ruin even the most generous of gestures. What began as a chance for us to "bond" (her words) had quickly morphed into a chance for me to perfect my skills as a live-in nanny, maid, and sous chef (my words). Two days ago, she asked if I wouldn't mind incorporating some fresh dinner recipes into my new nightly routine, as she felt that my staples of spaghetti, ham-and-cheese omelets, and grilled chicken were a bit "pedestrian." "Paul and I really want to expand little Pauly's taste buds," she had told me.

To be fair, if my kid wolfed down Play-Doh with the enthusiasm Pauly did, I might think about expanding his taste buds, too. Nevertheless, when my landlord called to tell me that it looked as if repairs would be at least another week, I felt a sudden weight on my neck that threatened to pull me to the ground.

The weight actually turned out to be little Pauly; he likes to launch sneak attacks on me (and just for the record, "little" Pauly is a misnomer; I'm beginning to suspect that Play-Doh is high in calories). Anyway, the realization that Kit wanted me to reprise my role of Mary Poppins this fall—with Pauly *and* a newborn—made me want to sit down with my head between my knees.

Happily, Aunt Winnie came to my rescue. "Oh, Kit, I would love to have you and the baby to the new place, but I couldn't in good conscience let you come before the repairs are completed. We're going to be gutting a large portion of the house. It'll be a dusty mess and God only knows what kind of toxic particles we might be unearthing. I wouldn't feel comfortable having a baby around all that dirt and grime. As soon as it's done, though, I want you to come."

Kit's lips pulled down into a pout, but she did not argue.

"Well, I guess I'll stay here alone while you all go off to Nantucket."

My self-restraint gave way and I laughed, saying, "Upon my word, I shall be pretty well off, when you are all gone away to be happy at Bath!"

Aunt Winnie smothered a smile. I think my mother did, too. Kit, however, glared at me. "Oh yeah?" she snapped. "You want to trade pithy quotes? Well, how about this? 'C is for cookie, that's good enough for me!' And I guess it'll have to be because no one seems to want to help me!"

My mother attempted to appease Kit with an indulgent pat on the back. "Now, Kit," she said soothingly, "that's not true. I told you that I would be happy to stay with you and help."

"And Kit, if you think gutting a house is fun, then you really do need a vacation!" added Aunt Winnie. "You come up once everything's ready. That way I can give you a proper vacation, pamper you, and show off my latest great-niece or great-nephew. Wait, is that right?" Aunt Winnie paused thoughtfully. "Would it be my great-great-niece or great-great-nephew? Would that make me a great-great-aunt? I don't know, it sounds weird."

"How about we just call you Extraordinary Aunt?" I said, laughing.

"Done," Aunt Winnie agreed. Turning back to Kit, she asked, "Do you have any idea what the sex of the baby is?"

"No," Kit replied. "We want to be surprised, but I keep having dreams that it's a girl."

Aunt Winnie smiled. "Oh, a little girl! How fun that would be!"

Mollified, Kit chatted happily about possible names for the baby if it was a girl until Aunt Winnie finally left to catch her flight. Giving me a final hug, she whispered in my ear, "Patience is a virtue."

"So's vodka," I whispered back.

With a laugh and a final wave good-bye, Aunt Winnie headed for her terminal. We watched her until she was swallowed up by the bustling crowd of fellow travelers before piling back into my mom's car.

"So, I was thinking that maybe sometime next week we all could meet for dinner somewhere," my mom said as she pulled out into the traffic, ignoring three separate cabbies' horns of warning. "I know that George would love to see you."

George is my mother's boyfriend. When our father died five years ago, our mom took it pretty hard. She left the house only for classes at the college where she taught English literature. In fact, if it weren't for her job, I don't think she would have left the house at all. To help, Kit and I had chipped in and signed her up for some spin classes at a local gym, thinking that the interaction might help ease her out of her loneliness. As fate would have it, George was the instructor. At first we thought it was cute when he'd asked her out, and we'd good-naturedly teased her about being a cougar. That was four years ago and it was no longer cute or funny. It isn't that George is a bad guy, mind you. He's nice enough. He is good-looking and in good shape. He is just dumb as an ox. The last time we all went out to eat at one of his favorite restaurants, I asked him if the turkey burger was any good. He answered that he didn't know because, and I'm quoting here, "I'm not one of those pansy vegetarians." He then flexed his biceps, *kissed it,* and added, "My guns need protein."

Really, not even Jane Austen would have a snappy comeback to that.

At my mom's mention of George, Kit and I exchanged glances of derision. It was funny, but after a lifetime of butting heads, we'd finally found one thing in common. We both found a night with George to be a damned tedious waste of an evening. But we love our mother, so we put up with him. The only reason we hadn't had to deal with him today was that he was at some cycling convention in Seattle, learning how to channel Lance Armstrong or something.

"Yeah, Mom, that would be great," said Kit. "Just let me know when it's a good time."

"I'm free all next week," I added.

"Except Tuesday," said Kit. "Don't forget, you're watching little Pauly for us next Tuesday night."

"I haven't forgotten. I'll be there," I mumbled. My social life had taken a hit lately, and Kit saw no reason not to take full advantage of this temporary lull. My best friend, Bridget, was newly married. She and her husband, Colin, had purchased a "fixer-upper" and now spent most of their time trolling Home Depot and poring over paint samples. As much as I love them both, I couldn't endure another conversation about whether "hushed hue" or "inner balance" would be a better color for the living room. (Seriously, do either of those colors suggest taupe to you? Why can't they just call colors what they are? In this case, "really light taupe" and "even lighter taupe.")

As for Peter, he was putting together a new business deal in

California, and we hadn't had much of a chance to get together. The result was that in addition to my other "Kit duties," I had now become her very own free babysitting service.

From the front seat, Kit suddenly gave a loud laugh. "Well, you'll be there unless they suddenly discover that Uncle Marty was murdered and you have to fly off to solve the case!"

I looked out the window and sighed, wondering for maybe the hundredth time just how bad exposure to mold was anyway.

CHAPTER 3

If there is anything disagreeable going on
men are always sure to get out of it.
—PERSUASION

I T WAS AROUND THREE when we arrived at Kit's house, a two-story, whitewashed colonial dating from the 1940s. Like many of the houses in Silver Spring, it retains a vintage charm in spite of being expanded and modernized over the years. Kit, of course, is hoping to move into one of those McMansions that line the Beltway.

As soon as Kit stepped inside, Pauly launched himself at her with an enthusiasm that bordered on violence. Pauly is a miniature of his father. He has curly brown hair, a round freckled face, and a sweet, lopsided smile. He has some of his mother in him, too. He doesn't like it when things don't go his way and isn't shy about letting people know it. I should know, I have bruises on my shins to prove it.

"Will you play Candy Land with me? Please? I'm so bored," he wailed, climbing up Kit's leg. Wiping his nose, he repeated, "Please?"

"Don't wipe your nose on your sleeve," Kit said automatically. "Are you feeling better, baby? Where's Daddy?"

A head cold had kept Pauly home from preschool today. Kit's husband, Paul, had stayed home from his job as a hot-tub salesman to watch him. Hearing our voices in the foyer, Paul wandered out from the living room, his cell phone pressed to his ear. Gesturing to Kit to wait a minute, he continued his conversation. "Yeah, Tom? Hey, listen, my wife just got in so I can get to the store after all. Tell them I'll be there within the half hour. Okay, thanks. Bye."

He turned to Kit. "Hey, babe. How was the funeral?"

While I tried not to laugh at the absurdity of the question, Kit put her hands on her hips and glared at Paul. "Did I hear you correctly? Are you going into the store? Today? Now?"

"Babe, come on. It's the high season for hot tubs. You know that. The store is packed today. As manager, I have to be there. This could mean a big bonus for us."

"You're really going to leave? I just came home from burying my uncle! I'm exhausted!" Kit cried.

"Oh, I'm sorry! I didn't realize that they actually made you dig the hole!" Paul shot back. "If you're that tired, take a nap. I'm sure Elizabeth can watch Pauly," he casually offered.

"But that's not the point," Kit began.

"Kit, he's right," I said. "I have the whole day off. You go take a nap. Let Paul go to the store. I can watch Pauly." Turning to Pauly, I said, "Come on, little man, let's go play Candy Land. But I get to be the blue guy."

"Deal!" said Pauly, breaking into a run to his room to get the game.

"Thanks, Elizabeth," said Paul. Looking back at Kit, he

said, "Babe, don't be this way. I have to go in to work. I wish I didn't, but I do. I'll try not to be too late." Giving her a peck on the cheek, he waved good-bye to me and yelled to Pauly, "I'm leaving now, Pauly. Love you, buddy. Play nice with your aunt Elizabeth!" Two seconds later, he was out the door. I turned to Kit, about to say, "Nursing does not belong to a man; it is not his province," but then I saw her face and thought better of the idea.

Kit frowned at the door Paul had just exited before storming up the stairs to her bedroom. "Men," I heard her mumble before shutting the door behind her.

"Sisters," I added under my breath before heading to Pauly's room for a rousing game of Candy Land.

Two hours later, after multiple trips to the Candy Cane Forest and Gum Drop Mountain and hanging out with Princess Frostine, I felt like a diabetic in need of an insulin shot. Happily, Pauly seemed as exhausted as I felt, and I had no problem convincing him to take a nap. I tucked him into his Pottery Barn Speedboat bed, which Kit paid through the nose for after getting into a bidding war over it on eBay. Given the final price of the bed, I suspected that Pauly would be stuck with it all the way through high school. But who knows? It just might have been wise parenting on Kit's part. I mean, I doubt the kid was ever going to try and sneak any girls into his room to make out on the plank detailing.

Once I was sure that Pauly was asleep, I headed for my room and flopped on my bed. Immediately, the lyrics to "I Wanna Be Like You" from Disney's *The Jungle Book* burst into my brain. It wasn't my fault. My room was the future nursery, and Kit had decided to go with a—you guessed it—jungle theme. Everywhere I looked animals of all shapes and sizes crowded together and gazed back at me. On the walls, painted monkeys and chimpanzees swung from twisted branches. From the closet doors, an elephant and a rhino peered out from behind a giant bush. On the ceiling, a giraffe leaned toward a full green leaf, its long blue-black tongue extended to take a bite.

I tried really hard not to look at the ceiling if I could help it.

When I'd moved in, Peter had taken one look at the room and reprogrammed the ring tone on his phone to play "Jungle Fever" every time I called. I did so now.

"Hey there!" he said. "I was just thinking about you. How are you doing?"

"Pretty good," I said, scooting back on the bed so I could rest my head on the pillows all the while keeping my eyes averted from the ceiling. "Aunt Winnie says hi."

"I'm really sorry I couldn't be there. But I think we're close to signing the deal."

"That's great!" I said. Peter was in San Diego overseeing negotiations for a new property. He'd promised to fly me out there for a getaway weekend if the deal went through. "When do you think you'll be done?"

"What's today? Tuesday? Probably by Friday. Think you can sneak away for the weekend? Or does Kit not let you take off weekends?"

"Doesn't matter. I've started a tunnel to the outside from my bedroom closet. I dump the dirt out of my pants pockets when

I take Pauly to the playground. By Friday, it should be ready. I already have the papier-mâché of my head completed."

"Excellent. I'll see you on the outside."

We chatted a little while longer until Peter had to go. Before he hung up, he once again tried to convince me to stay at his place while my apartment was being redone. "The commute can't be as bad as that tongue on your ceiling," he said.

"You might have a point there," I said with an uneasy glance upward.

"I do have a point. We'll talk more Friday."

"Okay. See you then."

"Hang tough. I love you."

My heart made that little flip-flop it did every time he said that. "I love you, too," I said.

I hung up and rolled off the bed. Stepping out into the hall, I listened for signs of activity from Kit's room but heard nothing. Peeking into Pauly's room, I saw that he was still asleep, curled up with an assortment of wooden trains.

Heading downstairs, I looked at the clock. Seeing that it was five thirty, I cleaned up the kitchen and living room for Kit and then started dinner. Around six o'clock, Pauly woke up and came stumbling into the kitchen, wiping the sleep from his eyes. A few minutes later, Kit emerged from her room as well. "Oh, thanks, Elizabeth," she said, when she saw that I'd started dinner. "I'm sorry you've been stuck doing so much. I just don't have any energy these days. This pregnancy is really taking a toll on me."

Sliding into a chair at the kitchen table, she pulled Pauly onto her lap. "We are very lucky to have Aunt Elizabeth staying with us, you know that, buddy?" she said, laying her blond head on his. Pauly nodded and grinned at me.

I smiled back and thought that Kit wasn't all bad. After all, she was eight months pregnant and undoubtedly exhausted. Taking care of Pauly and the house had to be draining even when enjoying the best of health. She then ruined my new-found goodwill by suddenly frowning at the stove and asking, "Wait. Are you making spaghetti? Again?"

Aunt Winnie's advice that "Patience is a virtue" popped into my head, reminding me of my own version of patience. I wondered where Kit kept the booze. Maybe I could make a nice vodka sauce for tonight.

Paul was home in time for dinner, which was good, as Kit tended to pout when he was late. Thankfully, he took over after dinner, cleaning up and giving Pauly his bath. While Kit prepared to snuggle in with Pauly and read him a Thomas the Tank Engine adventure, Paul turned to me and said, "Hey, Elizabeth, how about we go test out the new hot tub? It's the latest model, you know."

I did indeed know. It was a frequent topic of conversation. In fact, I think I could get a job at Paul's store with all the "portable spa" knowledge I'd amassed in the last week. For instance, the model that Paul had installed was the Vanguard. It boasted a gray spa-stone surround, four-zone multicolor lighting, an integrated MP3 sound system, and a total of thirty-two jets. It could comfortably hold six adults and four hundred gallons of water or the entire cast of *The Jersey Shore*. Hair gel was optional.

"That's not fair!" said Kit. "Elizabeth gets to use it before me! You know I can't go in while I'm pregnant!"

Paul shot her an irritated look and Kit realized how horrible she sounded. "I'm sorry," she said meekly. "I'm just grumpy, I guess. You guys go enjoy the tub. I'll get Pauly to bed."

I am not normally a hot tub person, but tonight it sounded like a good idea. I quickly changed into my bathing suit and stepped outside into the crisp evening air. As befitting a tub of this caliber, Paul had given it its own special area of the backyard. The tub was situated under a picturesque grouping of dogwood trees. The fall foliage provided a purplish-red canopy over it while elaborate stone flooring provided its base. It was all lit by a custom spotlight. As I climbed in the hot water, Paul fiddled with a few buttons and soon the lights and jets were both pulsing away. Hidden speakers were activated and Bruce Springsteen began to croon about a long-lost love and a car. Or it might have been about a long-lost love that *was* a car. I closed my eyes and leaned back, enjoying the quiet and letting the bubbling water ease away the tension in my shoulders.

"Hey, Elizabeth?"

I reluctantly pried my eyes back open and looked at Paul.

"I just want you to know that I really appreciate how helpful you've been these past few weeks."

I smiled. "I think I should be the one thanking you. You guys helped me out of a bind. I really appreciate the use of . . . your guest room," I said, thankful that I had stopped myself in time from saying "jungle land."

"Well, I'm not sure that we didn't get the better end of that deal," said Paul with a rueful look. "I know that Kit can be difficult at times." He paused and laughed. "Well actually, I don't think I need to tell *you* that. But this pregnancy has thrown her, somehow. She complains about *everything.* You've noticed, haven't you?"

I shifted uncomfortably in the tub. This wasn't the relaxing time I'd had in mind when I'd accepted Paul's offer. "Hmmm," I said noncommittally.

"Well, I was wondering . . . do you think you could talk to her?"

Although I had a vague suspicion of what he was referring to, I refused to believe it. "Talk to her about what?"

"About her constant complaining."

I opened my eyes wide in disbelief. "Are you serious? You want *me* to talk to her? About that?"

Paul sighed. "All right. Maybe it's a bad idea."

"Yeah, you think?"

"It's just that maybe if she heard it from *you* . . ."

"Oh, and she so loves my opinion as it is! I think you've spent too much time in this tub. It's melting your brain."

Paul opened his mouth to say something when Kit called out. "Elizabeth! Phone!"

"We will *not* continue this conversation later," I said with a laugh as I hopped out of the tub. Grabbing a thick terry-cloth towel off a patio chair, I rubbed myself dry before stepping back inside the house. Kit was waiting by the door. I could tell from her face that she was annoyed.

"Who is it?" I whispered.

"Ann," she answered, thrusting the phone at me.

Well, that explains the annoyance, I thought, taking the phone. Ann had asked for me and not her. Junior high all over again.

"Hello?" I said as Kit walked away pretending not to listen.

"Oh, Elizabeth, thank God I got you! Your cell phone keeps going to voice mail. I think it's dead." I was surprised when I heard her voice. Ann was agitated, an unusual state for her.

"What's going on?"

"They found a body!"

"What?! Who found a body?" Across the room, Kit spun around and stared at me.

"The new owners of the house in St. Michaels," said Ann. "Apparently they dug up the pool and found a body!"

"Holy shit, you've *got* to be kidding me!"

"Wait. It gets worse. The body. It's Michael. It's Michael Barrow."

CHAPTER 4

Our pleasures in this world are always to be paid for.

—NORTHANGER ABBEY

ICHAEL BARROW!" I gasped. "But that's ... that's impossible!" At the sound of Michael's name, Kit's eyes grew wide and her hand flew up to her mouth. Our eyes met in mutual horror. She made no pretense about not listening to the rest of the conversation.

"I know, I know," said Ann. "But nevertheless, it's true."

"But that means ... Oh, my God, that means ..."

"I know. I know. I can't even get my head around it," said Ann.

"Wait a minute. They found a body under the pool. How can they be so sure it's Michael?"

"They found his wallet. The police are going to do some ... tests, I don't know. But they seem pretty confident. Oh, God, this is like some sick nightmare."

Michael Barrow. It had been a long time since I'd thought about him. Movie star looks, intelligence, charm, and the morals of a sewer rat. My stomach turned in disgust now that I was forced to revisit the memory. A new thought occurred. "Reggie! Does Reggie know?" I asked.

"No. I haven't told her yet and I don't know *how* I'm going to tell her. I don't know how I'm going to tell *any* of them."

"Do you want me to come over?"

"Could you? I don't know what I'm going to do. I need someone here. If you can, maybe you could spend the night? Bonnie is absolutely no help." Lowering her voice, Ann added, "She still plans on going on that stupid spa retreat of hers. Can you believe it? She even packed the flag."

"Oddly enough, I can. I'll be over as soon as I can. Just let me grab some things."

"Okay. Thanks, Elizabeth."

I hung up the phone and stared at Kit, dumbfounded. "They found Michael Barrow's body under the pool at the St. Michaels house," I said.

"Dear God. Do they think he was murdered?" she asked.

"I didn't ask, but I can't imagine any other scenario. He had to have been murdered." It was testament to the severe shock that this news had produced that Kit didn't launch into some mocking speech about how I saw intrigue and mystery where there was none. But really, Michael didn't bury himself under the pool.

Kit sat down heavily. "But I thought that Michael stole all that money from Uncle Marty and then ran off," she said slowly.

"Yeah, well, it looks like he didn't run very far," I said. "I'll call you when I know more. Ann wants me to come over."

"Well, I should come!" Kit said. "After all I'm her cousin, too!"

I paused, unsure if Ann would want Kit to come. Kit didn't know the whole story of Michael Barrow and Ann, and I wasn't

sure if Ann wanted to make that story public. If you have a secret, Kit is the last person you should tell it to.

"Kit," I said calmly, "that's very sweet of you, but you should
stay here tonight. You're tired, you need your sleep. And besides, what about Pauly? He needs you here. I'll go to Ann's and
then I'll call you."

Kit stood up. "No," she said, in a firm voice that I knew from
experience brooked no argument. "I'm going. I've just as much
right as you to go. After all, it's my family, too." Turning on her
heel, she marched over to the sliding glass door that led to the
backyard. Yanking the door back, she stuck her head out and
yelled, "Paul! I've got to go out for a while with Elizabeth.
Ann's called and there's a family emergency. I'll be back as soon
as I can."

Turning back to me, she said, "Come on, get changed. I'm
driving."

I opened my mouth to protest but then thought better. I
couldn't change her mind even if I wanted to—and trust me, I
wanted to. With a sigh, I went and changed, thinking that like
Anne Elliot I had never submitted more reluctantly to the jealous and ill-judging claims of a sister; but so it must be.

I bet Jane Austen had a Kit in her family, too.

While Ann normally lived alone in a quaint two-bedroom
house in Bethesda, she had been staying at Uncle Marty's house
in Georgetown. Ann had been required to make this temporary move because even though the family had hired a nurse for
Uncle Marty (the infamous Mata Hari aka Rona Bjornstad),
there were still gaps, gaps that Bonnie on her best day couldn't

fill. On her best day, Bonnie couldn't keep a plastic houseplant alive. Now that Uncle Marty had died, Ann was still needed at the house. The task of organizing and distributing the many items Uncle Marty had willed to various friends and family had been left to Ann. Ann, of course, did all this with her usual grace and continued to stay at the house and commute to her job. Several years ago she received her doctorate in English literature from Cambridge and now worked at the Folger Shakespeare Theatre in D.C.

Kit had to park a few blocks from the house, as parking in Georgetown is always a nightmare, and we walked in silence to the house. I was still annoyed at her for barging uninvited into Ann's crisis and frustrated at myself for not stopping her. At least I didn't tell her that I was spending the night, which was the only reason Kit hadn't stashed a change of clothes and a toothbrush into her tote like I had.

The night was cool, and after a minute Kit said, "This weather has been really unbelievable this week. So warm, but I think that's all about to end." I should mention that Washingtonians are convinced that their weather is like no other and spend inordinate amounts of time discussing it. While the past week had been lovely and, as such, much discussed, it had also been the last bloom of summer. Signs of fall were inescapable. From the earlier sunsets to the leaves on the trees that were now tinged with gold and red, it was clear that the warmth of the summer was giving way to the dying time of year.

Within minutes we turned onto Uncle Marty's street, which was lined with both ancient trees and elegant homes, most of the latter dating from the early 1800s. Each of the Georgian façades boasted perfectly proportioned dormers and brightly painted paneled doors, flanked by flattened columns and topped with filigree fanlights. The houses faced the street, with little to no front yard. However, the backyards were the real jewels of the neighborhood. Unexpectedly large gardens, pools, and well-tended lawns were nestled behind the high fences that kept both neighbors and pedestrians at bay.

Soon we were in front of Uncle Marty's three-story house. We made our way up the curved brick staircase. I had scarcely touched the bell when Ann flung open the door. She was still wearing the black sheath she'd worn to the funeral, although she was in her bare feet. Her normally rosy complexion was pale and her auburn curls hung in disheveled lank tendrils around her face.

The greeting she had planned died on her lips at the sight of Kit standing on her front steps with me. Through some eye twitching, I tried to convey that Kit's presence was not my idea. I'm not sure if I got that exact point across. She may have just thought I'd developed a nervous facial tic since lunch. After a startled blink, Ann recovered, merely saying, "Oh, Kit. You've come as well. Thank you."

Hearing this, Kit, of course, shot me one of her standard I-told-you-so looks, before saying, "Well, of course I came, silly! Where else would I be? You're family!"

I shot Ann an apologetic look while she stood aside and politely waved us into the house.

I love Uncle Marty's house. It has an effortless kind of charm that I knew from my own decorating attempts was anything but effortless. Mahogany wood floors run through the main level of the house, although most of those are covered with thick Oriental rugs in various muted hues. To my left was the dining room, where an antique Waterford chandelier hung from the ornate tray ceiling. The gilded mirror atop the stone fireplace sent the glittering light from the delicate crystals dancing on the white paneled walls. To my right was the living room, where Ann now led us.

Like the dining room, it too had a tray ceiling and a stone fireplace, atop of which was another large gilded mirror. The innate sophistication of the room had been tempered with the simple blue-and-white décor, largely inspired by the Wedgwood plaques set in the fireplace's mantel. Kit and I sat on the ivory brocade couch and looked expectantly at Ann.

"Can I get you something to drink?" she asked, seemingly now reluctant to discuss the reason for our visit.

"*I'm* fine," said Kit, with a dismissive wave of her hand. "Now tell me, what exactly happened? Elizabeth wasn't very clear on the details."

My blood pressure jumped a few notches and my stomach tightened. Leave it to Kit to make it sound like I hadn't gotten the details accurately. I had. Annoyed that she had pushed herself unwanted into the situation, I simply had refused to give her anything other than the barest information. I was childish, perhaps, but *not* inaccurate.

With a brief glance in my direction, Ann sighed and sank into one of the matching blue club chairs opposite the couch, her posture one of weary resignation.

"Well," Ann began, her voice low, "as you know, Father sold the house in St. Michaels a few weeks ago. The family that moved in decided that they wanted to expand the pool. They began construction this week and yesterday they found . . ." Ann paused. Taking a deep breath, she continued, "They found a body. It was decomposed, of course, but apparently there was ID on it. According to the police, the ID belongs to Michael Barrow. Obviously, they believe that the body is Michael. I guess they're going to check dental records for confirmation, but for now that's the assumption."

"I see," said Kit in a matter-of-fact tone. "And has his next of kin been notified?"

I stifled a groan. Kit was so excited to be a part of this tragedy that she was trying to appear more knowledgeable than she was, throwing around absurd pseudolegal terms like "next of kin." Next she'd be spouting off about the "alleged murder." Kit watches a lot of *CSI*.

Ann shook her head. "As far as I know, Michael had no family. His parents died years ago, before we ever met him. I believe he was an only child."

"Oh, that's right," Kit said quickly. "I'd forgotten that. I remember now. So I gather that the police are treating this as an alleged murder investigation, correct?"

Told you.

"I . . . uh . . ." Ann's face crumpled a bit at Kit's question. I couldn't blame her. If Michael had been "allegedly" murdered, as Kit put it, there were many people in the Reynolds family who would have to answer some very tough questions.

A noise on the stairs diverted our attention. It was Bonnie. For once, her entrance was a welcome distraction. Scarlett, her little Pomeranian dog, bounded excitedly into the room ahead of her. There used to be another dog, aptly named Rhett, but just as aptly, he ran away. Nobody blamed him.

"Oh, hello, my dears," she said when she saw us. Unlike Ann, Bonnie had obviously had time to change out of her funereal garb. Although she was still wearing black, she no longer appeared as Vivien Leigh's understudy from *Gone with the Wind*. Instead she was wearing a rather chic outfit consisting of lightweight wool trousers and a snug turtleneck. It not only hugged her curves but also emphasized her slimness. At sixty, Bonnie still had a great figure and wasn't shy about showing that off.

Kit and I both stood and hugged her while Scarlett jumped on our calves. "I thought I heard the doorbell ring," Bonnie continued. "Have you come to see me off?" Although I was used to Bonnie's flakiness, it still took me by surprise how quickly she could switch gears. Just this morning she was inconsolable with grief over Uncle Marty's death. Now she was all preoccupation over her impending trip.

Ann's jaw clenched in annoyance. "They're here because I called them, Bonnie. I told them about the discovery at the house. You remember? The body?"

"Oh, yes," Bonnie replied, crinkling her nose in distaste. "Nasty business. Poor Michael. If it *is* Michael. Though I can't imagine it *isn't*. After all, they found his wallet. I mean, if it wasn't Michael, I'd imagine that he'd have come looking for his wallet long before this."

"Yes, well, thank you for clearing that up for us," said Ann. I glanced at Ann in some surprise. Normally, she wasn't so openly rude to Bonnie. However, seeing the lines of worry clustered around her hazel eyes, I couldn't really blame her. After all, she'd had more than her fair share of stress today. This morning, she buried her father; this evening, she was dealing with a potential homicide investigation.

"Well, I don't see why you're so upset, Annabel," Bonnie said. "He was a thief. And a common thief at that. No one here is mourning his passing."

I wondered if Michael had been an *uncommon* thief it would be a different story. Would Bonnie have mourned him then? But what exactly was an uncommon thief? All that came to mind was Cary Grant in *To Catch a Thief.* I considered the matter. While I normally don't agree with Bonnie, I had to admit she might be right about this one. If I had a John Robie in my life, I'd probably mourn his passing.

Bonnie continued on. "The only one I can see being upset by this news is Reggie. After all, it was Reggie who was engaged to Michael."

"Didn't she break it off with him, though?" asked Kit, as she bent down to pet Scarlett, who, in turn, helpfully presented her belly. "A few months before the wedding?"

Ann nodded. "She broke it off and . . ."

"And then Michael disappeared," finished Bonnie. "But I guess he didn't, did he? You don't suppose he killed himself because Reggie broke it off with him, do you?"

Although Bonnie's lack of a filter between thoughts and speech was no secret, it still managed to catch you by surprise from time to time. Ann briefly closed her eyes before answering. "No, Bonnie. I don't think that Michael killed himself and then buried himself under the pool's foundation."

"Well," Bonnie said with a slight shrug of her shoulders,

"when you put it *that* way, I suppose it doesn't work. Well, don't worry yourselves about it, my dears. That's what the police are paid to find out. I've no doubt that they can handle our little mystery. Like I always say, we can worry about that tomorrow. After all, tomorrow is another day." Shooting us a bright smile, she moved for the doorway. Scarlett paused, as if torn between staying with us and following her mistress. Just like her namesake, she opted for the decision that would suit her best: she sat down with us. Heading for the curved staircase that led upstairs, Bonnie paused and turned back to us. "Do you think you should mention Marty's death to the police? Do you think there could be a connection?"

"No, Bonnie," Ann said firmly. "I don't."

Bonnie looked unconvinced but said, "All right. Well, I've got to finish packing. Now remember, Ann, I'll be gone one week. I've left all the instructions for Scarlett on the hall table. Take good care of her; you know how delicate she is." We all looked at Scarlett, who was busy cleaning herself with great abandon. "When I get back, we can have that party for Marty. Why don't you check the club and see if it's available?" Almost as an afterthought, she called over her shoulder, "And just think! By then, this whole thing might be solved!"

Ann winced at Bonnie's words. "That's just what I'm afraid of," she whispered. Scarlett stopped cleaning herself long enough to look up and bark.

CHAPTER 5

The old well-established grievance of duty
against will, parent against child.
—SENSE AND SENSIBILITY

So SHE'S JUST GOING TO LEAVE? Now?" asked Kit in amused disbelief.

"It would appear so," said Ann, her face resigned. "Although, when I stop to think about it, I can't say that I'm surprised. Sensitivity isn't exactly Bonnie's strongest quality. But I'm fine. Actually, it will be easier if she's *not* here. There's so much I have to do before I can go back to my own place."

"What do you need to do? Can I help with anything?" I asked.

"That would be great, thanks. I've got to sort through Father's papers, catalog everything, and then distribute the various items that he left in his will. There's an oil painting upstairs that Frances was always fond of. I know Father wanted her to have that. There are also a few china figurines that were set aside for Reggie." She paused as Scarlett jumped at her knees. "And, of course, I've got to take care of Scarlett here." Her lip sneered ever so slightly as she said this. Not that I blamed her. Scarlett is a pint-sized diva.

"Speaking of Reggie," said Kit, "I gather you haven't told her yet."

Ann shook her head. "No. I'll have to, and soon, but I don't seem to have the mental capacity tonight to figure out exactly what I'm going to say."

"How do you think she'll take it?" Kit asked with ghoulish interest.

Ann's forehead wrinkled in confusion. "She'll be upset, of course. To what extent, I can't say."

"Well, obviously!" Kit gushed. "No, what I mean is, why exactly did Reggie break it off? I could never figure that out. At that point, Michael was still Mr. Perfect. No one knew about the embezzling yet. Uncle Marty loved him—I mean, wasn't he grooming Michael to take over the business?"

Ann nodded, almost as if the movement caused her pain. "I believe he was, yes," she replied in a near whisper.

"And you all loved him, right?" Kit asked.

Only a fool couldn't see that this was a subject that Ann didn't want to discuss, but Kit nevertheless pressed ahead with her investigation. As horrible as it may sound, I have to admit that sometimes I wished that my mom would come to me and tell me that Kit wasn't really my sister, that she found her in a wicker basket on the front porch. Hell, I'd even be okay if my mom told me that I was the result of a sordid affair. Even then, we'd only be half sisters, and I could soothe myself with the knowledge that we were *not* produced by the same gene pool.

"It was after Michael's disappearance that Uncle Marty turned to Scott as a successor, wasn't it?" I asked, hoping to change the subject.

"Yes," said Ann. "Frances had always wanted Scott to take over the business anyway. She felt that since he'd been in the family and at the company longest, it was only fair. I don't think Scott cared as much about it as she did."

"Well, she's always been the more intense of the two about Scott's career," I said.

"So, *why* do you think that Reggie broke it off?" Kit interrupted, reverting back to her line of questioning.

"She didn't think it would work," Ann replied. "She didn't go into the details with me."

"Do you think she was still in love with him? I mean, sometimes couples get into fights and say things they don't mean, especially right before their wedding. It can get pretty stressful. I know Paul and I had a couple of doozies."

"I don't know anything about that. All Reggie said was that she told Michael she didn't want to marry him. She seemed pretty certain about it."

"Right." Kit nodded her head as if this proved her point. "But Michael disappeared right after that. I just wondered if she regretted her decision."

"I don't think so," said Ann. "After all, it was right after he disappeared that Father discovered that the money was missing."

"Do you think Reggie could have known about the money?" asked Kit, her voice a conspiring whisper. "Do you think that's why she broke it off?"

While Ann's eyebrows shot up in surprise, my patience snapped. "Kit! Of course Reggie didn't know that Michael was embezzling from Uncle Marty! Use your head. She would have said something!"

Kit swung to face me, her eyes narrowed in anger. I knew I'd pay for my outburst later, but right now I didn't care. She was making the situation worse. Granted it was unintentional, but nevertheless I had to get her to stop.

"I'm only asking a question," she retorted. "I wasn't implying anything and, besides, I imagine that it's a question that the police are going to ask as well."

"You are *not* the police," I said through clenched teeth.

Kit gave a shrill laugh. "Oh, I get it. You think you're the only one in this family who can ask questions about a murder?"

I took a deep breath. "No, Kit. That's not what I'm saying. The police don't know Reggie, but *we* do! Can you really see her not telling Uncle Marty if she knew Michael had embezzled the money?"

Kit shrugged. "I'm not *saying* she knew. All I'm saying is that love can do funny things to people sometimes."

Mercifully, her cell phone rang just then, putting an end to the conversation, at least for now.

"Paul?" Kit said into the receiver. "What's the problem? Well, I can't right now. I'm busy." Holding one finger up to us as a signal to wait, she shifted her body away from us. "Paul, it's not that hard. Just get him some of his trains, that'll settle him down. What? They're downstairs in the bin." Pause. "No, the other bin. I don't know! Get him Thomas, Gordon, and Percy. No, Gordon is the long blue one; Henry is the green one. No, that's James. For goodness' sake, Paul, it's not that difficult!" Long pause. "All right. Fine. Uh-huh. Okay. I'll be there soon. Bye." With an irritated click, she snapped the cell phone shut. Turning back to us, she said, "I have to go. Pauly's not feeling well. Ann, I'm really sorry about all of this. Please let me know what I can do. I mean it."

"Thanks, Kit, but I'll be fine."

"Well, the least I can do is bring over some dinners for you. You've got enough to worry about without adding cooking into the mix." With a smile she added, "No pun intended."

I suddenly felt like a jerk. Kit meant well, she really did. She was just one of those annoying souls who always manage to put a foot in it.

Ann nodded. "That would be great, Kit. Thanks. I really appreciate your coming over tonight. It's nice to know you guys are here for me when I need you."

"Of course we are!" replied Kit. "You should know that by now! That's what family is for!" Giving Ann a big hug, she turned to me. "Are you ready?"

With a fair amount of dread, I said, "Oh, uh, actually, I'm going to stay here tonight. I brought a change of clothes. I'll leave for work from here in the morning. I thought I'd help Ann tonight."

Kit looked like I'd slapped her, and for a second I saw a hurt little girl in front of me. I felt horrible. Kit had always had a hard time making friends. Kit didn't try to help people because they needed her help. Kit tried to help people so she could feel better about herself. When her offers of help were refused—even politely refused—Kit took it as a personal affront.

"Kit . . ." I began.

"Nope, it's fine. I'll just see you tomorrow," she said with artificial briskness, but I heard the catch in her voice. My heart sank.

"Kit—"

She cut me off. "I'll be sure to bring over some meals tomorrow, Ann," she said. "Lord knows, if you let Elizabeth do the cooking, all you'll end up eating is spaghetti!" Still laughing at her little joke, she left.

I sighed. Same old Kit.

Ann turned to me. "Would you like some tea?"

"If by 'tea' you mean Chardonnay, then yes," I said, following her to the kitchen. Scarlett scampered along beside me. Located in the back of the house, the kitchen was a large modern room with stainless-steel appliances, white cabinets, and white marble countertops. During the day, the back windows provided a view of the landscaped backyard and pool below.

I sat on one of the yellow cushioned stools at the counter, while Ann pulled out a chilled bottle from the refrigerator. Scarlett settled at my feet.

"How are you *really*?" I asked.

"About how you'd expect," she replied, getting down two glasses from the cabinet. "You know what my feelings about Michael were, but to know that he's dead, and not only dead but dead and buried under the pool we all swam in . . ." She broke off with a low moan of disgust and covered her mouth with her hand.

"You can't think about it like that," I said briskly, getting up and easing her into my chair. "You'll only make yourself sick. None of you knew that then."

Her head in her hands, she said, "Someone knew."

Fitting the corkscrew over the neck of the bottle, I pushed

down the lever and pulled out the cork. Pouring us each a glass, I slid Ann's across the counter to her.

Cradling the glass in her hands, her head low, she said, "Thanks, Elizabeth. I'm sorry. I shouldn't have said that."

"No, it's a fair comment. You're right. Someone did know."

Ann raised her head, her gaze direct. "I'm scared. Michael wasn't a nice man. He hurt a lot of people. He hurt people in my family."

I nodded. I didn't say what we were both thinking, that Michael had also hurt Ann. As I remembered the detail, my hands gripped my glass with unnecessary strength. Out of precaution, I put it down.

"Ann?" I asked. "When did the pool go in?"

"Eight years ago last July. Two months before what would have been Michael and Reggie's wedding. They were going to have the reception at the house and Reggie wanted a pool. Not to swim in, of course. She just wanted to float candles and flowers in the water. She thought it would look pretty."

"She always was a mini-Martha, wasn't she?" I said with a laugh.

Ann nodded in agreement. "That she was. And of course, Dad denied her nothing. He absolutely doted on her. She was so much like him." She took a sip of wine. "Anyway, the pool went in right around the time that Reggie broke it off with Michael. Right around the time he disappeared." She paused. "Obviously."

"That was right after your dad's Fourth of July party, right?"

Ann closed her eyes and nodded. "Yup, right after that horrible night."

I took a sip of my wine, unsure if I should continue. "Ann?"
She looked up. I took a deep breath. "Did you ever tell anybody
what happened at the party?"

Ann gave a rueful twist of her mouth. "You mean, did I ever
tell anybody that Michael tried to rape me?"

I nodded.

"No." She stared at the glass in her hands. "No. I never did.
You're the only one who knows. I don't know why I never
said anything." She put the glass down and twisted a lock of
hair around her finger and continued. "Maybe it was because
right after that, Reggie said she'd ended things with him. God,
I was so relieved when she told me that. I honestly don't know
if she would have believed me if I had told her. Then Dad discovered that the money was gone and that Michael took it."

"And then Michael was gone," I added.

She nodded. "And then Michael was gone. Except now it appears that he wasn't. Not in the way we all thought, anyway."
Propping her elbows on the counter, she rested her head in her
hands. "What are the police going to think when they hear all
this?"

"I don't know," I said honestly.

Neither of us said anything else, drinking our wine in silence. After a few minutes, however, I said, "Ann?"

"Hmmm?"

"If Michael's dead, what happened to the money?"

CHAPTER 6

*Nobody, who has not been in the interior
of a family, can say what difficulties of any
individual of that family may be.*

—EMMA

ANN'S BROWS KNIT TOGETHER. "I don't know. I imagine it's still sitting in whatever bank he dumped it. Why? Do you think we could get it back?"

"I don't know what your options are legally if you ever find it. I guess what I really meant was, could Michael have had an accomplice? Someone from the company, maybe?"

Ann leaned back, considering my question. "I never thought about that. Do you mean that whoever he was working with could have double-crossed him and killed him?"

"It's a possibility."

Ann mulled this over. "I just can't think of who would have done that." She sighed. "But then, I was surprised to find out that Michael had stolen the money in the first place. Guess I'm not the best judge of character on that count. But I'm sure I can call Scott and get hold of the company records from back then and check who was working. I should probably talk to Miles, too; I bet he'd have some insight."

"Oh, good idea," I said.

Miles Carswell was Uncle Marty's old partner and good friend. They had run the business together almost from the beginning. A few years back, Miles had left the construction business and started his own landscaping company. He and Uncle Marty had stayed close, continuing to work together, referring clients to one another, and doing joint projects.

"I saw him and Laura at the funeral," I said, "but I didn't get a chance to talk to them. How are they doing?"

"They're fine. Laura's been wonderful, calling me all the time to see how we're doing. I wanted them to come with us to the luncheon, but Bonnie insisted that it only be family." She sighed. "It's ridiculous, of course, because honestly Miles is like an honorary uncle and Laura . . . well, for Pete's sake, she was Mother's best friend in college!"

Over the years, Laura had served as a kind of godmother to the girls, trying to fill the void left by their mother. She loved them all but perhaps was closest to Ann. Probably because of all the girls, Ann most resembled her mother.

"Why do you think Bonnie didn't want them there?" I asked.

"She's never gotten along with Laura," said Ann. "I think she feels that Laura judges her and compares her to Mother— which is probably true."

"And Miles?"

"That's harder to explain," said Ann, with a tip of her head. "But honestly, I think that Bonnie *liked* Miles; you should have seen how she'd flirt with him. It was embarrassing. If you ask me, one of the reasons that Miles left to start up his own company was so he wouldn't have to deal with Bonnie chasing after him all the time."

"You never told me any of this!"

"Well, I'm not sure I'm right—it's only a hunch. But after Miles married Laura, Bonnie seemed to find fault with both of them. It sure sounded like jealousy to me."

"This is fascinating! I never thought of Bonnie as lusting after anyone, least of all Miles!"

"Yeah, well, I think it came as something of a surprise to Miles, too."

"Do you think your dad ever noticed?"

Ann shrugged. "Who knows? You know what he was like."

I nodded. Uncle Marty loved his business and his kids—in that order. I doubt if Bonnie was even in the top ten. Half of the time he ignored Bonnie; the other half he mocked her. Once the kids were grown, Bonnie was no longer necessary to Marty's plan. As a faithful Catholic—at least to the rules, if not the intent—divorce was not an option for Marty. He simply ignored her. I wondered if Marty would have cared if she'd run off. Probably if it were with anybody other than Miles, he wouldn't have.

"Well, I think it's a good idea to call him tomorrow and see if he can help by remembering any disgruntled employees from back then."

"And then what do we do?" she asked.

"Oh, I'm not suggesting that we *do* anything. I just thought that it might be worthwhile passing that information on to the police."

"Meaning that we should do everything we can to point the

police to the idea of an accomplice, someone outside the family," she said.

I tilted my head in acknowledgment. "Something like that. I don't think the police are going to ignore the family or the effect that Michael had on everyone. I just think it might be a good idea to give them more than one option."

Ann stared back at me, her eyes worried. "I'll call Scott and Miles first thing in the morning and then see if I can't get those records."

Up in my room, I called Peter. I ended up with his voice mail so I left him a brief message to call me when he had a chance. I didn't go into the details of my day. I couldn't begin to fathom how I would even phrase that message: *Hey, Peter, it's me. Funny thing happened today. Remember that guy Michael who embezzled all that money from Uncle Marty? Well, he was just found dead and buried under the old family pool. Anyway, hope all is well with you. Give me a call when you have a sec. Love ya!*

My call to Aunt Winnie was more successful. She answered on the second ring, and her surprise at hearing from me so soon gave way to stunned silence as I launched into my tale. When I finished, she said, "I always thought Michael was a little shit. I see that I wasn't alone in that sentiment."

"Any idea on who that might have been?"

"No. Both Marty and Reggie were besotted with him. I tried to warn Marty when I realized he was grooming Michael to take over the company, but he wouldn't listen to me. Nothing unusual there."

"I was wondering if Michael might have had a partner in the embezzlement scheme."

"And you think that person double-crossed him and killed him?" she asked.

"Something like that."

"It's not out of the realm of possibilities, that's for sure. What bothers me is that he was put under the pool. That's a little too close to home. And speaking of home, how is it there? How's Bonnie been?"

"Well, she's still leaving for her spa retreat as planned. No surprise there. Considering she planned a trip for the day after Uncle Marty's funeral, I don't think anyone expected that a little thing like Michael's body being discovered on the old property would deter her from her trip."

"Yes, well, her going might not be a surprise, but it still makes me want to smash my forehead on the table. Or better yet, smash *her* forehead on the table," said Aunt Winnie. "How's Ann holding up?"

"Pretty well. You know Ann. She's the kind of person the rest of us want to be when we grow up. She's had so much dumped on her and yet she still manages to keep it all together."

"Still, I'm glad that you can be there to help her. I imagine she's going to need all the help she can get over the next few days."

"I'm happy to stay here and do whatever I can," I said with what I hoped was the proper measure of humbleness.

Of course, Aunt Winnie saw right through *that*. "Oh, please," she said with a snort. "I know you want to help Ann, but let's be honest! You jumped at the excuse not to have to stay with Kit!"

"Well, I don't know about 'jumped' . . ." I began.

"Skipped, bounced, hopped. Whatever verb you prefer, you did it. I know it and you know it."

"Yeah, well, if you had to deal with Kit, Pauly, and the Jungle Room, you'd have done it, too," I muttered defensively.

"Oh, don't get me wrong! I'm not judging you—far from it. Just be aware that Kit probably knows it, too. Be nice. You know how she can get."

"Better than anyone," I said. "But you're right. I'll try to be nice."

"Good girl."

We talked a little more, and I hung up after promising to keep her posted on the case. Curling up onto my side, I thought about what Aunt Winnie had said about Kit. I made a sleepy resolution to be nicer.

Sleepy resolutions, I've found, are always the easiest.

Although I awoke as I had for the last few weeks—to the tinny clanging of my cell phone's alarm, this morning there was a marked difference. Gone was the sensation that I was in the middle of some safari gone terribly wrong. No monkeys swung above me, no elephants sat before me, no hippos peered out at me. And the ceiling! It was a glorious, crisp, *sensible* white; nary a blue-black tongue in sight.

Really, it's the little things in life that give you the most joy.

I rolled over and languidly stretched in the queen-size bed. I was in Uncle Marty's guest bedroom: a bright, airy room that faced the back of the house. I walked to the window and pulled back the white linen drape. It was another perfect autumnal day.

Azure skies, crisp leaves, and cool air greeted me. All that was missing to make it perfect was Peter. And a cup of hot coffee.

I couldn't have Peter, but at least I could have the coffee. Throwing on my robe and favorite (and only) well-worn bunny slippers, I headed down to the kitchen to start the coffee. Halfway down the stairs, I was greeted by the rich aroma of a pot already brewing. In the kitchen, I found Ann, up, showered, and busily bustling around. Scarlett was up as well and happily eating from her bowl. Actually, I should say she was happily eating from her Waterford bowl. I guess if my day started with breakfast out of a Waterford dish, I'd be happy, too.

"Morning!" Ann said. "Coffee's ready. I know you're not a morning person. Can I speak, or do I have to wait until you've had a cup?" She didn't wait for an answer and broke into a stream of questions. "Can I get you something to eat? We've got bagels, English muffins, and toast. How'd you sleep? Would you prefer a fruit salad? What's your pleasure? You take your coffee with cream and sugar right?"

"Uhh . . . good morning?" I said slowly. I knew something was up but, unfortunately, I *did* need my coffee before I could figure it out. "Don't worry about me, I can get my breakfast," I said, making my way to the breadbox. I picked out a poppy seed bagel and plopped it in the toaster. Ann hovered anxiously nearby. I wondered if she had mistakenly taken Bonnie's medication.

"Did you by chance take Bonnie's medication this morning?" I asked.

"No, why?"

"You're very chatty. And busy. And chatty. Speaking of Bonnie, is she up?"

"No. She usually doesn't arise before ten. Would you like some coffee?"

"Yes, please. But Ann, honestly, I can get all of this. You don't need to wait on me."

Ann ignored me, pouring a large amount of steaming coffee into a blue-and-white polka-dotted ceramic mug. Handing it to me, she said, "Cream? Sugar?"

I took the cup. "Enough already! You keep spoiling me like this and I'll never leave. I'll be like Sheridan Whiteside in *The Man Who Came to Dinner*."

"Somehow I can't picture you as an annoying guest."

"You haven't had my spaghetti yet," I reminded her, adding a liberal dose of both cream and sugar to my coffee, before taking a much-needed sip. The bagel popped up from the toaster and Ann rushed to get it.

"Ann! *Please*. I can get this! You don't need to wait on me." She put the bagel on a plate and handed it to me. It was then that I saw the worry in her face and belatedly remembered that, like me, Ann gets chatty when she's nervous. Taking the plate, I said, "What's wrong? What's happened?"

Her shoulders slumped. "I got a call from the police this morning," she said, wringing her hands. "Homicide. They want to send someone out here later today to get a statement or something. They want to talk with all of the family."

"Oh. Well, that's not too surprising. I mean, we knew that the police were going to treat this like a murder investigation. It's only natural that they would want to interview the family."

"I know. I'm just scared."

"Don't be. You've nothing to be afraid of. Everything will be just fine," I said confidently. "Did you get a chance to call Miles yet?"

"Yes, he and Laura were horrified to hear about Michael. They said they'd come over later."

"That's good. You can talk to him about past employees then. In the meantime, call Scott and see if you can get those employment records."

"Okay." Ann fell silent, tracing some invisible line along the counter with the tip of her finger. After a moment, she said, "Elizabeth, do you think you could be here when the police come? I could use some moral support. If it makes it easier on you, you could stay tonight as well. In fact, you can stay as long as you like. That is, if you think Kit won't mind."

"Absolutely, I'll be here and I'm sure Kit won't mind. She'll probably be happy to have a break from me and my 'pedestrian spaghetti.'"

We joked a little more, pretending that everything was fine even though we both knew it wasn't. Michael Barrow had been murdered and buried underneath the pool at the Reynoldses' house in St. Michaels *and* he had "allegedly" embezzled almost $1 million from the family's company before his death. Add to that a broken engagement with one sister and a drunken attack on another, and the picture became even grimmer.

Any hope I might have entertained about organizing my thoughts on Michael's murder during the day flew out the window within seconds of sliding into my desk chair. Sam Wallace, another of our staff writers and probably my closest friend in the office, sidled up to my desk. More than one female head turned his way as he did. Sam is hands down the best-looking guy in the office. Of course, the competition isn't too fierce; the guy in second place is balding with stubby fingers and a paunch. Still, with his broad shoulders and chiseled features, Sam's not too shabby. Over the years, Sam's friendship with me has prompted a few catty comments, but that's all we've ever been—friends. He's been happily dating a girl named Amanda for over a year. However, even though Sam has Amanda and I have Peter, that doesn't stop the office gossips from making their assumptions.

"Don't get too comfortable, Parker," Sam said with a smirk. "Hannigan's here. Apparently he's got some brilliant new idea. Come, the conference room awaits us."

Shit. Richard Hannigan—or Dickey as we subordinates call him when he is out of earshot—is the managing editor/owner of the paper. Once a month or so he appears unannounced armed with some new idea that he guarantees will revitalize the paper's "chi" (his word) and boost circulation. The staff is then herded much like cattle into the conference room Dickey commandeers whenever he visits, where we listen in rapt silence to this new idea. These sessions last anywhere from two to four hours. Lunch is *not* served.

My eyes darted from Sam to the conference room to the elevators. Did I have time to sneak out unnoticed and then call in sick? Before I could bolt, Sam anticipated my move. "Don't even try it, Parker. I will rat you out in a heartbeat. Sharon already knows I'm here. If I have to waste my day in there, then so do you." To prove his point, he called out, "Sharon? Elizabeth is here. We can get started when you're ready!"

"You bastard!" I said, laughing. I couldn't be mad at him; I would have done the exact same thing if the situation were reversed. Sam and I depended on each other during those meetings, mainly to help one another stay awake, although sometimes a quick sanity check was in order.

Grabbing my notebook, I trudged into the room behind Sam and took a seat at the large oval table next to him. While the rest of the staff filed in, I studied the walls for any new additions.

As Dickey used the conference room as his office, he decorated it as if it was his as well. Therefore, there was the standard vanity wall—or in Dickey's case, *three* vanity walls. For those unfamiliar with such walls, every inch is covered with framed pictures of celebrities from all fields—politics, entertainment, sports, you name it. Most of them have meaningless inscriptions scrawled across the bottom, such as "Dear Richard, You're the best! Keep up the great work!" Although most of the pictures are standard publicity head shots, Dickey does feature in a few of the pictures himself, "caught" at some function yakking it up with some bigwig. These pictures are usually the same, a group of people standing around at some cocktail party all grinning foolishly at the camera. Dickey's always easy to spot. First of all he's completely bald, five foot five and a good deal north of two hundred pounds. He's also usually on the edge of the crowd, looking like he just ran over in time for the shutter to snap, which, knowing Dickey, is probably the case.

However, the first time you see Dickey's vanity walls, you tend to be impressed. You believe that he actually knows all these people. I did, anyway, until we received a publicity still of Angelina Jolie along with a form letter thanking Dickey for his fan letter. Two days later I noticed the picture on the wall—

framed—complete with an inscription that Dickey presumably had added himself. Although it could have been signed by his secretary, Barbara Clark. For unknown reasons she adores Dickey and probably would give him her kidney if asked. I should also mention that Barbara lives alone with six cats.

Of course, I wasted no time relaying that story to Sam. Since then we've taken turns trying to sneak celebrity photos onto the walls—complete with inscriptions—to see if anyone notices. Last month, I hung a head shot of Steve Carell with the inscription, "Thanks for the inspiration!" Before that, Sam hung a picture of Renée Zellweger that read, "You complete me." So far no one has noticed either one.

Sitting at the head of the table, Dickey clapped his hands to get everyone's attention. "All right, everyone! Let's get started!" My immediate boss, Sharon, sat to his right. While Sharon isn't my favorite person, I did feel for her. Whenever Dickey descended on our office, her whole day went out the window. She sat quietly, her long face immobile and her gray-green eyes appearing resigned to her fate. Turning to her, Dickey said, "You're going to want to write this down." Sharon dutifully nodded at the blank tablet in front of her and held up her pen as evidence of her readiness. "Oh, right," said Dickey. "Well, everyone should write this down."

Around me everyone pulled out pads and pens in lackluster anticipation of Dickey's pronouncement. When he saw that we were all ready and waiting, he leaned forward, cleared his throat, and said, "Significant Human Beings." Then he sat back.

Nobody wrote anything down. Nobody spoke, either. Really, what could any of us say? Sharon was the first to venture a response. "Um, well, you certainly have our attention Di . . . er, Richard. How do you see us going forward with this exactly?"

Dickey beamed at her. Spreading his hands, palms outward, and eyeing us with almost maniacal pride he said, "Our new feature! Every week we'll run a story on some person, a Significant Human Being. You know, someone from the community who is making a difference. We'll run a picture of him or her—with me, of course—and then tell the story. I was thinking we could call it Significant Humans in Town." He punctuated each word by high-fiving the air in front of him.

"But wait, there's more," he added, like one of those TV commercials for a gadget that promises to change your life (but doesn't). "I have a brilliant idea for our first article. He was a great man who, sadly, recently passed, and who has a special connection to our little staff here." A nasty feeling of apprehension slid down my spine. Glancing at Dickey, I saw that he was beaming in my direction.

"It is my pleasure to announce that our first Significant Human in Town will be none other than the late Martin Reynolds, who as you all probably realize was the great-uncle of our very own Elizabeth Parker."

All heads swiveled my way. Shit, I thought with appropriate vulgarity, Uncle Marty was to be, as it later became known, our first SHIT.

By the time Dickey adjourned the meeting, my legs were numb, my deadlines were looming, and I was being pestered by the rest of the office for details on my dearly departed uncle. I spent the rest of the day hunched over my desk frantically trying to get everything done and deferring personal questions.

When I'd finally finished, my neck ached, my shoulders were sore, and my fingers were cramped from holding my red editing pen.

I sighed and rubbed my eyes. I was in a lousy mood and was finding it hard to cheer myself up. My apartment was still infested with mold. I was living with my bossy pregnant sister. I hated my job. My boyfriend was constantly traveling. Oh, and let's not forget—my extended family was wrapped up in (another) murder investigation. Given all that, Sam's invitation to get a drink and "shoot the shit" seemed a perfect idea. Glancing at my watch, I saw that I had enough time for a quick drink before I headed back to Ann's.

We headed for the DC Grill, a little bar/restaurant down the street from the office. It's not bad and it's not great; mainly it's convenient and sometimes that's all you need for success. Sam and I headed to the crowded oak bar and ordered. As I still had to drive to Ann's, I ordered a Diet Coke. Sam opted for a beer.

When our drinks came, I raised mine. "What shall we toast to? SHIT, my Uncle Marty, or both?"

Sam laughed. "I vote we toast Dickey. But don't toast my glass. It's bad luck to toast with a nonalcoholic drink."

"Who told you that?"

"I don't know, it's just one of those things people don't do."

"By 'people,' I take it we're referring to drunken frat boys?"

"Hey, drunken frat boys are people, too," he said, pretending to look hurt.

"Yes, I believe that is the literal translation of Alpha Gamma Delta."

Sam laughed at me. "That's a sorority, not a fraternity."

"Does it matter?"

"I take it you didn't pledge."

I shook my head and took a sip of my Diet Coke. "Nope. I went to an all-girls Catholic school. They don't need sororities. It's already one big giant sorority, complete with hazing and drunken pledges to be friends forever."

Sam cocked an eyebrow at me. "You seem jaded."

I dipped my head in acknowledgment. "Another by-product of the all-girl Catholic school experience."

Sam started to say something when his attention was caught by someone behind my left shoulder. From his frankly appraising expression, it was an attractive someone.

"Who are you gaping at?" I asked, turning to scan the room. "Need I remind you that you are dating a lovely girl named Amanda?" While there were several attractive women in the bar, I instinctively knew which woman held his attention. She wore a backless tangerine dress that hugged every one of her curves. Her shapely tanned legs were supported by four-inch pumps, the kind with that sexy ankle strap. Her glossy black hair hung in heavy waves down her Nautilus-defined back. I knew it was a Nautilus-defined back, because I knew the owner of the back. It was none other than my cousin Reggie.

"That's my cousin Reggie," I said.

"Oh, yeah? I can see the resemblance," said Sam with false politeness. I laughed outright at the absurdity of the idea. "Who's that with her?" he asked. "Her husband?"

"No, she's not married. At least she's not currently married. That's a status that frequently changes with her, though." I craned to get a better look at the man on whose brawny arm Reggie now hung. He was tall, tan, and muscular. His dark hair was cut short, as was his beard. He was also no one I'd ever seen before. However, from the way they were talking, this did not appear to be a casual first meeting at a bar. His head was bent down low to hers. From their somber expressions, their conversation appeared anything but casual. My cell phone went off just then, preventing me from catching Reggie's eye and waving hello. It was Peter. I turned my body toward the bar and pressed the phone against my ear so I could hear better.

"Hey, there. Where are you?" he said.

"I'm out having a drink. Then I'm going to head over to Ann's. You wouldn't believe the day I had. Dickey took over the day with another one of his harebrained ideas."

"You have my sympathies. Who are you out with?"

"Sam. So get this—Dickey wants us to write a fluff piece each month of some local bigwig. Guess who he picked! Uncle Marty, that's who! He's got this really stupid acronym for it, too. He's calling it Significant Humans in Town. So it's basically SHIT."

There was the briefest pause before he answered. "Sounds pretty dumb. Well, I don't want to hold you up. I just thought I'd call and say hi. I've got to run back into a meeting. I'll call you later, okay?"

"Oh, okay. I'll talk to you later then. I love you."

"Love you, too," he said, but he said it kind of fast. I hung up wondering if Peter could actually be upset that I was out with Sam. I pushed the idea away, dismissing it as silly. Peter knew we were just friends; after all, Sam was the guy I went with to see those chick flicks that Peter couldn't stomach. Looking back up for Reggie, I saw that both she and her date had left. The weird thing was, she would have had to walk right past me to get out. Had she not wanted to interrupt my phone conversation with Sam, or had she simply not wanted to be seen? Reggie had never been unfriendly toward me before, leaving me to wonder if her avoidance had more to do with the man than with me. God, I hoped he wasn't married.

Traffic being what it was, it took me almost an hour to get to Uncle Marty's house. Ann answered my knock almost instantly. "How are you doing?" I asked as I stepped into the foyer. She was wearing black tailored pants and a lightweight lavender cashmere sweater. This color normally looked great on her. However, today it would take more than a complementary hue from her color palette to liven up her ghostly complexion.

She shrugged. "As well as can be expected, I guess. I got a message that the detective in charge of the case will be here around seven thirty. I called Reggie and Frances and told them everything. They said they'd be here to talk to him."

"I actually just saw Reggie, but I don't think she saw me," I said. "How did she take the news?"

Ann shook her head. "I couldn't tell, to be honest. She got very quiet. I'll have a better idea once I see her."

I glanced at my watch; it was a quarter to seven.

"Come on," said Ann, "help me get the living room ready. I figured we could all sit in there."

Within minutes, Ann and I had made what little adjustments were necessary. We brought in a few extra chairs and arranged them around the coffee table. Once done, Ann turned to me and said, "Do you think I should put out cheese and crackers or anything?"

I thought about it. "I don't think so. A, we want this over as quickly as possible; no need to encourage the police to linger; B, we don't want to appear like we're not taking this seriously; and C, this isn't a social meeting."

"Agreed," she said. "God, I could use a drink, but I doubt that's a good idea. I should have my wits about me for this."

"I'll tell you what," I said, giving her arm a friendly squeeze. "Once the police leave, I'll take you out and buy you all the drinks you want."

"Deal," she said with a faint smile.

There was a brief knock on the door before it swung open. It was Reggie. There was nary a hint of distress on her perfectly made-up face. Looking calm and cool, she was wearing the same tangerine dress I saw her in earlier. The only difference was that she had pulled her hair back into a smooth, tight bun. She even made that look sexy.

Scarlett ran excitedly to the door. However, seeing that it was Reggie, she turned and walked away. Scarlett did not care for Reggie. Inasmuch as Reggie sneered when she saw the little dog, I assumed that the feeling was mutual. After a perfunctory greeting to me and Ann, Reggie said, "So I take it Bonnie went on her silly spa retreat anyway?"

"Yes," said Ann. "I drove her to the airport this morning. She . . . she didn't seem overly concerned about any of this."

Reggie scoffed. "She wouldn't be overly concerned if the house fell down around her, just so long as it didn't interfere with her five o'clock martini. Is Frances here yet?"

"No," said Ann, "but I expect her any minute. I thought we could use the living room for when the police come."

Reggie nodded. "Right. Well, I may as well make myself comfortable. Is there any wine in the fridge, Ann?"

"Uh, yes, there's some Chardonnay. Do you really think it's a good idea to have a drink, though?"

"Why in the name of God shouldn't I have a drink? Hell, if there was ever a time when one *was* warranted, I think it would be when your ex-fiancé turns up dead and buried under the family pool."

"I have to say, I think that's a fair point," I said.

"Exactly," Reggie said, nodding in my direction. Without a word, Ann turned in the direction of the kitchen, presumably to get Reggie her wine.

"Lord," said Reggie, "whatever are the police going to think? You know they're going to think one of us did it."

"Not necessarily," I said, more out of politeness than any real conviction.

"Well, if they don't, then they have no imagination." She turned on her heel and glided into the living room. With almost feline grace, she made herself comfortable on the couch.

A confident knock sounded on the door, and it opened. It was Frances and Scott. Frances was wearing one of her standard A-line tweed skirts with a red blouse. Scott was casually dressed in jeans and a T-shirt. Unlike Reggie, neither presented a calm façade. "Dear God," said Frances when she saw me, her voice shrill, "this is just like a nightmare! Who would have ever believed that all these years Michael was actually *dead*!" Next to her, Scott did not speak. He stood awkwardly with his hands jammed into the pockets of his jeans, his body tense. "Is Reggie here?" Frances asked.

I nodded and gestured to the living room.

"Reggie, I just can't believe this," said Frances, rushing over to her sister. "How are *you*? Are you all right?"

Reggie sighed with annoyance. "Of course, I'm all right, Frances. Please don't be melodramatic. We already have enough drama as it is. Besides, you seem to forget, *I* broke it off with *him*. It's not as if he left behind some lovesick pale copy of the girl he loved. Besides, that was *eight* years and *three* marriages ago."

"Yes, but he's dead!" Frances said. "You can't be happy that he's dead!"

Reggie rolled her eyes in disgust. "Frances, I didn't say I was *happy* that he was dead. I'm just not crying into my hankie. There's a difference."

Frances looked unconvinced but said no more. There was a loud, officious knock on the door, immediately followed by a collective intake of breath around me. The police, it would seem, were here. Frances and Reggie looked at me, while Scott stared at the floor. Apparently I had just been appointed official greeter.

I am by no means someone my friends would describe as being calm under pressure, but I was still taken aback at the surge of adrenaline that swiftly raced through my veins. With shaking hands, I grabbed the cut-glass doorknob and swung open the door.

Before me stood one woman and one man. The former was in a crisp, blue uniform, her light blond hair tucked underneath her hat. I couldn't tell you much else about her other than the fact that she had blue eyes and a trim figure, because my real focus was on the second person.

He hadn't changed much. No gray marred his thick, dark hair. From the way his Burberry overcoat clung to his broad shoulders, he appeared to be as lean and fit as ever. Seeing me, a flash of recognition appeared in his blue-green eyes, but no welcoming smile accompanied it.

Before I could speak, I heard Ann approaching from behind. Turning, I saw her just as she saw him. The color drained from her face and her grip on the glass of wine tightened, turning her knuckles white.

With a strained whisper, she got out his name. "Joe!"

CHAPTER 7

Surprizes are foolish things. The pleasure is not enhanced, and the inconvenience is often considerable.

—EMMA

Joe's response to hearing Ann utter his name was a brief tightening of the muscles in his jaw. With an overly polite nod in her direction, he said, "Actually, it's Detective Muldoon now."

Ouch. It was clear that even after all these years, Joe hadn't forgiven Ann. I glanced at her to see how she was taking all this. From the stricken look on her face, I deduced not very well. Ann blinked and pressed her lips together tightly, her face etched in silent misery.

I stuck out my hand, "Hello, Joe . . . er . . . Detective Muldoon. I don't know if you remember me, but I'm—"

"Elizabeth Parker," Joe said, briefly taking my hand in his and giving it a formal shake. "Of course, I remember you." Turning to the officer next to him, he said, "This is Sergeant Erica Beal."

I nodded at the sergeant. Scarlett gave a happy bark and jumped up and began to paw at Joe's leg. He looked down at her in confusion. "Scarlett, go away," I said, nudging the dog away. Scarlett ignored me and began to lick Joe's pant leg. I bent over and scooped up the dog while she squirmed in protest. "Scarlett, you are no lady," I said before looking back to Joe. "Well, the family is all here." I gestured toward the living room. "I'll show you in." Leading them into the room, I wondered what Reggie's and Frances's reactions to seeing Joe again after all these years would be.

"Everyone," I said, "this is Sergeant Beal and Detective Muldoon."

Reggie glanced up, her expression calm. However, seeing Joe, her eyes quickly darted to where Ann still stood in the foyer. When she returned her attention to Joe, there was a wary expression in her eyes. With the briefest nod of her head, she said, "Detective Muldoon. Sergeant Beal."

Frances was less composed. "Joe? Is that really you? Why, you've hardly changed a bit! You're a detective now?"

"As you see," he said.

Scott moved toward him, his hand outstretched. "Joe, it's good to see you again."

Joe shook the proffered hand. Beside him, Sergeant Beal's face was unreadable. She didn't seem particularly surprised to find that her detective was on such familiar terms with the family. I wondered just how much Joe had told her.

"I'm sorry to have to disturb you," he said now, "especially so soon after your father's funeral." He paused. "I was sorry to hear of his passing. You have my condolences."

I have to admit, hearing Joe say that aroused my darkest forebodings. Joe *hated* Uncle Marty. And to be fair, it wasn't without reason. Uncle Marty did everything he could to make

Joe feel unwelcome and unworthy to be a member of the Reynolds family. But all those years ago Joe had an open face that was easy to read. However, the way Joe offered his condolences just now, you would have thought that he really had liked Uncle Marty. It didn't bode well, in my humble opinion.

Seeing Ann still standing in the foyer helplessly clutching Reggie's glass of wine, I said, "Let me go get some coffee for everyone." I hurried out, still clutching Scarlett in one hand, and firmly grabbed Ann by the elbow with the other and steered her to the kitchen.

"It's Joe!" she said numbly. "Jesus, I can't believe this. After all these years, he's here. In this house. Oh, my God." Frantically running her hands through her hair, she tried to see her reflection in the chrome toaster. "I look like shit!" she wailed.

"Would you put the toaster down? You do not look like shit," I said, as I deposited Scarlett on the floor and then yanked open cupboards in search of the coffee. As I said this, though, I realized that to a certain extent Ann's looks had suffered somewhat since her breakup with Joe. For lack of a better phrase, she'd lost her glow. When Joe left, a part of Ann had faded away. As no other man had ever come close to Joe in her estimation, the glow had never returned. However, this obviously wasn't the time to address that. "Pull yourself together. Where the hell is the coffee?" I asked.

"Top shelf, left," she said automatically. "Did you see the way he looked at me? Like he was looking *through* me or something."

"He was just trying to be professional, that's all," I said, quickly pulling down the package of whole beans, which then slipped from my hands. The bag landed with a crash on the kitchen floor, sending tiny brown beans flying everywhere.

"Oh, crap, crap crap!" I said as I scrambled to clean up the mess. Seeing Ann's stricken face, I joked, "Hey, look! The cops are here and I spilled the beans!"

Either Ann didn't hear me or was politely ignoring me. It was probably the latter, because you have to admit, it *was* a funny joke. "Now, I know I said no crackers and cheese," I said, as I gathered all the beans together and dumped them into the trash can, "but I've changed my mind. How about you get out a platter while I get the coffee going?"

There was no answer as I scooped fresh beans into the grinder. "Ann?" I said, looking over my shoulder at her. She was still standing where I'd left her. Her head tipped back, she was rapidly draining the glass of wine. "Or you could just chug the wine," I said. "Yeah, that's a better idea. Why don't you do that and I'll get the cheese."

Once the coffee was made and Ann had finished her liquid courage, we emerged from the kitchen, coffee and cheese and crackers in tow. Scarlett tagged right along and ran straight to Joe, who was sitting on one of the chairs, his coat off and neatly folded on his lap. He was wearing a blue suit that fit him like the proverbial glove. Scarlett plopped herself down directly in front of him and barked happily. Sergeant Beal stretched out her hand and attempted to pet Scarlett, but Scarlett ignored her. Scarlett, like her namesake, preferred the company of men. Joe reluctantly scratched Scarlett behind the ears.

I placed the crackers and cheese on the table while Ann poured the coffee. Nobody spoke. Finally, Joe pulled back from Scarlett and said, "Well, you know why we're here. Michael Barrow's body was discovered earlier this week under the foundation of the pool of the house your family used to own in St. Michaels. I don't have the medical examiner's final report yet, but it seems pretty clear that he died from blunt force trauma to the head."

"Could he have fallen into the hole and struck his head?" Frances asked hopefully.

"As I said, I am still awaiting the medical examiner's report," came the reply. "I wondered if you all could tell me when you saw him last."

"Are we under suspicion?" asked Scott.

"Right now, we're just collecting information," Joe replied. "Ms. Reynolds," he said, turning to Reggie, "why don't we start with you. I believe you were engaged to the deceased."

Reggie smoothed out her dress and uncrossed her shapely legs. Sergeant Beal's eyes narrowed, and I noticed she glanced at Joe to gauge his reaction. I wondered just how close Joe was with Sergeant Beal. "Actually," said Reggie, "it's Ms. Ames now."

"I'm sorry. *Ms. Ames,* could you tell me the last time you saw Mr. Barrow?" asked Joe.

Reggie responded promptly. "The last time any of us saw him was at my father's Fourth of July party eight years ago. It was at that party that I told him I didn't think we should go through with the marriage."

"When was this, exactly?"

"Just after the fireworks ended. I told him and then I went to bed."

"And what was the reason for the breakup, if you don't mind me asking?" Joe asked.

Reggie shifted slightly. "His drinking, for one. It was getting completely out of hand."

Joe nodded. "I see. And what was his reaction to your ending things?"

Reggie paused. "Well, he was upset, naturally. He begged me to reconsider. I told him to go to bed and sleep it off. I said that we could talk more in the morning, but by that time, he was gone. I assumed that his pride was hurt and he'd left for his house. When I didn't hear from him, I figured that he was waiting for me to call. Of course, I didn't."

"And you didn't wonder why you never heard from him?" Joe asked, with a dubious expression.

"Well, no. I just thought he was pouting, but within a week or so afterward, we discovered that Michael had embezzled almost a million dollars from Daddy. We all assumed that he had hightailed it somewhere. So no, I never wondered why I never heard from him," said Reggie.

"Yes, I have the copy of the report your father submitted regarding the embezzlement," said Joe. "Did anyone see Mr. Barrow after that Fourth of July party?"

We all shook our heads.

"Don't forget, Joe," said Frances, "you were at that party, too. With Ann," she added unnecessarily. Beside me, Ann flushed crimson. Joe cleared his throat. Sergeant Beal shot Joe a searching look.

"Yes, thank you, Mrs. Phillips," Joe said. Turning to Ann, he said, "An . . . excuse me, Miss Reynolds. It is still Miss Reynolds?"

he asked. Ann gave a quick nod. Joe continued, "Did you have any contact with Mr. Barrow that might be relevant?"

Ann didn't answer right away. I knew she was wondering if she should reveal Michael's attempted attack on her. After a moment, she said, "He was extremely drunk. But I don't really have any information other than that."

Joe regarded her silently. At one time, Joe and Ann were so in tune with each other they could practically read each other's minds. I found myself fervently hoping that Joe had lost that ability. After a brief pause, he said, "I see." Clearing his throat, he continued, "Did any of you have any contact with Mr. Barrow at the party? Or notice anything out of the ordinary?"

"I had a couple of drinks with him," Scott said cautiously.

Joe nodded at him encouragingly. "And . . . ?"

Scott looked down at the carpet before answering. "And nothing, really. We had a few beers on the back patio and then . . . I went to bed. Michael was still outside when I went inside."

"Any idea what time this conversation was?" Joe asked.

Scott shot Joe an incredulous look. "Are you kidding me? It was eight years ago!"

"Fair enough. Was it a friendly conversation?"

Beside her husband, Frances stiffened. Scott paused. "Friendly enough, I guess. I don't remember the details." Frances shifted in her chair and glanced quickly at Scott and then at her lap. Was I missing something?

"You were staying at the house, I take it?" Joe said.

"Yes," said Scott. "We all were."

"Including Michael?"

Scott nodded. "Yes. Although I remember he wasn't there in

the morning. His car was gone. I just assumed that he'd already left."

"When did you leave?"

"The next morning, the fifth. We all did," Scott said, looking around the room. "Construction was to start on the pool and . . ." Scott abruptly stopped talking as he realized what must have happened.

Joe looked at the rest of us. "Did any of you see Mr. Barrow the next morning?"

We all shook our heads. "As I told you," said Reggie, "no one saw Michael after that party."

Joe leaned back in his chair, the barest of smiles on his lips. "Although my mother always told me never to argue with a lady, I think I'm going to have to disagree with you there."

The doorbell rang, breaking the sudden tension Joe's words caused. Ann jumped from her chair and hurried to open the door. Scarlett abandoned her post at Joe's feet and ran after her. It was Miles and Laura Carswell. A former marine, Miles had stayed in excellent shape, so much so that those who met him thought him a good decade younger than his actual age of seventy-three. To me, he looked like Cary Grant in his later years: round pleasant face, snow-white hair, and black-framed glasses. Laura was an elegant woman with brown eyes and short brown hair that was flecked with gray ("You wouldn't believe how much it costs to realistically 'fleck' one's hair," she once told me). Her clear complexion and high cheekbones gave her a more youthful appearance than her actual age of sixty-nine.

Scarlett's yips of excitement increased upon seeing Miles. He bent to pet her while Laura focused on Ann. Seeing her flushed face, Laura stepped into the foyer, her brown eyes filled with concern. "Ann!" she said. "Are you all right?"

A noise from the living room alerted her to our presence. Turning our way, her eyes landed on Joe. Her mouth pulling into a faint frown, she said, "Good Lord. Is that Joe?"

Eyeing Laura with a cool, appraising glance, Joe merely said, "Mrs. Carswell. We meet again."

CHAPTER 8

An occasional memento of past folly, however
painful, might not be without use.
—NORTHANGER ABBEY

ILES STEPPED FORWARD. "Hello, Joe. I'm not sure if
you remember me . . ."

"Mr. Carswell," Joe replied with a genuine smile; seeing it was
a brief reminder of his former self. Joe stood up and extended his
hand. "Of course, I remember you. It's good to see you, though
I'm sorry it's under these circumstances. How have you been?"

"Pretty well, pretty well," Miles replied. Miles had always
gotten along great with Joe and, in fact, had been his strongest
champion to Uncle Marty. But as close as Miles and Uncle Marty
were, Miles still couldn't convince him of Joe's merits. Eight years
ago, Joe was just starting out on the force. He was, in Uncle
Marty's words, "nothing but a blue-collar cop," and as such he
viewed the match as "degrading" for both him and his daughter. It didn't help that Laura agreed with Uncle Marty. Laura
adored Ann—just as she had adored her mother. She wanted
the best for Ann and, unfortunately, that didn't include a marriage to Joe at age twenty-two. Ann found herself opposed by

both her father and the woman she looked to almost as a mother.

"We were told that Michael's body was found on the St. Michaels property. Don't tell me that you are on this case," said Miles.

Joe nodded. "I am, sir. I'm a detective, now."

Miles smiled. "Congratulations. I always knew you'd go places."

Joe nodded briefly, the compliment seeming to remind him of those who didn't have such confidence. Ann stared at the floor, clearly uncomfortable.

Joe deflected the awkwardness of the situation by introducing his associate. "This is Sergeant Beal," he said. "Sergeant Beal, this is Mr. and Mrs. Carswell."

"Pleased to meet you," she said.

"And you as well," Miles said with a smile. "My, but sergeants have definitely gotten prettier since my day." Sergeant Beal smiled coyly at this and threw a challenging glance at Joe. Yup, I thought, she likes him. And if I had to interpret that glance she gave him, I would say she wonders why he doesn't like her.

"Well, we might as well sit down," Miles said. Joe moved aside so he and Laura could find a seat. Ann came and sat next to me. Her hands were nervously twitching. I reached over and grabbed one, giving it a reassuring squeeze.

"What do you need to know from us?" Miles asked.

"From what we know so far, it appears Mr. Barrow died of blunt force trauma to the head. His remains were found under the foundation of the pool. We are trying to gather information as to when he was last seen. Do you remember when you last saw him?"

Miles frowned as he thought over Joe's question. "I think it must have been at Marty's Fourth of July party," he said. "Is that right?" he asked, looking quizzically at Laura.

She shook her head apologetically. "I couldn't tell you, Miles. Remember, I was out of town that weekend, visiting my mother."

"Oh, yes, I'd forgotten. Well, I think it was at the party." Miles looked over to where Reggie sat. "I believe it was soon after that that we learned the money was missing." Reggie nodded. Miles continued, "I remember thinking that it was a good thing I was out of town when I found out what he'd done because I'd probably have . . ." Miles abruptly stopped.

"Killed him?" said Joe.

Miles gave a rueful smile. "Well, that's a stupid figure of speech under the circumstances. But I probably would have done my best to mar that pretty face of his. You've no idea what his theft did to the company. I left the day after the party and was in New York for two weeks for a meeting with a potential client. By the time I got back, everything was in utter disarray."

"I understand it was a large amount—one million dollars?" said Joe.

I forced myself to take a sip of coffee mainly to hide my wholly inappropriate smirk. Every time they mentioned that amount all I could hear was Dr. Evil's voice from *Austin Powers*.

Miles nodded. "It was all the worse because it was Michael who took it. Marty loved that boy like a son; he thought he was the perfect pick to run the company one day."

At this, Frances made a noise and Scott shifted uncomfortably in his seat. Miles glanced in their direction, wincing slightly as he realized his gaffe. Joe noticed as well and quickly asked Miles, "Why were you not considered to take over, sir?"

"Oh, Marty knew that I was going to branch out by then. I had decided to start my own landscaping business. We would still partner for various projects, but I'd no longer work for Reynolds Construction."

"This was an amiable break, then?" Joe asked.

"Perfectly. In fact, Marty was responsible for setting up the meeting in New York back then and later for steering several clients my way."

"Did you talk to Michael at the party?"

"Of course, but about what, I really couldn't say. Nothing important—just chitchat."

"And was that the last time you saw him?"

Miles nodded. "Yes. As I said, I had to go to New York City the next day for a business trip. I was gone about two weeks. Laura called and told me what had happened, both with Reggie ending the engagement and with Michael's embezzlement."

Joe nodded. "And how about you, Mrs. Carswell," Joe said. "Do you recall the last time you saw or spoke with Michael?"

"I believe that it was the week before the party. I had lunch with Reggie and Michael. We discussed some of the details of the wedding. They were going to be married at the house, on the back lawn. We'd ordered the bridal canopy and were discussing the flowers for it. I remember that Reggie wanted it covered in pink and white roses." She glanced over at Reggie with a melancholy smile. Reggie studied her manicure, pretending not to notice Laura's look. "Anyway," Laura continued, "everything seemed fine. I had no idea what Michael had done or what he was planning. It came as an utter shock to me. I can't tell you how devastated I was to learn the truth. Michael had us all fooled."

"Yes, it must have been upsetting to learn that your instinct was wrong," said Joe to no one in particular.

Laura flushed. Beside her, Miles said, "Easy, Joe."

"My apologies," said Joe, suddenly standing up. "Well, I think I have everything I need for now. I'll be in touch with you again once I get the coroner's report. And of course, I'll want to interview Mrs. Reynolds when she returns from her trip." With the barest glance in Ann's direction, Joe said, "Again, please accept my condolences. I'm sorry that this investigation must take place so soon after your loss."

Ann stood to walk him to the door, but Joe anticipated her. "No need to disturb yourself further on my account. I'll see myself out." He turned and headed for the door. Sergeant Beal jumped to her feet and hurried after him. Seconds later, we heard the front door open and shut.

There was a collective sigh of relief at their departure. No one spoke at first; no one looked at each other. It was Reggie who broke the awkward silence. "Ann," she said, "you really are a crap hostess. You forgot my glass of wine. Now, if you please, I think you'd better bring me the whole bottle."

CHAPTER 9

Where so many hours have been spent in
convincing myself that I am right, is there not
some reason to fear I may be wrong?
—SENSE AND SENSIBILITY

I FOLLOWED ANN into the kitchen, where she immediately collapsed limply into a chair. "Oh, God!" she moaned into her hands. "He hates me! Hates me!"

"He doesn't hate you," I said, as I pulled out a chilled bottle of wine from the refrigerator. "He's just proud. You didn't expect him to act any way else, did you? Here, open this." I handed her the bottle. "I'll get the glasses."

I reached into the cabinet behind me and took down several glasses. By the time I'd turned around again, Ann had eased the cork out and was in the process of pouring the contents down her throat.

"Hey!" I yelled, as I grabbed the bottle away from her. "What the hell are you doing?"

Ann grabbed the bottle back. "Trying to get drunk, thank you very much. Now if you'll stop interfering, I'd like to get back on task." She took another sip, but I grabbed the bottle back again before she could drink any more.

"Would you please stop doing that?" she said, trying to snatch the bottle back. "It's really annoying!"

I held the bottle away from her. "Ann, you don't drink. Not like that, anyway. You are the personification of a lightweight. Need I remind you of what happened at Reggie's second wedding? You had three drinks and ended up puking in the bathroom for half an hour."

"That's not true," Ann said with a haughty lift of her chin, "I threw up after I caught sight of myself in the mirror wearing that hideous bridesmaid dress."

She had a point. Reggie had hired some famous designer (who I dearly hoped was in a different line of work now) to create her dress and the coordinating bridesmaid dresses. Hideous didn't even begin to describe the resulting creation. Think dominatrix meets Scarlett O'Hara—in strip-pole pink. If I recall correctly, there were even little chains on the corset portion of the dress.

"Well, I'm not letting you get drunk," I said firmly. "It's not going to solve anything."

Ann rested her head in her hands. "I never said it would solve anything," she mumbled. "It just would let me forget for a while that he hates me."

I put the bottle down (well out of her reach) and went over to her. Gently putting my hand on her back, I said, "He doesn't hate you, Ann. But you didn't expect him to come here all smiles, did you? Besides, he didn't come on a social visit. He had to keep it impersonal and professional."

"Well, he succeeded at that, all right. He was nothing *but* impersonal and professional. In fact, if I didn't know otherwise,

I'd say that he didn't even recognize me. He treated me like he would a complete stranger!"

"Ann . . ."

"We used to be able to practically read each other's thoughts," she continued in a soft voice, almost to herself. "We could just look at one another and *know* what the other was thinking. But tonight . . . it was like staring at a blank wall. I don't know him anymore."

"Ann, I know this is hard, and I don't want to sound insensitive, but I think we have a bigger problem here than how Joe feels about you."

She stiffened at my words. "You're right. I'm being silly. I almost forgot. Michael."

"Yes, Michael." Trying to lighten the mood a bit, I added, "Some people are always troublesome, I guess. Even in death."

Ann gave a wry smile. "Yeah, well, that would be Michael." She stared at the table for a moment and then said, "The police think one of us did it, don't they?"

"I . . . um, I . . . think . . ." The words caught and I couldn't finish.

"Yeah." She sighed. "That's what I thought."

By the time we returned to the living room, Frances was holding court, talking loudly and gesticulating with enthusiasm. Reggie was tapping her well-shod foot in obvious annoyance. Seeing the wine, she muttered, "Oh, thank God," and practically leaped out of her chair. Grabbing the bottle out of my hand and a glass out of Ann's, Reggie quickly served herself.

With a half glance over her shoulder at Frances, she said in a low voice, "I swear to God, if she doesn't shut up, I'm going to belt her."

"Honestly, it's been so long since I thought about Michael," Frances was saying, oblivious of Reggie's annoyance. "But I have to say, I never liked him. There was something about his face—his eyes were too close together, for one thing. I tried to warn Daddy at the time, but of course no one wanted to listen to *me*."

I glanced over at Ann in time to see her roll her eyes heavenward. Reggie raised her glass to her mouth—and kept it there a very long time. Taking the bottle back from Reggie, I offered wine to the others.

"Well, he had *me* fooled," said Miles after accepting a glass. "I was never more surprised than when I found out what he'd done." He glanced down at his hands, his face etched with regret. "I always felt that I let Marty down somehow. I should have noticed what was going on."

Laura grabbed his hand; it looked almost childlike against Miles's large and calloused one. "This is *not* your fault," she said firmly. "No one suspected Michael of being a thief." Frances shifted in her seat and appeared to be about to speak, when Laura shot her a quelling look and repeated, "No one."

Frances sniffed and turned her face, but at least she took the hint and didn't reiterate her ludicrous claim.

"What I can't believe is that he's dead," said Laura. "Murdered, in fact!"

Frances twisted her lips. "Well, I can't say *I'm* surprised now that I've thought about it. He was a criminal. Criminals usually come to a bad end. And to think that Joe is in charge of it all!" Looking to Ann, she asked, "Did you know he was going to be on the case?"

"No. I was as surprised as anyone."

"He hasn't changed much, has he?"

"No," said Ann, "he hasn't," her face starting to crumple.

Laura saw this and quickly changed the subject. "Well, what I wonder is, who do you think could have killed Michael?"

Frances shrugged. "He probably had an accomplice or something. Maybe Michael tried to double-cross him or something."

"I wonder if the police will ever find the killer," said Scott. "I mean, *can* they after all this time?"

"I doubt it," answered Frances.

"Well, in any case, I think we should consult with a lawyer," said Miles. "I would imagine that we haven't seen the last of the police."

"Miles, don't be absurd!" Frances scoffed. "We don't need a lawyer! No one who knows us would ever think that one of us could have had anything to do with this!"

"I agree. As soon as we hire a lawyer, we'll look guilty," added Reggie. Frances nodded in agreement.

"I don't know," said Scott, "I think Miles has a point. It's a precautionary move and I don't necessarily think it indicates guilt."

"But we're Reynoldses!" said Frances. "Our family has an excellent reputation. That must count for something."

"Frances!" Ann burst out. "Our name might mean 'quality construction' to some, but that hardly translates to inculpability!"

"Girls! This isn't getting us anywhere!" said Miles, raising his hands. "I think we need to face the very real possibility that the police are going to want to ask all of us a lot more questions and will view us with more than a little suspicion. Having a lawyer on hand to guide us will only help us, not hurt us."

"I agree," Scott said, to the obvious annoyance of Frances, who crossed her arms across her chest and shot him a mutinous look.

"Why don't I call Stephen Guilford?" said Miles. Stephen Guilford had been the family lawyer for years.

Scott nodded. "He's a good guy. He'll know what to do. He was really good with Reggie's first divorce."

"And her second," added Frances.

"And her third," said Ann with a smile.

Reggie good-naturedly rolled her eyes. "And no doubt one day he'll be wonderful with my fourth. Point taken, ladies."

"So I'll call him in the morning?" asked Miles.

"Fine. Call him. But the publicity is going to be awful. I just know it," said Reggie. "The *Post* is going to have a field day with this. I can see the headline now: *Is D.C.'s Best Wedding Planner a Black Widow?*" Looking over at Ann, she added, "I guess hindsight is twenty-twenty, but it might have been a good thing if you'd stayed with Joe after all. At least we'd have someone in the police department on our side."

"Reggie, don't be absurd," snapped Laura. "Ann made the right decision and you know it."

Next to me, Ann bent her head low and said nothing.

CHAPTER 10

It was a delightful visit;—perfect,
in being much too short.

—EMMA

N HOUR LATER, the rest of the family left Ann and me surrounded by dirty dishes and empty glasses. Scarlett, who clearly had no Mammy to advise her to eat like a bird in front of others, freely gobbled up the scraps of food left behind. Miles had promised to call Stephen Guilford in the morning, although Frances and Reggie remained unconvinced of the wisdom of that plan. Pouring the last of the coffee into Ann's cup, I said, "How are you holding up?"

After taking a sip, she said, "I don't even begin to know how to answer that. It's bad enough to have to remember that horrible night with Michael, but then to have to process the fact that someone killed him and buried him under our pool! And who's in charge of it all? Joe!"

"Yeah. I guess it was kind of a stupid question. I was thinking, though, about something Scott said. He mentioned that Michael's car was gone the morning after the party."

"So?"

I paused. "Well, I just wondered what happened to it. Did

Michael leave and then come back another way, or did someone else drive the car away?"

Ann considered the question. "Does it matter?"

"I think it might. Did his car ever turn up?"

Ann frowned at her coffee cup. "I believe the police eventually found it at the airport in Baltimore." She nodded as if to confirm this fact. "Yes, they found it at BWI. I remember thinking that the only reason Michael would have left that car behind was if he'd left the country. Do you remember it? He had that Mercedes. I've never seen a man love a car so much. I wouldn't be surprised if he rubbed it nightly with a diaper."

I did remember the car. It was a C-class Mercedes, which a boyfriend of mine at the time had referred to as a "starter Mercedes." It was perfect for Michael. Image was all-important to him, and he thought that his car labeled him as an up-and-comer in the world. I remember laughing at the time at how wrapped up into cars guys can get. All I noticed about the car was that it was black. Of course, men probably would say the same thing about women and shoes. Silly men.

"Well, Michael obviously never left the country," I said. "I guess whoever killed him drove his car to the airport to make everyone think that. The question is, *when* did that person put it there?"

"I don't see how the timing really matters," Ann said.

"It might not, but there are only a few options. One, Michael left St. Michaels the morning of the fifth and then returned later for some unknown reason. Two, Michael left on the fifth, was killed, and *then* brought back. Three, Michael never left St. Michaels the morning after the party, meaning . . ."

"Someone who was at the party must have driven it away," finished Ann, realization dawning.

"It would look that way."

Ann stared at me. "Shit," was all she said.

It wasn't a terribly elegant thought—but wholly accurate. We didn't say much after that, about the murder or anything else, for that matter. We were both too caught up in our own thoughts. I imagined that Ann was trying to process the sudden reappearance of Joe in her life and the grim possibility that someone we knew had killed Michael. I was wondering how Michael's car ended up at the airport. I debated bringing it up again, but seeing Ann's drawn face, I decided that she'd already dealt with enough tonight.

As we cleaned up the dishes, I found myself working out various scenarios in my head, scenarios revolving around different people killing Michael and hiding the body in the construction area for the pool. Could someone have really buried a body there without being seen? Was more than one person involved? I thought about Scott. He was familiar with the construction site and might have resented Michael, but was that really a motive for murder? Hell, I hadn't liked Michael even before I found out about his attack on Ann, but I still couldn't fathom someone killing him. Unless, I thought with a sick feeling, Michael's attack on Ann was the very reason for his murder. I quickly glanced over at Ann, wondering if she'd thought of that. Her face, as she dried the cheese platter and put it away, was unreadable.

We said good night around ten o'clock and went upstairs to bed. I called Peter and quickly brought him up to speed on what had happened. After quietly listening to my tale, he said,

"Another murder? Jesus, Elizabeth, I hardly know what to say. For a fact checker, you certainly have a fair amount of excitement thrown your way. Well, at least this time, thank God, you have no reason to get involved."

When I didn't answer right away, Peter said, "Elizabeth? You're not actually thinking of getting involved in this, are you?"

"Well . . ." I paused, unsure how I really felt.

"Elizabeth! No! Please, no! I know you've been thrown into investigations in the past, but in those cases it was because the murder happened when you were there!"

"But in a way, I *was* there! I was at the Fourth of July party and no one saw Michael after that—or at least no one is admitting to it. After the party, Michael disappeared, and about a week later it was discovered that he'd embezzled Uncle Marty's money. For all we know, he might have been killed during the party!"

"Yes, but he might *not* have. I don't see why you think you need to get involved! Let the police handle this!"

"But this is family! I think Ann wants me to help—"

"Did she ask you to?" Peter interrupted.

"No, not in so many words but—"

"Did she ask in *any* words?"

"Peter! What is your problem? Ann is upset; she needs me now!"

"Fine! Hold her hand, talk to her, listen to her, but don't play detective!" Peter took a deep breath and continued in a calmer tone. "I know you helped the police in the past, but Elizabeth, that doesn't make you some kind of expert."

"Hey, if it wasn't for me, the police would have never figured out who killed Gerald Ramsey! I helped clear Aunt Winnie's name!"

"And you also came very close to getting yourself—and me, I might add—killed!"

I squirmed a bit when he said that. I preferred to gloss over that part when I thought of my first success at sleuthing. "Peter, I'm not doing anything dangerous—nor am I *going* to do anything dangerous," I quickly added, hearing him about to interrupt again. "I am just helping Ann while the police conduct their investigation. It's bad enough for her that they discovered Michael's body on the old property, but knowing that Joe is in charge of the whole investigation is pushing her over the edge. I am merely here for moral support right now."

Peter groaned. "Right. Until you decide that moral support isn't enough." I had a sudden image of him resting his forehead on his desk in frustration. "Elizabeth, I don't like this. I know you, you can't *not* get involved, and I'm afraid that you're going to get hurt!"

"How can I get hurt with you coming home to protect me?" I joked, hoping to lighten the mood.

"That's just it—I won't be home for at least another week."

"Why? What's going on?"

"Oh, it's a long, complicated, and ultimately stupid story," Peter groused. "But I've got to stay out here awhile longer to get it all straightened out."

"So I guess I won't be coming out to see you this weekend?"

"It doesn't look good. I'm sorry."

Disappointment washed over me at the thought of Peter gone another week. "Oh. Well, that stinks."

"I know. Just please promise me to be careful and not to get involved in anything beyond giving the police a statement. Just because this man was killed eight years ago doesn't mean that his killer won't do it again if threatened."

A faint chill ran down my spine when he said that. "I promise," I said softly, mentally amending "to be careful" to that statement. We talked a little more, but I think Peter sensed that I was bent on involving myself beyond his comfort level and was more than a little annoyed—both at being across the country and at not being able to convince me otherwise.

After we hung up, I changed into my pajamas and thought about that Fourth of July party all those years ago.

It had been a beautiful night. The day's warmth had given way to a crystal-clear, balmy evening. Uncle Marty's house, a white two-story colonial, sat on a manicured lawn that gently sloped down to the Miles River. Once night fell, we'd dragged wool blankets out onto the lawn and lain on them, idly watching the multicolored display of explosives above. The fireworks barge was so close that some of the debris from the explosions floated down to us like burned confetti. After the show was over, we'd watched the lights from the boats anchored on the water tip back and forth, gently rocked by the river's current. After a while, the guests wandered off in various directions. Some, like Ann, Joe, and I, walked down to the water; others, like Frances, went inside to tend to the twins (Thing One and Thing Two), who were still nursing. Ann, Joe, and I sat on the dock, talking while we dangled our feet in the cool water. After a while, I walked back up to the house and headed to the bedroom that I was sharing with Ann. Sometime later, I heard the

Things crying. When they didn't stop after a minute or so, I got up to check on them. Scott was asleep on the bed—or rather, passed out on the bed. I had just started to soothe the boys when Frances came into the room and took over. Only seconds after I returned to my room, Ann came in disheveled and visibly shaken. It was then that she told me what had happened.

After Joe said good night, she'd remained on the dock, trying to decide if she should break it off with Joe before she left for England. Although she didn't want to, she was being pressured by both her father and Laura to do so. As she sat there, Michael approached her. He saw that she was upset and made an effort to console her, putting his arm around her shoulders. Although Ann realized that he was drunk, she didn't know just how drunk until he made his sudden declaration of love, a love he claimed to have always felt for her and not Reggie. He said Reggie was proud and shallow, but Ann was the real thing, going so far as to call Reggie a pale copy of Ann. He then further shocked her by trying to kiss her. When Ann pushed him away, he grew angry and tried to do much more than kiss her. His inebriation kept him from doing any real harm, but he was still bigger and stronger, and it was several desperate minutes before Ann was able to punch him and wrestle herself away. Without looking back, Ann ran blindly for the house and to our room. She was horribly shaken and upset. I wanted to tell Uncle Marty and Reggie, but Ann refused. I think on some level she knew that by telling her father and Reggie, she would be destroying Michael's life. Even though he'd tried to attack her, she was loath to destroy him. She had some idea of talking to him in the morning and insisting that he get help and, of course, cancel the wedding. However, in the morning Michael was gone and Reggie announced that she'd broken it off with him. Ann saw no reason to tell Reggie the rest of it. A week or so later, Ann left for England and Michael's embezzlement was discovered and we all thought we'd seen the last of him.

Which was sort of true.

But what had really happened? Had Michael left and come back? And if so, with whom and why? And why was he killed? Was it the money, or was it because of his attack on Ann? Or was it for some completely different reason? There was something there that bothered me, something I was missing. But every time I tried to pinpoint what it was, it swam out of reach.

As I continued to mull everything over, I realized that Peter was absolutely right. I *was* planning on injecting myself into this investigation. But why? Crawling under the bed's thick duvet, I frowned at the ceiling. Was Kit (God forbid) right? Did I secretly see myself as a modern-day Nancy Drew, coolly stepping in to solve the crime when the local police force found themselves baffled? Did I actually possess a kind of knack for solving crimes, or was I merely a twenty-eight-year-old who was bored out of her skull with her current life? That last thought struck a tender nerve somewhere in the not-so-deep recesses of my head. Could that be my problem? True, I didn't particularly enjoy my job, but so didn't loads of other people and they didn't run off and push themselves into murder investigations. For the first time in my adult life, I was in a mature, stable relationship with a great guy. Hell, just being in a relationship with a guy who wasn't cheating on me, sponging off of me, or stealing my patent leather pumps for reasons best left unexamined was a first. True, a lot of my friends were getting married lately, and I could navigate both the Williams-Sonoma bridal registry and Babies "R" Us sites with my eyes closed. But did I want to get married and start a family? I loved Peter, but I didn't know if I was ready for that step. Among other things, I always figured I should know how to balance my checkbook before I got married, let alone start a family.

No, I thought, squaring my shoulders as much as one can square shoulders in a bed with a down mattress, I refused to believe that I was focusing on these investigations to distract myself from a boring, but nevertheless secure, job and a life that seemed to have no real direction.

Then again, I'd believed in the Easter Bunny until I was almost twelve. I don't even *want* to go into the whole Santa Claus debacle, except to say that childlike naïveté begins to resemble undiagnosed lead poisoning when it hits late adolescence.

I pulled the bedspread up to my chin and curled onto my right side. As I listened in silence to the soft, rhythmic ticking of my bedside clock, I decided the reason I found police investigations so fascinating wasn't the issue. The issue was that a man—a man who was once considered a part of the family— had been murdered and buried under the family pool.

Don't ask me why, but I found myself remembering the lines from *A Charlie Brown Christmas*, the scene where Charlie Brown confides to Lucy that he's feeling let down about Christmas. Lucy assertively tells him, "You need involvement. You need to get involved in some real Christmas project. How would you like to be the director of our Christmas play?" To which Charlie Brown excitedly replies, "Me? You want *me* to be the director of the Christmas play?"

Well, no one had asked me to be the director of this investigation, but I had to admit that there was something enticing about setting an overlooked wrong to right.

CHAPTER 11

It is very difficult for the prosperous to be humble.

—EMMA

HE NEXT MORNING, Ann and I ate a quick breakfast before we headed off to our respective offices. I wasn't at my desk five minutes before I realized that it was going to be one of those workdays that ended with me wanting to drink my feelings. Every article that landed on my desk had a same-day deadline and most appeared, by my addled brain anyway, to be written in Greek. Using both FactCheck.org and large amounts of coffee, I was able to get a majority of the work done. Unfortunately, it was a little ditty written by one Arthur MacArthur (if that was indeed his real name) that was my undoing: a two-thousand-word opus on the migratory habits of the Baltimore oriole. It took me a good five hundred words in to realize he wasn't talking about the baseball team. By the time I finished, I had a headache, my neck hurt, and I had taken a real dislike to both Arthur MacArthur and his stupid birds. That's about the time Kit called, wanting to know when I was returning to her house and if I could babysit Pauly that night. She wasn't happy with either of my responses. "I don't see why Ann thinks she needs you there," Kit groused. "I hope you haven't been pretending that you can actually find out who killed Michael. I'd hate to think that you're staying there under false pretenses."

"False pretenses! I'm helping her organize the items that Uncle Marty specified in his will and offering moral support while the police conduct their investigation."

"Ha! You're pretending to be Jane Marple is what you're doing," she shot back.

"I am doing no such thing," I angrily bit out. Jane Marple. Please. Granted, she was a brilliant detective, but she also was a frail old woman who enjoyed bird watching and knitting. If I was going to emulate any of the women sleuths from the Golden Age, it would be Adela Bradley. Mrs. Bradley was breezy, fashionable, and devastatingly clever; she also drank gin and, perhaps more important, had no earthly desire to knit. Or maybe it was the other way around.

Kit ended the call by tersely reminding me that I'd promised to babysit next Tuesday. I forced myself to respond pleasantly and almost pulled a muscle in the process. I hung up, refusing to let myself dwell on the call. After all, I was a very busy and important career woman with much to do. For instance, I had to organize a birthday celebration for Sharon. I knew she'd like the idea because she actually e-mailed me the suggestion. The one hiccup in the plan was that on the likability scale, Sharon runs a close second to Dickey. However, lured by the anticipation of cake, the staff dutifully crowded around the conference table and sang an off-key rendition of "Happy Birthday." Unfortunately, they all left with empty stomachs and grumpy at me because Sharon is on a diet and refused to let me buy a cake. We celebrated with celery sticks and carrots. Yeah. Happy birthday, Sharon.

I was still irritably pulling celery strings from my teeth when Ann called. However, within a matter of seconds my irritation with the celery was replaced by another emotion—uneasy foreboding.

"Joe called," Ann said without preamble. "The coroner's report came in. It's official. Michael was murdered."

"I'm sorry, Ann," I said. "I really am."

She sighed. "I don't know why I'm surprised. I mean, I didn't really think it was an accident that he wound up under the pool, but still . . ."

"It would have been nice to hear that it was all some terrible mistake," I finished. "I know. I wish it was a mistake, too. Did Joe say anything else?"

"Yes," Ann said after a moment's pause. "He wants to talk to us again, at the house tonight. Actually, I think he really just wants to talk with Reggie again, but he's covering that by asking to meet with us all."

"Why do you think Joe wants to talk to Reggie in particular?"

"I don't know. It was nothing he said, it was just that . . ."

"You just know him," I finished.

"Yeah, something like that," she said with a sigh. "Can you . . ."

"I'll be there as soon as I can."

I left work as soon as I could, stopped by Kit's to grab some more clothes, and rushed back to Uncle Marty's house. The rest of the family had already arrived. I heard a tangle of raised voices—Reggie's, Frances's, Scott's, Laura's, and Miles's—coming from the living room. As I peeked in, Ann saw me and made her way toward me, her shoulders slumped. "Thank God you're finally here," she muttered. "They're driving me crazy with questions. Like *I* know anything!"

"Is Joe here yet?" I asked, shrugging out of my coat.

"No, but I expect him any minute."

No sooner were the words out of Ann's mouth than there was a rap on the door. The voices fell silent and Ann turned to me, her eyes wary. "Showtime, I guess," she said and reached to open the door.

As expected, it was Joe who stood uneasily on the front steps. At his side once again was Sergeant Beal. From the thoughtful way she eyed Ann, I suspected that she knew of Joe and Ann's past. I didn't get the impression she viewed this information through unbiased eyes.

"Hello, Joe. Sergeant Beal," Ann said, opening the door wider. "Won't you come in? Everyone is in the living room."

"Thank you," Joe said. He shot Ann a quick look that seemed to express discomfort at having to be here at all. Ann ducked her head in silent acknowledgment before proceeding into the living room.

The uneasy silence that pervaded the room abruptly ended with Joe's arrival. Scarlett gave a happy bark and scampered over to him while Frances snapped, "Why exactly have you asked to talk to us again? Nothing has changed since last night."

"Well, actually one thing has changed," Joe said as he dodged Scarlett's advances. "I received the coroner's report. Michael was definitely murdered. His skull was fractured. It appears he was hit with something hard and heavy."

A brief silence met these words. After a beat, Frances shrugged and said, "Well, did anyone really think it was anything other than murder? I mean, the man was buried under the pool, for God's sake!"

"If I recall correctly," said Sergeant Beal with a studied glance at her notebook, "*you* were the one who asked if Michael's death could have been the result of his falling and hitting his head." Sergeant Beal looked up from her notes with a studiously bland expression. Frances pressed her lips into a hard line and breathed loudly through her nose.

"I do apologize for the inconvenience," Joe said evenly, "but in light of the report, I wanted to make sure that I had everything I needed from you. Then I can move on with the investigation."

Ann moved out from behind Joe. "Won't you two have a seat?" she asked, indicating the empty couch. Both Joe and Sergeant Beal sat down. Ann and I found seats as well. All eyes turned questioningly to Joe, but it was Sergeant Beal who began the interview.

"Ms. Ames," she said, turning to Reggie and glancing down at her notebook, "I wanted to go over again the last time you saw the deceased. You said that you ended the relationship with him because of his excessive drinking. Is that correct?"

Reggie smoothed the lines of her skirt before answering. "Yes, that's right. I felt that his drinking was starting to change him. I didn't like it."

Sergeant Beal nodded sympathetically. "I can imagine. What was his reaction to your ending things?"

Reggie's eyes narrowed. "He was disappointed, of course. I already told you this."

"I know," said Sergeant Beal with an apologetic smile. "Please forgive me, it's just for the report. I have to get every detail."

From the way the corner of Reggie's mouth curled, I don't think she was buying Sergeant Beal's whole "good cop" routine.

"So," Sergeant Beal continued, "you say he was disappointed. Was he anything else?"

Reggie stiffened. "What else would he be?"

Sergeant Beal spread out her hands. "Well, was he perhaps angry? I mean, I would imagine that he'd be pretty angry. By ending your relationship with him, wouldn't you also be ending his shot to take over the company? I mean, I don't know about *your* dad, but *my* dad certainly wouldn't want to hand his company over to someone I didn't trust."

Reggie's eyes narrowed until they were mere slits. "What exactly are you getting at?"

Sergeant Beal's hands fluttered as if she was trying to find the right words to express herself. "Just that if he thought that he was not only losing you but also the chance to control the company, he might react with an emotion stronger than disappointment. He might, in fact, have been angry. Very angry. Since by your own account he was drinking very heavily that night, he might not have been able to control his anger."

"And?" Reggie bit out the word with barely suppressed rage.

"And he might have reacted physically." Sergeant Beal softened her voice and leaned forward. "He might have tried to attack you. If that were the case, and you fought back, it would be self-defense."

Reggie sat perfectly still. Her face drained of color. Her eyes, however, did not. They blazed with unbridled fury. "How dare you! How dare you! You think I killed him! I loved that man. I would never kill him." My stomach twisted in anticipation of something terrible. Reggie's temper was not something you wanted to see. Frances apparently agreed with my assessment, because she immediately spoke up.

"Reggie, calm down. This is silly. No one thinks you had anything to do with Michael's death. Besides, you couldn't have. You said you broke up with him right after the fireworks and then went to bed."

Sergeant Beal turned to Frances, as Reggie tried to get her emotions back under control. "And why does this mean that Ms. Ames had nothing to do with Mr. Barrow's death?"

"Because Michael was alive and well long after the fireworks ended. I saw him myself."

"And where was this?" Sergeant Beal asked with an edge in her voice.

"Down by the docks. With Ann," Frances replied.

Sergeant Beal's eyes swung toward Ann. "Really? Well, that *is* interesting. I don't believe you mentioned this in your earlier statement, Ms. Reynolds. Would you care to explain why that was?"

Ann tried to speak but couldn't seem to find the words. "I . . ." was all she got out. I moved over and crouched next to where she sat. Taking her hand, I said quietly, "Ann, it's got to come sometime."

Ann looked at me and nodded. Looking back at the room, I saw that Frances looked confused and Reggie curious. Only Joe seemed to sense Ann's deep level of disgust and discomfort. The words still stuck in her throat, so I said what she couldn't.

"Michael came down to the dock after Joe left and I'd headed for bed. He talked to her a bit about her plans for school, and then he . . . he told Ann that he was in love with her." Frances gasped in horror at this. Reggie didn't move, her face pale with surprise or fury. "When Ann rebuffed him, he . . ." I paused and looked to Ann, unsure how to continue.

Taking a deep breath she said, "He attacked me. He tried to . . ." The words stuck in her throat. Ann wrapped her arms around herself. "He attacked me," she repeated. "He . . . he caught me by surprise, but once I realized what was happening . . . well, I fought as hard as I could."

Joe's face was like granite and he gripped the arms of his chair. "Did he . . . ?"

Ann shook her head. "No, I stopped him." I tried to catch Ann's eye and caution her to stop, but she wasn't looking at me. Her eyes were firmly fastened on Joe. "I pushed him away," she continued, saying the words I feared she'd say. "Michael was so drunk that he lost his balance and fell back. I ran like hell for the house and didn't stop until I got to my room." Joe relaxed slightly, but his expression was still murderous. I thought once again that it was a good thing Michael was already dead.

"Why didn't you ever say anything?" Reggie asked, her eyes wide with horror and shock.

"I was going to," said Ann. "But then I guess I wanted to pretend it never happened. In the morning Michael was gone and you announced that you'd ended things with him. Then we found out about the embezzlement and it seemed pretty clear that he was out of our lives forever. It was hard enough for

MURDER MOST PERSUASIVE 13 111

you already. I couldn't see how telling you what he'd done to me would help."

"Oh, my God, Ann, you poor thing!" cried Frances.

Reggie crossed the room and wrapped her arms around Ann, hugging her tight. "I'm so sorry. I didn't know. But why didn't you tell me?"

"You'd been hurt enough," Ann said. "I didn't want to add to it."

"Oh, Ann. How horrible. I had no idea!"

"It's okay. How could you have?"

Reggie shook her head sadly. "I don't know . . . I just somehow feel responsible. I'm so sorry."

Ann grabbed Reggie's hands. "Don't be. It's over. I'm fine now. But I'm sorry you had to find out. He hurt a lot of people in his life."

"Well, at least he can't hurt either of us anymore," said Reggie.

"Amen to that," said Frances.

I would have felt much better about this little family catharsis if it hadn't been for the way Sergeant Beal gazed at Ann like a hungry cat eyeing a trapped mouse.

CHAPTER 12

A woman, especially if she have the misfortune
of knowing anything, should conceal it
as well as she can.

—NORTHANGER ABBEY

"SO I TAKE IT YOU FOUGHT BACK against Michael when he attacked you?" Detective Beal said blandly. Joe blanched at her words. However, if Sergeant Beal noticed, she ignored it.

Ann nodded, not picking up on Sergeant Beal's real meaning. "Yes, I told you. I pushed him back and ran for the house."

"You must have pushed him pretty hard for him to fall back," Sergeant Beal said.

Ann finally realized where Sergeant Beal was taking the conversation. Her eyes widened. "I pushed him from me and yes, he fell back, but he wasn't hurt. He was just drunk and I took him by surprise."

"By your own account, you just said that you pushed him off of you hard enough that he fell down and that you ran for the house and didn't look back. How do you know he wasn't hurt?"

"Because I was there. I saw him fall. It wasn't the kind of fall that injures people."

"You'd be surprised the damage a simple bop to the head can produce," Sergeant Beal continued.

Next to her, Joe said, "Erica . . ."

"Erica" held up her hand to stop him. "I understand your reluctance to see someone you were once . . . friends with come under scrutiny like this, Detective. And I know you would hate for it to seem that you were biased in this investigation. But the fact remains that we have a dead man. A dead man who this woman claims she attacked."

Ann's jaw dropped open. So did most every one else's, for that matter.

"Now wait a damn minute!" cried Miles. "She did not say that she 'attacked' Michael. She said that she pushed him off of her and he fell back! I don't know how you got to be a police officer if that's how you interpret facts. Any fool can see that Ann not only didn't kill Michael but that she simply didn't have the strength to do him any real harm. Michael was a big man. Ann is a petite woman. Her pushing him couldn't have done any real damage."

"Oh, I would agree with you there. In fact, I don't see how he could have fallen if it was just a push," said Sergeant Beal.

"What the hell does that mean?" snapped Ann.

"It means that you were scared and probably mad. Furious, even. Who wouldn't be? He's your sister's fiancé—practically part of the family—and he's attacking you? No one would blame you if you, let's say, picked up a tree branch or a log and bashed the guy's head in," Sergeant Beal said evenly.

Ann opened her mouth, but it was Miles who spoke. "Don't say a word, Ann. Not one more damn word. Not until we've gotten you a lawyer. This interview is over." He stood up and marched over to Sergeant Beal. Looking down, he said firmly, "Let me show you out. We'll be in touch."

Sergeant Beal didn't answer or move right away. It was Joe who nudged her into action. "As you wish," she said, but if it was in response to Miles or Joe, I couldn't tell. She bent her head to tuck her notebook back into her pocket. As she did so, she missed Joe catching Miles's eye and pointedly mouthing "Thank you."

I gave a sigh of relief. At least Joe still believed Ann. I just hoped it was enough.

Miles was on the phone to his lawyer seconds after the front door shut. The rest of us circled around Ann, not that any of us really knew what to say. It was all so absurd. But it seemed clear to me that in her haste to discredit Ann in front of Joe, Sergeant Beal had squarely put Ann in the position of number one suspect. Not with any of us, or with Joe for that matter, but the rest of the police department might not see it as we did.

"Scott," I said, "can you get those records for us? The ones listing all the employees from Michael's time at the company?"

Scott nodded. "Absolutely. Do you think they'll help?"

I shook my head. "I really don't know. But we have to do something. We can't let Sergeant Beal railroad her theory about Ann without a challenge. Maybe the list will provide some other ideas."

"That woman . . ." said Ann, "that woman thinks I killed him, doesn't she?"

"Who cares what she thinks?" I said. "She's an idiot. The fact is that you didn't kill Michael and we're going to prove that."

Ann looked up at me and said one word. "How?"

"*We're* going to find his killer," I said. Apparently, I was going to direct the Christmas pageant after all.

CHAPTER 13

Seldom, very seldom, does complete truth belong to any human disclosure; seldom can it happen that something is not a little disguised, or a little mistaken.

—EMMA

FTER EVERYONE LEFT, I put Ann to bed. She was in a state of semishock. Once she was settled, I called Aunt Winnie and told her the news. She was horrified, of course—both at the fact that Michael had attacked Ann and that she was now suspected of killing him. Peter had much the same reaction. However, knowing me as he did, he was doubly upset because he knew that I was now bound and determined to help prove Ann's innocence. "I'll be home as soon as I can," he said. "Just promise me not to do anything stupid—at least until I get there."

"I promise to save the stupid for until you get here," I said. He didn't laugh.

When Ann got up the next morning, she was still reeling from Sergeant Beal's accusation. I tried to talk her out of going to work, but she insisted that it was the very thing she needed to keep her mind off things. We agreed to meet for dinner at six at the Old Ebbitt Grill. As Scott had promised that he would get us the list of past employees this afternoon, we planned to discuss it over dinner.

Work was a blur of meetings and deadlines, but finally, that magical number six appeared on my desk's digital clock. Actually, it looked like a fishhook as depicted by Salvador Dalí because the display is broken, but I knew how to read it. I leaped up from my desk and went to meet Ann. Located on 15th Street in downtown Washington, the restaurant's beaux arts façade was once the entrance to the B. F. Keats theater and is something of a D.C. landmark.

As it was a Friday, the bar was packed with the happy hour crowd. Luckily, Ann had made us a reservation and was waiting for me in one of the wooden booths in the main dining room. Sliding onto the green velvet bench, I saw that she had a pile of papers in front of her. "Scott got you the records, I see. Have you looked through them yet?" I asked, as I opened my menu.

Ann nodded. "I think I may have found something, too." Tapping the top paper, she pointed to a name. "Donny Mancuso."

I looked at her blankly. "Who's Donny Mancuso?"

"Reggie's boyfriend before Michael. In fact, she dumped Donny for Michael. He wasn't too happy about it, if I remember."

"And he worked at the company?"

"Yes, but wait, it gets better. He not only worked at the company, he worked on the design of the pool. He might have even been there when it was put in."

"Where is he now?"

"He's got his own pool business. It's out in Rockville."

"Really? This is great!" I said, then caught myself. "Well, not *great,* but well, you know what I mean."

"I know exactly what you mean. It means that the police can focus on someone other than me, and *outside* the family."

"Right. Especially when you consider that Donny has his own business. I mean, it takes a fair amount of capital to start something like that. Add in his connection to Michael, and the police will have an interesting suspect. Speaking of the police, what did they say when you told them what you found?"

The waitress appeared to take our order just then, delaying Ann's answer. Ann ordered the Thai shrimp while I opted for the Niçoise salmon salad. As soon as the waitress left, I returned to the topic at hand. "So," I said after taking a sip of ice water, "what did the police say about Donny? Did you talk to Joe?"

Ann paused and traced an imaginary design on the crisp linen tablecloth. "No. I didn't call them yet."

Something in her voice aroused my darkest suspicions. I put down my glass and stared at her. "But you are going to, right?"

"Hmm? Oh, yes. But I want to talk to Donny first."

I gaped at her, dumbfounded. "Are you crazy? Why on earth would you do that?"

Ann ducked her head. "What if he's innocent? I mean, I'd hate to throw him to the police for no reason. I know how that feels, after all, and I wouldn't wish that on my worst enemy."

"But what if he's the killer?" I yelled. Despite the noise in the dining room, several heads turned our way. "But what if he's the killer?" I repeated in a calmer voice. "Michael Barrow was murdered and Sergeant Beal wants to pin it on you! Here's a guy who might have had a grudge against Michael. We've got to tell the police about him! Not only did he have a motive; apparently he also had an opportunity to bury the body!"

"I know," said Ann, "but I'd just feel better about it if I saw him first. Look, I don't know how to explain it. Donny was a nice guy and Reggie treated him pretty poorly. I doubt he had anything to do with it. I just want to go talk to him first."

"So because of that you feel you owe him a heads-up on the police investigation?" I sputtered.

"No . . . yes . . . I don't know. I just want to see him." Her voice was determined. "I'll tell the police about him, but not until I see him."

"And when are you planning on seeing him?"

"I thought I'd go tomorrow."

"Don't!"

"Don't what?" she asked.

"Don't go back to Rockville, what else? Don't go see Donny!"

"Ha-ha! Very funny. Please, be serious."

"I *am* being serious. I don't like this."

"Then don't come with me. But I am going whether you like it or not. However, I would like you to come."

I sighed. "Fine. Stupid but fine. I'll go with you, but I want you to promise me that the second we leave, you'll call Joe and tell him about Donny."

"Okay, deal. Thanks."

"Don't thank me," I grumbled. "I'm on record as stating that this is a stupid idea. I'm beginning to see why Peter gets so mad sometimes."

Ann's eyebrows pulled together. "What are you talking about? What does this have to do with Peter?"

"Nothing," I mumbled, taking another sip of water.

The next morning I went downstairs to find Ann in the kitchen, hunched over the paper and drinking coffee. Scarlett was curled up under one of the chairs. Seeing me, Ann pointed at the coffeemaker. Mercifully, she was silent.

After pouring a large cup, adding cream and sugar, and drinking enough to jump-start my brain, I was capable of conversation. "So, any chance a good night's sleep made you see logic and abandon this absurd idea of going to see Donny Mancuso? A man, by the way, who sounds like an extra from *The Sopranos*."

Ann didn't bother to look up. "Nope."

I sighed. "Thought so."

Ann kept reading the paper. Suddenly, she gave a startled gasp.

"What?" I asked.

"Reggie was right," she said, tapping the paper. "The gossip page has everything about the discovery of Michael's body and Reggie's relationship with him."

I leaned over her shoulder to read. It was the *Post*'s "Reliable Source" column. "Do they call her a black widow?" I asked.

"No, thank God, but she's going to freak when she sees this."

I had just taken another sip of coffee when the doorbell rang. "I'll get it," I said to Ann, as I padded down the hallway with Scarlett right behind me. Swinging open the door, I was surprised to see Kit standing on the front steps. She was wearing maternity jeans and a blue polo shirt and a smug smile. In her hands was a large casserole dish. Scarlett was interested in neither and so turned back to return to the kitchen.

"Hey, Kit! I didn't know you were coming over this morning," I said in surprise.

"I promised Ann that I would bring her a meal, remember? You aren't the only cousin who is capable of helping," she said as she pushed past me into the house.

"I never said I was," I began.

She ignored me. "And besides, if Ann needs help organizing Uncle Marty's things, *I'm* the one who should be helping her. Everyone knows how disorganized you are."

I opened my mouth to defend myself, but Kit wasn't finished. Shifting the dish in her hands, she smiled slyly at me. "Unless, of course, you aren't really here to help her organize. The way I look at it, whether or not you are here to help organize, Ann needs *real* help in that department. So I decided to offer my services."

I stared at her, uncharacteristically at a loss for words. She was actually so upset Ann had asked me for help and not her that she simply decided to barge in and foist herself on us using what smelled to be chicken piccata as cover. I paused. Kit's chicken piccata was really good. "But what about Pauly? Who's watching him?" I asked.

"I hired one of the neighborhood girls to babysit him."

From the kitchen, Ann called out, "Elizabeth? Who is it?" A second later she appeared in the foyer, coffee cup in hand. Surprise registered on her face when she saw Kit. "Kit! What are you doing here? Is everything okay?"

Kit let out a little laugh. "Everything is fine, silly. Didn't I promise you that I would bring you some food?" Kit held out the glass dish as proof. "I made you my chicken piccata."

Ann politely accepted the dish. "Oh, Kit, that was very kind of you. But really, you didn't have to go to all that trouble."

Kit brushed this away. "Don't be silly. It was no trouble at all. Besides, I love to cook." I shot Kit a pointed look. This love of cooking was certainly news to me, as she had told me just two days ago that cooking dinner had become "a gastric nightmare" for her due to the pregnancy. Gastric nightmare, my ass. Then, as if the idea had just occurred to her, she added, "Hey, Elizabeth was telling me you needed help organizing all of Uncle Marty's things. I'm actually free today. Why don't I help? After all, family should come together in times like these," she said sweetly.

My teeth began a slow grind. She wasn't fooling me for a minute. The only motivation behind the chicken piccata was to make sure that I wasn't "playing detective," as she'd so sneeringly referred to it a few days ago. On the slight chance that I *wasn't* doing just that (no comment, thank you very much), she decided to try and show me up with her superior organizational and cooking skills. I didn't know whether to laugh at her or smack her upside her smug little head.

Okay, who was I kidding? I knew *exactly* which one I preferred.

I squeezed my hand shut to ensure better self-control and shot Ann a look of frustration. To her credit, Ann did not appear nonplussed at Kit's offer. Instead, she smiled brightly and said, "Well, Kit, that's very sweet of you. But I think we have everything under control here. Actually, we were getting ready to run an errand or two. But since you're free today, how about we all meet later for lunch?"

As far as dodges go, it was nicely done. Unfortunately, it didn't fool Kit for a second. Over the years Kit has become quite an expert at thwarting dodges. "Don't be silly," she said firmly. "Since I'm already here, why don't I just go on the errands with you?"

"It's a long ride," I ventured.

"I adore long rides," she said, giving me a smile that offered me a view of the majority of her teeth. It was a little like being smiled at by a piranha who'd been afforded excellent dentistry. "Besides, it'll give Ann and me a chance to catch up," she continued. "So where are we going?"

Ann's smile dimmed a bit. "Um, well, Bonnie was thinking about updating the pool out back a bit. I promised to get her some quotes while she was gone."

Kit's perfectly groomed brows pulled together in confusion. "She isn't going to use Uncle Marty's business?"

"Um, probably. I mean, most likely. She just thought it would be interesting to see what else is out there."

Kit didn't respond at first. I could practically see her mind's gears furiously twisting and turning as she tried to work out why Bonnie wouldn't use the family business to update the pool. She had suspected our errand had something to do with the investigation. Finally she spread her hands and said, "Well, lead the way. I'm at your disposal. You've got me for the whole day."

The whole day? The very thought made me want to lie down in the fetal position. Although Kit truly wanted to help Ann, she also just as sincerely wanted to make herself look better in comparison to me. That meant she'd spend a fair amount of time trying to score points off me. I sighed. Spending the whole day with Kit when she was in one of these moods was like a sudden attack of the twenty-four-hour flu. You knew it was only temporary, but it was sheer hell while it lasted.

Thirty minutes later, we piled into Ann's car and set out for Rockville, Maryland, and Donny's pool company. Figuring that he'd probably be in the office on a Saturday, she decided to try there first. Like she did with Kit, Ann planned to pretend that she was just getting some quotes about updating the pool at Uncle Martin's. It wasn't the best plan in the world, but as I could neither talk her out of it nor come up with a better one, it was the one we were stuck with.

As we drove, Kit entertained us with every aspect of her pregnancy thus far (and trust me, there was *no* detail considered too trivial to mention). To hear her, you would think she was the first of our species to reproduce. My only solace was that she couldn't act as if this baby was the second coming since she had done *that* the first time. I think there's a rule that you are allowed to give birth to only one Messiah. Fortunately, her conversation didn't necessitate participation from Ann or me. Kit talks a great deal but very seldom requires a response.

We found Donny's office with little trouble and parked the car in an adjacent parking lot. The building itself was rather nondescript: a redbrick exterior with a green-and-white awning over the glass door. A blue neon sign in the window read MANCUSO's POOL SYSTEMS.

"My goodness," said Kit as she stepped out of the car, "this certainly is a long way to go to get additional quotes. How did you ever hear of this place, Ann?"

"Oh, you know," Ann answered vaguely, "word of mouth."

Kit eyed Ann and then the store dubiously. "Uh-huh," she said, clearly unconvinced.

With an air of determination, Ann crossed the small parking lot and pushed open the store door. A bell attached to the back of the door announced our arrival. A low teak table to our right held numerous brochures that seemed to equate pools with a better life. Four matching teak chairs, each with a green-and-white seat cushion, surrounded the table. A young woman sat at the receptionist desk, her round face exhibiting evidence of massive boredom or a recent head injury, as she languidly filed her long pink nails.

Seeing us, she reluctantly put down the nail file and said, "Good morning. Welcome to Mancuso's Pools. I'm Lindsay. How can I help you?" Her voice held all the warmth and sincerity of a dishwasher.

"Uh, yes," said Ann. "I wanted to talk to someone about expanding our current pool."

"Please excuse me a moment while I get one of our specialists to assist you." Lindsay picked up the phone and pressed a button. "Tim? Are you available to meet with a customer?"

Great, now we were going to have to chat with the wrong guy about our imaginary pool addition. I glanced over at Ann in annoyance. She ignored me. The receptionist nodded to the chairs behind us. "If you would care to have a seat, someone will be with you in just a moment. May I offer you a cup of coffee or tea?"

"Oh, no thank you," said Ann as she sat down. Kit and I declined a drink as well. Lindsay shrugged. Her patently memorized speech for interacting with potential clients had come to an end. She resumed filing her nails.

I sat down next to Ann. "Now what?" I muttered under my breath, while I pretended to study one of the brochures. On the front was a woman, blond and impossibly stacked, sitting in the pool with a man. From the looks of his pumped biceps and bulging veins, he had recently completed some horribly intense upper-body workout. Her eyes closed, the woman leaned back into the man's chest, her full lips curved in a contented smile. The man stared outward, his face dreamily satisfied. Below it read, *"And they thought they were only getting a pool . . ."* I quickly put the brochure down. Truth be told, I felt a little dirty.

Before Ann could answer my question, a man in a white company shirt and blue slacks came out of a back office. He had sun-bleached blond hair, a spray tan, and a lean, athletic build, qualities that probably are essential for pool salesmen. "Hello," he said, extending his hand first to Ann and then to me and finally to Kit. "I'm Tim. I understand you ladies are interested in discussing adding on to your current pool?"

I stayed quiet and let Ann handle this. After all, it was her imaginary construction. Kit stood silent as well with an avid expression of interest on her face.

"Yes," said Ann. "Are you the Mancuso of Mancuso's Pools?"

Tim shook his head and smiled. His teeth were very white. "No, that's Donny. He's the owner, but I'm happy to help you. Why don't we go into my office so you can tell me what you're interested in?"

The door jingled again and a large man with jet-black hair and a short beard entered the store. Like Tim, he also wore a white polo and blue pants. However, next to this man, Tim's lean build looked pubescent. The man's arms were a rocky, muscular terrain of deeply tanned skin, and his wide chest stretched the Mancuso logo until it was almost unreadable. From the little noise Ann made when she saw him, I guessed that this was Donny. It was also none other than the man Reggie was with in the bar the other night. Tim's next words confirmed my assumption. "Oh, hey, Donny. These ladies are here to discuss an addition to their pool."

So Reggie and Donny had apparently renewed their friendship. I wondered exactly when this had happened and, more important, why. From their body language the other night, they had been discussing something serious. Could it have been the discovery of Michael's body?

Ann stepped forward, a slightly puzzled look on her face. "Donny?" she said. "Donny Mancuso? I'm Ann Reynolds. Didn't you work for my father once? Martin Reynolds?" I had to give Ann credit; she carried off her little speech very nicely. It sounded almost believable. Next to me, Kit's eyes lit up as the penny dropped and she realized the true reason behind our visit. She shot me a knowing smirk before turning her attention back to Donny and Ann.

An expression passed over Donny's face that I didn't have time to interpret before he pasted a wide smile on his face. "Well, hello, Ann," he said, wrapping his large hand around her small one. "How are you? It's been a long time. How's the family?"

"Well, I don't know if you'd heard, but Dad died last week.

He'd been pretty sick with cancer and it finally was too much for him."

"Oh, I'm sorry to hear that," said Donny, his voice dropping to a suitable somber tone. "He was a nice man and a good businessman. Here, why don't you come into my office? We can catch up in there." Turning to Tim, he said, "I'll handle this, Tim. Thanks."

"Whatever you say, boss," Tim replied amiably before disappearing back into his own office.

We followed Donny into a large office consisting of a mahogany desk, opposite which sat four office chairs upholstered in the same green-and-white fabric as the ones out front. Posters touting the many benefits of pools covered the wall. Apparently, this was what was missing from my life; here lay the answers to all my problems. From what I could gather, having a pool would not only transform my body into a sleek, sun-kissed form but would also ensure familial and spiritual contentment—and all for only $35,000!

As Ann, Kit, and I slid into the chairs, Ann introduced us. Donny nodded courteously. "Pleased to meet you," he said. Taking a seat behind the desk, Donny pushed aside a newspaper. "So what's happening to the company now?" he asked.

"My brother-in-law, Scott, has taken over," said Ann. "I don't know if you remember him. He's married to my sister Frances."

Donny nodded. "I remember him. He's a good guy. Now, if you don't mind me asking, why are you here for pool work? Don't you guys do pools anymore?"

Ann flushed slightly. "Somewhat. I wanted to get some fresh

ideas. I know what our firm offers. I wanted to check out the competition."

From the way Donny cocked his head slightly, I wasn't sure that he was buying it. I think Ann sensed that, too, because she abruptly steered the conversation to the real reason we were there. "Speaking of pools, though, did you hear about what happened with the pool at the St. Michaels house?"

Donny shook his head but didn't speak. Ann continued, "Well, do you remember Michael Barrow?"

Donny's jaw tightened at the name of the man who replaced him in Reggie's affections. "I do."

"Then you know what happened?" I held my breath wondering how Donny would answer.

A faint expression of confusion crossed over his tanned face. "What do you mean what happened? About the money? I had heard that he ran off after embezzling money from your father."

Ann shook her head. "Yes, well, that's what we all thought until last week. We recently sold the St. Michaels house and the new owners decided to dig up the pool. The workers found a body under the foundation. It was Michael's."

I watched Donny closely for his reaction to this news. I don't know what I was expecting, but whatever it was, it wasn't coming. "Oh, that's terrible. I had no idea," Donny said in a flat voice, his face expressionless. "Do the police have any ideas what happened?"

Ann shook her head. "No, they don't. It's pretty awful, though."

"Well, I'm sure they'll figure it out. In the meantime, let's

talk about pleasanter things," said Donny, changing the subject. "Tell me, what are you thinking about your pool?"

For the next fifteen minutes, Ann rambled on about hot tubs,
lighting, and widening the deck. Donny took notes and asked
appropriate questions. I sat quietly and tried to look like I found
both my surroundings and the conversation fascinating. I also
ignored Kit, who I could tell was quivering with anticipation
of shouting, "I told you so!" at me the first chance she got. Then,
finally, thankfully, the interview came to an end. As we stood to
say our good-byes and shake hands, I saw something of note.

On Donny's desk was today's *Post,* open to the "Reliable
Source" article on Reggie.

So much for not knowing anything.

CHAPTER 14

Every man is surrounded by a neighborhood
of voluntary spies.

—NORTHANGER ABBEY

ONCE OUTSIDE and safely back in the car, Kit did just as I expected. "Elizabeth Jane Parker!" she exclaimed shrilly. "I knew it! Not only are you playing detective, but you've somehow convinced Ann to play along as well! You have no business involving yourself in this investigation, let alone our cousin! You have no special skills or talents for crime!"

"For your information, coming here was Ann's idea, not mine," I shot back just as Ann said, "Kit, I asked Elizabeth to help me, not the other way around. The police seem to think that I may have had something to do with Michael's death."

Kit's eyes grew wide. "You! But that's absurd! Why on earth would they think that you had anything to do with it?"

Ann ducked her head and didn't immediately reply. Then she quietly told Kit of Michael's attack and Sergeant Beal's suspicion. When she finished, Kit slumped back against the seat. "Dear God," she said, "how horrible. I'm so sorry, Ann. I had no idea. What a rotten bastard. But I still don't see why they think you had anything to do with it! I mean, do they think that you killed him and then later came back and buried his body? Why on earth would you do that? It makes no sense."

"I know," said Ann. "But unfortunately it seems to be a theory that Sergeant Beal is considering."

Kit fell quiet for only a moment. "So what are you thinking about this Donny guy? Do you think he was involved in Michael's murder? Why would he want to kill Michael?"

"He used to date Reggie," said Ann, as she steered the car out onto the busy road. "In fact, Reggie broke up with him for Michael. He was, if I remember correctly, furious. And he was also on the crew that installed the pool."

Kit's brows pulled together. "So you think he might have killed Michael out of jealousy? You know, I saw an episode of *CSI* where something similar happened."

I believe I may have mentioned that Kit watches *CSI*. A lot.

"But he didn't seem to know anything about Michael," Ann said.

"Well, that's not exactly true," I said. I quickly explained that I'd seen the newspaper on Donny's desk open to the "Reliable Source."

"So what does that prove?" Kit asked.

"There was a blurb in today's column about Reggie and the discovery of Michael's body on the property at St. Michaels. Donny had to have seen it. Therefore, it stands to reason that he was lying to us."

"I totally missed that!" said Ann. "Well done, Elizabeth!"

"That's not all, I'm afraid. The other night I went out for a drink after work with Sam. While I was there I saw Reggie. She was with Donny."

"What?" Ann cried.

"They were together, and from the looks of it talking about something pretty serious."

"What do you think it was?" asked Kit.

"I have no idea. Peter called me and I got distracted. When I looked back to where they were, they'd left."

"Do you think she saw you?" asked Ann.

"I don't know. She might have. But in any case," I said, "you need to call Joe right now and tell him what we found."

"What about Reggie? Should I tell him that she was out with Donny?" Ann asked.

"I don't know," I said. "That's your call. Maybe talk to her about it first."

"Okay," Ann said. "Um, but do you think you could call Joe? I don't think I can talk to him."

"You want *me* to call him? And say what exactly? That you got the list of old employees, saw Donny's name, and then— against my expressed advice, by the way—went to see him on a completely trumped-up reason?"

"I suppose it really doesn't matter what you say. He already hates me. Thinking I'm an idiot on top of everything else won't matter much now." She turned her head, but not before I saw her eyes well up with tears. Kit reached over and soothingly patted her arm. Looking back at me, she mouthed, "Call him."

I sighed. I was no match for tears. "Fine, I'll call him." I took the card Joe had left with us from my purse and punched his number into my cell phone. He answered almost immediately. "Detective Muldoon," he said.

"Hi, Joe. I mean, uh, Detective Muldoon. This is Elizabeth

Parker. I, uh, thought you should know something." I paused, unsure how to continue.

"I'm listening."

"Ann was able to get a list of employees from around the time that Michael worked for Uncle Marty's company." I glanced over at Ann. Her face was red with anticipated humiliation. Oh, hell. Time to take one for the team. "Well, a name on the list jumped out at me. Donny Mancuso. He used to date Reggie. In fact, he dated Reggie right up until Michael came on the scene. He was also on the crew that put in the pool at St. Michaels."

"Hang on." I heard Joe rummage on his desk for a pencil. "Donny Mancuso. M-A-N-C-U-S-O?"

"Yes. Anyway, I looked him up and he, uh, owns a pool company, Mancuso's Pools, in Rockville. I thought it might be interesting if I went to see him. So, uh . . . I did."

I shut my eyes as the icy silence on the other end of the phone lengthened. "I'm sorry," Joe finally said. "You did what?"

"I went out and met with Donny." From the front seat, Ann shot me a grateful look. I rolled my eyes and looked away.

"What exactly did you say to him?" Joe asked.

"Nothing really. I pretended to be interested in a pool and that it was just a coincidence that it was Donny's business I went to. We chatted a bit, and I told him about what happened to Michael. He claimed not to have heard anything about it, but as we were leaving I noticed today's *Post* on his desk—it was open to the 'Reliable Source' story about Reggie and how Michael's body had been found. I just thought you should know that." There, I did it. Done.

"Back up a second," Joe said. "You said you noticed the paper when 'we' were leaving. Who, may I ask, is 'we'?"

Shit, shit, shit. "Um, well, now that you mention it, Ann and Kit were with me." Hearing this, Ann hunched up her shoulders in embarrassment.

"I see. And when we took down everyone's addresses the other night, I seem to recall you saying that you were living with your sister while your landlord dealt with some mold issues at your apartment."

"That's right."

"Interesting. I must say, I've heard of renters who've taken it upon themselves to update certain aspects of their apartments, but I've never actually encountered one who contemplated putting in a pool. Seems to me it would have made more sense for Ann to have asked about potential pool work, seeing as there actually *is* one at her father's house."

The man clearly hadn't made detective just based on his looks. "It might have," I mumbled.

"I want you back at the house by noon. I will be there to pick up that list and enlighten you on what it means to interfere with police business."

I assured him that we would indeed be there. I didn't tell him that he needn't bother with the lecture as I already had vast experience with interfering with police business. Somehow I doubted that would help my case any.

"You didn't have to take the blame," Ann said as soon as I tossed the phone back into my purse. "I feel terrible! What did he say?"

"Oh, I wouldn't feel too bad. He didn't buy my story about it being my idea. For one thing he remembered I live in an apartment and so therefore would be unlikely to have reason to put in a pool."

Ann grimaced. "Oh."

"Yeah. 'Oh' is right. He wants to see us. He's going to meet us at your dad's house at noon. He wants the list of employees." I looked out the window. "And he may want to provide us with a brief tutorial on what constitutes interfering with police business."

"I told you!" Kit crowed.

I ignored her.

"What the hell was I thinking going to see Donny?" Ann moaned. "Did Joe sound very mad? Never mind, don't answer that. I don't want to know."

We rode the rest of the way in silence. From the way Ann constantly chewed on her lower lip, it was clear she was nervous about her conversation with Joe. Truth be told, I wasn't too keen on the idea myself.

We arrived home around eleven thirty. The answering machine was blinking on the hall table, so Ann went to listen to it while I headed into the kitchen to put on a pot of coffee. Kit followed me.

While I busied myself grinding the beans, Kit got down the mugs. After a minute, Ann came into the kitchen. "That was Laura," Ann said. "She called to check in and see if I need anything and to invite us over for dinner tonight. I hope you don't mind, but I called her back and accepted."

"That sounds like fun, actually. What time?"

"Eight. Kit, would you like to join us?" Ann asked.

"I'd love to," Kit said. "Let me call Paul and see if he's working." Kit pulled out her phone and called Paul. From the disappointed side of her conversation, it was clear that tonight was not a good night for Paul.

"He's working," Kit said with a sigh as she snapped her phone shut. "But thanks for asking me."

"Sure," said Ann. "If you guys will excuse me, I'm going to change real quick before Joe gets here." She glanced down at her jeans and T-shirt.

When she left, Kit turned to me. "What do you think is going to happen to her? Do the police really think she was involved?"

I shrugged and filled the coffeemaker with water. "I don't know what to think. I don't think Joe believes it, but that sergeant of his certainly is entertaining the idea. If you ask me, she likes Joe and is happy to paint Ann in an unfavorable light."

"Well, we'll just have to make sure that the real killer is found," Kit said.

That got my attention. " 'We'? I'm sorry, but aren't you the sister who constantly mocks me for my so-called pretensions of assisting the police?"

Kit dismissed my words with a casual wave. "That's not the point. The point is that we need to help Ann. We need to clear her name."

I stared back at her, dumbfounded. I don't know what was more daunting: the task of clearing Ann's name or of doing it with Kit.

Twenty minutes later, there was an official-sounding rap on the front door. As Ann was still getting ready and Kit had gone out back to make a call, I answered it. As expected, it was Joe, and as expected Scarlett was at my side eager to greet him. She was really starting to get on my nerves. Joe was wearing jeans and a faded blue oxford shirt with the sleeves rolled up. He looked very handsome; from the hard set of his jaw, he also looked very mad. I invited him to have a seat in the living room. "Ann will be out in a minute," I said, as he took a seat on one of the chairs. "Can I get you something to drink?"

"No, thank you," he said as he bent to pet Scarlett.

"You're only encouraging her," I said.

Joe laughed. "She's a pretty little thing."

"No, she's an annoying little thing. So how have you been?" I asked, mainly to start a conversation that didn't involve our trip to visit Donny.

"Fine," he replied somewhat quietly. "And you?"

"Good, thanks."

Joe said nothing else, nor did he seem inclined to do so. Frantically, I tried to think of something to talk about before the silence between us grew unbearably awkward. "Are you still sailing?" I finally asked, remembering how much Joe used to enjoy that sport.

"I am. I really started to focus on it more after . . . well, um . . . I just really got into it over the past couple of years."

I nodded. Over the past eight years, I'd guess if I had to.

Joe continued, "I sailed in a regatta this summer."

"Wow. That's great. Do you still have the same boat? What was it called, again?"

"*The Asp*," Joe replied with a nod. "No, unfortunately it was ruined in a storm a few years back. I've got a new one now."

"That's great. Is it the same kind of boat?"

"No, it's a Catalina."

"Oh, nice," I said, not having any idea what kind of boat a Catalina is but nodding as though I did.

"You don't know what a Catalina is, do you?" said Joe with a smile.

"Uh, no. Not really. No," I admitted.

"It's a brand of sailboat. Mine's a thirty-foot. It's a little bigger than *The Asp* was."

"Oh." The silence returned. I thought he was about to ask about our visit to Donny, so I quickly said, "Where's your sergeant today?"

Joe flushed. "I don't know. I didn't tell her about your visit."

"Does she really think Ann could have killed Michael? It's ludicrous!"

Joe shrugged. "Erica . . . Sergeant Beal isn't a bad cop, but she has a tendency to be impulsive. I admire her spirit, but sometimes she lacks good sense."

As I tended to be one of those souls who leaned more toward impulsivity rather than good sense, I chose not to comment. Instead I asked, "You don't think Ann did it, do you?"

Joe shook his head. "No. The Ann I knew would never do anything like that." He paused. "Lord knows people change. I mean Ann . . . well, the other night I hardly recognized her . . ." Joe stopped, seeming to realize what he was saying. "But no matter what has happened, I know that Ann could never kill anyone."

"Well, can't you tell your sergeant that?"

"The problem is that Erica knows about Ann and me. For

me to tell her to back off of her theory would look bad. It could actually make it worse for Ann."

I thought about what he said. As much as I hated to admit it, he had a point. "Have there been any additional developments on Michael?" I asked.

Joe shook his head. "I'm afraid not. Unfortunately, the people who had the most against him are the Reynoldses. Michael didn't seem to have any friends or family that I can find. His whole life seemed to revolve around Reggie and the business."

"But—"

Joe raised his hand. "I don't want to believe anyone in the family killed him, Elizabeth. In fact, I'm doing everything I can to find another answer. Trust me. The last thing I want is to hurt An . . . the family," he amended.

I understood him. He might still be angry at Ann for ending their relationship, but he was not unfeeling. He didn't want to see her suffer and would do what he could to prevent it. My hopes that they might be able to reconcile rose. Joe might still be resentful, but he was also here. That alone was an excellent start.

"I'm here to help, too," I said. "I don't want to see Ann hurt any more than you do. She hasn't been very, well, *happy* in a long time. I'd hate to see her get hurt *again* because of her family."

Okay, that last bit might have been too obvious, but I've found it pays to be direct.

Joe shot me an odd look. "What are you talking about?"

So maybe my idea of direct doesn't always jibe with everyone else's.

"Uh, well, you know . . ." I began, suddenly at a loss for

words. Luckily, Ann joined us just then. For a moment, it was like the past eight years had never happened. It was like looking at the old Ann. She was wearing a green-and-tan cotton sheath. Her hair was freshly curled, and makeup had been artfully applied. I didn't think Joe would be looking through her today. Upon seeing her, I was happy to notice that Joe's expression softened and I doubted he still thought she'd changed beyond recognition. That he still cared for her, I was sure. But whether his pride would let him admit that was another story.

"I've just made some coffee," I offered. "Can I get everyone a cup?"

This time my offer was accepted, and I ducked back into the kitchen where Kit was readying the tray.

"Is Joe here?" she asked. When I nodded, her face twisted into a grimace. "Well, let's see if we can't convince him to look for Michael's murderer elsewhere."

"I don't think it's him we need to convince. It's that sergeant of his. Thankfully, Joe didn't bring her today."

Kit and I took our time in the kitchen, hoping to give Ann and Joe a moment alone with each other. When we finally emerged with the tray laden with the coffee, cups, cream, and sugar, Ann and Joe were quietly talking. When they saw me and Kit, they fell silent and Joe got to his feet.

"Here, let me help you with that." He took the tray from me and actually smiled at me. Wondering what had prompted the change in his mood, I glanced at Ann, but she was staring at the floor. Her cheeks, however, appeared to be a bit rosier than they'd been minutes before.

Kit and I seated ourselves and I poured out the coffee. After everyone was served, I said, "Joe, I'm sorry about going to see Donny. It's just that Ann didn't like the idea of telling the police about him until she saw him first. But he's lying, I know he is. He knew about Michael before we got there."

Joe nodded. "Well, I appreciate the tip. Just next time—"

"Don't let there be a next time, right?"

With a grim smile, he nodded. "Exactly."

"The problem is," said Kit, "that it seems there are some in your department who think that Ann might have been involved in Michael's murder. I don't know if you know this, but Elizabeth has helped the police in the past." I gaped at her. Just days ago she mocked the very idea that I had provided any real assistance to the police. Now she was touting my skills.

At Joe's inquisitive glance, I explained. "I've been involved in two murder investigations. Last year, a guest at my aunt's inn was murdered, and this past fall, a guest at my friend's wedding was murdered."

"In both cases, Elizabeth was fundamental in helping the police solve the crimes," Ann added loyally.

Joe glanced curiously at me before saying, "Well, obviously I'd appreciate any tips you might have, but as I said before . . ."

"I know, I know. Nothing but complete honesty from now on," I said.

"Our point is," continued Kit, "that we'd be happy to offer our services."

I gaped at her. "*Our* services! What are you, my broker?"

Kit gave me a level look. "We're family. I think we are obliged to help. Besides, I've always been good at finding things out, too. I can help."

"Kit! Just because you're a good gossip doesn't make you a good investigator!" I snapped.

Kit's brows pulled together and her lips pursed. She was about to say something, but Ann spoke first. "I'll take all the help I can get. I really appreciate both of you helping me." Turning back to Joe, Ann said, "Does your sergeant really think I killed Michael?"

"I think that she's young and wants to impress. But Ann, why didn't you tell me about Michael?"

"I don't know," she said softly. "I thought that I could handle it. I'm not sure what I would have done if Michael hadn't disappeared. But when he did, the problem seemed to disappear with him. Oh, what a mess I've made of things! What must Reggie think?" she said, putting her head in her hands.

"Ann, this wasn't your fault." Joe leaned forward and put his hand on hers. Color rose in her cheeks and she looked down at his hand like it was a long-lost friend. Joe continued, "How could anyone be angry with you for something Michael did? And Reggie *didn't* marry him—thank God. She broke up with him *before* his attack on you. Who knows, maybe he was trying to get back at her. Anyway, it's not as if you kept quiet about him and let Reggie marry the bastard. Only then could you have a legitimate regret." Joe's voice strained a little as the thought occurred to him of another regret Ann might—or might not—have. He pulled his hand back. Ann's glance slid away and her cheeks grew even redder. "All I'm saying," said Joe, "is that Reggie *knew*

Michael was a creep. He stole from your father. Finding out about this attack on you only confirms what she already knew."

Ann fingered the handle of her coffee cup. "I guess you're right, Joe. I just wish it had all been different."

"So do I," Joe said quietly.

CHAPTER 15

My idea of good company is the company of
clever, well-informed people, who have a
great deal of conversation.

—PERSUASION

OE STAYED a little while longer. Kit and I busied ourselves in the kitchen as much as possible. Despite Ann's
earlier protestations that she didn't want to be left alone with
Joe, she didn't seem to notice our frequent absences. Or if she
did notice, she didn't seem to mind.

While I was in no way eavesdropping, I did overhear a few
snippets of their conversation. They talked mainly about their
jobs. Ann told Joe about some of the projects she'd worked on
lately, and Joe detailed some of his more interesting cases. At one
point Ann responded to something Joe said with, "No, never.
You?" He, too, responded with a negative. Were they discussing
marriage histories?

Joe left around one o'clock with a promise to call us if he
learned anything new. After that, Ann, Kit, and I decided to go
into Georgetown for lunch. We headed to Martin's Tavern, a
favorite haunt of locals and tourists alike. The two-story tavern,
which opened in the early 1930s, has hosted every president

from Harry Truman to George W. Bush. John Kennedy used to be a regular. In fact, he proposed to Jackie in booth number three. In the main dining room, foxhunting prints and black-and-white baseball photos hang on paneled walls while Tiffany-style lamps dangle overhead.

We slid into one of the high-backed hardwood booths that afford a view of Wisconsin Avenue and studied the menu in silence. "You know," Ann said, after we'd decided on our orders, "I was thinking. Maybe I should get in touch with Nana."

At the mention of Nana, I looked up in surprise. Nana (aka Sara Myerson) had worked for years for Uncle Marty as a kind of housekeeper/nanny. She had been brought in to pick up Bonnie's slack. As you might imagine, it was a full-time job. Nana kept the house organized, the kids supervised, and Marty in good humor. Not an easy task, but Nana tolerated no foolishness, and under her watch the household ran with a machine-like precision. Despite her strictness and no-nonsense manner, all of the kids adored Nana and remained close to her well after her retirement. She now lived in St. Michaels, not far from the family's old summer house.

"Nana?" said Kit. "Why would you call her? Didn't you just see her at Uncle Marty's funeral?" When Ann didn't answer right away, she peered closely at her. "Oh, I see," she said. "You want to call her to find out about Michael."

"But Ann," I said, "Nana wouldn't know anything. She wasn't even at the Fourth of July party."

"No, but she helped set it up," Ann said. "And even if she wasn't there, she always seemed to know everything that was happening. Sometimes before it happened." With a knowing smile, she added, "She certainly busted us on numerous occasions."

"That she did," I agreed. "Remember the time we brought those guys back to the pool?"

Ann laughed at the memory. "That's right! I'd almost forgotten. I don't know what we were thinking."

I shook my head. "When she called down to us, asking what all the noise was, you told them to duck under the water so she wouldn't see them."

"Okay, so I wasn't thinking too clearly. I forgot she was calling down to us from the *upstairs* window. Not my finest moment, I grant you."

Beside me, Kit shifted in her seat, clearly annoyed. I felt a pang of guilt. Regardless of how irritating she could be at times, it wasn't very nice of me to talk about past events where she hadn't been included. I shot Ann a quelling look. She caught my meaning and quickly changed the subject.

"Anyway, all I'm saying," said Ann, "is that maybe Nana saw something that we missed. In any case, she should talk to the police."

Kit leaned across the table and said in a conspiratorial tone, "Or maybe she should talk to *us*. You know how older women can be—somewhat suspicious and uncomfortable around policemen. If we talk to her first, it could put her mind at ease."

"Whoa! Wait one second!" I said, making a time-out sign with my hands. Turning to Kit, I said, "What's with the 'us' business all of a sudden? Need I remind you that up until today you spent a fair amount of time and energy, not to mention oxygen, making it very clear that you thought my involvement in police business was, and I'm quoting here, 'disgraceful'?"

Kit bristled. "I—" she began, but I cut her off.

"And you," I said, pointing an accusatory finger at Ann, "you just promised Joe not one hour ago that you wouldn't meddle in this investigation anymore! Or have you already forgotten that?" While I wanted to do everything I could to help Ann, I also didn't like this feeling that I'd just been cast as the den mother for the Bobbsey Twins.

"No, I haven't forgotten," Ann replied defensively. "And I don't believe that I suggested anything akin to meddling. I merely said that Nana should talk to the police." She paused, then added, "I think I'll drive out to see her tomorrow. I can talk to her about it then. In any case, it's been awhile since I've been out to see her. I owe her a visit."

"Uh-huh. Are you forgetting that you just saw her at the funeral?" I responded.

It was Kit who waved this argument away with a brisk flip of her wrist. "Oh, please," she said dismissively. "You know funerals are just like weddings. You never really have time to have a proper chat with anybody."

"Exactly," said Ann with a knowing smile. "That's all it is, a social visit. I'll see her and then put her in touch with Joe."

Joe. Now I understood Ann's desire to stay involved in this case. She wanted every reason possible to stay in touch with Joe. That I got; that I would cheerfully help her with. But I wasn't going to let her endanger herself.

"We'll all go with you, Ann," said Kit. "You need your family around you at a time like this."

I stared at Kit in astonishment. She sat calmly, a satisfied smile playing on her lips. As I said, I got Ann's desire to get involved. It was Kit's sudden desire for involvement that I didn't get. At first. Then it hit me: she wanted to show me up. Even though she had just blasted me for "playing sleuth," she was quite prepared to play the same game if she thought that it would win her points with Ann. An even stronger motivation was her desire to beat me. It was just like the summer after my first year of college. Friends of mine were having a keg party. Kit, of course, was appalled. "Underage drinking is not only stupid but it's illegal!" she'd scoffed. Until, that is, she got invited. Suddenly it wasn't such a moral dilemma after all. She went happily and then spent the better part of the night puking in the bushes after doing a keg stand.

I didn't know what she was planning this time, but I didn't want to get stuck holding her hair again while she emptied the contents of her stomach.

After lunch, Kit headed back to her house full of promises to see us again tomorrow for our drive out to St. Michaels. Ann discussed the details with Kit, as I was so disgusted with her that I didn't trust myself to get out a civil word.

A little before eight that night, Ann and I headed to Miles and Laura's house. They, too, lived in Georgetown, only a few quaint cobblestone streets over from Uncle Marty's house. It was starting to get dark earlier now, and dusk had settled by the time we got there; the last of the sun's fading rays brushed the clouds with a faint blush of indigo and purple. A soft maze of ivy crisscrossed the house's classic three-story Georgian façade, the once green leaves now a warm red. Shallow steps led to a white paneled door above which a fanlight glowed with hospitable brightness. Laura answered our knock, swinging open the door with a welcoming smile. She was wearing a black A-line dress with cream piping and a simple strand of pearls. "Hello, dears," she said, waving us inside. "Miles got hung up with some client at the office, but he should be here soon. Come on in."

Ann and I stepped into the large foyer lit by an antique crystal chandelier. We followed Laura across the thick jewel-toned Oriental rug into the living room. Here Laura's love of flowers was on full display, from the freshly cut tulips, roses, and lilies spilling out of thick vases to the brightly colored botanical patterns on the furniture. I took a seat on a yellow club chair emblazoned with red cabbage roses, while Ann and Laura sat on the couch, which was red with yellow roses.

"What can I get you to drink?" asked Laura, indicating the drink tray on the low mahogany coffee table in front of the couch.

"I'll have a glass of Merlot, please," said Ann, after studying her options.

"I'll have the same," I added.

Laura poured the wine, plus a glass for herself, then settled back on the couch. Turning to Ann, she said, "So, kiddo, how are you holding up?"

Ann shrugged before answering. "I'm not sure, actually. I feel a little like my whole world just got turned on its head over the past few days. Losing Dad was bad enough, but then add in

Bonnie's bizarre behavior and the discovery about Michael and the *memories* of Michael and then to have the police think that I . . . I mean, it was bad enough having to see"—Ann paused, taking a sip of wine—"Joe again after all these years, but under these circumstances, it's all the worse somehow. My defenses are already down."

Laura nodded in understanding. "I know, darling. I can only imagine how difficult this has been for you. No one believes for one minute that you had anything to do with his murder. The whole thing is just ridiculous. Miles is already working on it. And I can sympathize with your feelings at seeing Joe again." She paused and toyed with the long stem of the wineglass, apparently trying to choose her next words carefully. "I think one reason this is so hard is that you've devoted yourself to the family—perhaps more so than is healthy. You've made this family your universe. You need to be a little more . . . well, *selfish* for a change. Go out more. See more of the world. Meet more *people*." It was clear that by people, Laura meant men. Ann looked down at her lap. "By expanding your horizons," Laura continued, "these kinds of setbacks won't prey on you as much. You'll be able to keep them in perspective."

Ann shook her head. "Laura, I know you mean well, and I know you *meant* well before, but . . . don't get me wrong, I do love you, but . . ." Ann's voice dropped. "But I honestly think I would have been happier if I'd stayed with Joe."

Laura directed a melancholy smile at Ann before shaking her head as if to negate this thought. "Ann, you were young and about to begin a new life as a student abroad studying Shakespeare. Do you really think that was the best time to become engaged?"

"'The time is out of joint,'" Ann muttered. "'O cursed spite.'"

"Come on now," Laura said with an indulgent chuckle. "Look at you now. You have a wonderful job, doing exactly what you one day hoped you'd be doing. You're working at the Folger! Do you really think that would have happened if you'd settled down in St. Michaels as the wife of a policeman? Don't get me wrong: Joe is a very decent sort of man, but I don't think he is in your league."

I kept my mouth—for once—firmly shut. I liked Laura. She had a good heart and she meant well, but she was a dreadful snob at times. Brought up in a wealthy family that not only extolled the virtues of higher education but also socialized primarily with other wealthy intellects, Laura had grown up equating wealth with refinement and intellectual curiosity. As such, she viewed (incorrectly) Joe's humble beginnings and subsequent career choice as evidence of an inelegant mind.

"And speaking of work, are you still seeing Ben Wicks?" Laura asked Ann, referring to the coworker she'd gone out with a few times. Ben Wicks was a sweet, shy guy who was something of an expert on Shakespeare's sonnets. Ann had taken him under her wing when he started at the Folger and I think he'd been grateful for her friendship. However, while they had a mutual passion for Shakespeare, it hadn't translated into one for each other.

Ann shook her head. "No, I think we're better as friends. Besides, he started seeing this grad student, Devon, who worked for him this summer. Ben thought he'd discovered a lost sonnet of Shakespeare's. He and Devon got very close while they researched it."

I already knew this story and so giggled and said, "They fell in love over poetry!" Ann laughed.

"That doesn't mean it's necessarily over," said Laura.

"Devon's a guy," Ann added drily.

"Oh, well in that case, then it probably *is* over," Laura amended with a smile. "I'm sorry. Is there anybody else you're interested in?"

"Not really," said Ann. "Most of the guys I know are taken. They're either happily married or happily divorced and now dating pubescent young things, or they're gay. I hate to say it, but there are times when I wonder if there's any truth behind that stupid statistic." She looked at me for confirmation. "You know the one that says if you haven't married by age forty—"

"You're more likely to die in a terrorist attack than walk down the aisle," I finished. "Yes, I know it."

Laura burst out laughing. "What utter nonsense! First of all, Ann, you are all of thirty, and second of all, look at me. I didn't marry Miles until I was well past my fortieth birthday. And it wasn't some case of two old fogies coming together out of mutual loneliness: It was—and is—true love."

Ann sat seemingly lost in thought, staring at her glass of wine. Laura turned to me. Her brow was furrowed in concern at Ann's mood. However, she switched topics. "Ann tells me that you are seeing someone now, Elizabeth," she said.

I smiled. "Yes. His name is Peter. Like you, I never thought I'd meet a nice guy. Most of my ex-boyfriends seemed to wander off on me; either with other women or personal items of mine."

"I've been there," Laura said sympathetically. "I'd gotten so used to that particular type of behavior that I actually began to anticipate it. I even thought Miles was about to break up with me."

Ann looked up, astounded. "Miles? You thought Miles was going to break up with you? He's adored you from the day he met you! When was this?"

"Oh, a long time ago, back when we were dating. But actually, now that I think of it, it was right before we got engaged— which shows you how clueless I was. I remember I was out of town one weekend visiting my mother and when I came home there he was at the airport with a huge bouquet of roses and a ring." Laura smiled softly at the memory. "He was actually getting on a plane himself in the next hour, but he said he didn't want to waste one more minute not engaged to me." Almost as an aside, she said, "I remember I was so relieved that I burst into tears right there in the middle of Gate Twenty-four."

"Why were you relieved?" I asked.

Laura appeared embarrassed. "Well, I didn't talk to him at all while I was away that weekend, and I guess I got worried that he'd gotten tired of me. But we'll have been together nine years in July," she said happily. "And I'm as happy today as I was then. Miles is one of a kind."

As if on cue, the front door opened and Miles strolled in. Shrugging out of his blue blazer and loosening his green paisley tie, Miles apologized for his lateness, explaining that he'd had to meet with a difficult client. Apparently the woman had recently been to France, where she visited Versailles. Enchanted with Marie Antoinette's Petit Trianon and gardens, she wanted to create something similar. "A friggin' hamlet in a tiny town house backyard is what she wants me to create," Miles fumed. "A place where, like the young queen, she can, and I'm quoting here, 'escape her burdens.' Burdens! This from a woman who spends her day spoiling her silly dogs! Ten to one, I'm going to want to behead *her* after another month of this," he predicted.

Laura poured him a generous glass of wine and rose from her seat. She greeted him first with a kiss then the wine.

Smiling, Miles returned the kiss and said, "Well, thank you! I'll have to be late for dinner more often! What was that for?"

"Oh, just for being you," she said. "I was just telling Ann and Elizabeth about how you proposed to me at the airport."

"One of the best days of my life," he said with a nod. Miles sat down in the chair next to mine. "And now look at us—an old married couple."

Laura grimaced. "Speak for yourself, old man."

Two hours later, we were sitting in the dining room enjoying Laura's homemade peach kutchen after having a wonderful dinner of rack of lamb, peas, and orzo. The conversation had drifted to the discovery of Michael's body.

"The whole situation is simply horrible," Laura said to Ann. "I feel especially terribly for you and Reggie—it's almost like you both have to relive Michael's deviousness. We all thought so highly of him, your father in particular! Afterward, well, I can only guess at the betrayal Marty must have felt. And Reggie! I sometimes wonder if her subsequent rash of marriages wasn't somehow a result of the whole debacle with Michael."

"How so?" I asked.

"Well, Reggie was *really* in love with Michael," said Laura. "When she met him, it was as if she was suddenly struck with Cupid's arrow. Don't you remember? She was all hot and heavy with that boy . . . oh, what was his name?"

"Donny Mancuso," Ann offered.

"That's right! What a good memory you have!" Laura said. I studiously refrained from looking at Ann. "Anyway," Laura continued, "she dropped Donny like a hot potato. I never was a big fan of his, a bit of a jug head, I always thought, but was he ever devastated. He pined after her for months, but Reggie never gave him a second look after meeting Michael." Laura paused and took a sip of coffee. "You know, I don't think she's ever really loved anyone the way she loved Michael. She didn't like him just because he was heir to the business. She liked him for himself. Afterward, it was as if she put up a kind of emotional wall; she wasn't going to let herself get hurt again. In every relationship she's had since him, she's the one who has ended things, not the other way around. I really think that for each one of those relationships, Reggie was really trying to get Michael out of her system."

"Well, if that's the case, that boy must have really clogged up her system," Miles said with a smirk as he took a bite of the kutchen.

Ann hid a smile and said, "But Laura, you're forgetting, Reggie broke it off with Michael, too."

Laura dipped her head in acknowledgment. "I know, and thank God she did given all we've learned about the kind of person he turned out to be. But I don't think Reggie really thought it was over until Michael took off and then money was discovered missing. She may have ended things with him hoping that he'd sort out his drinking issues and then come back to her. When he didn't, and she learned of the embezzlement, she was devastated." Ann looked down and said nothing. "You had left for England so you weren't here for the aftermath," Laura continued, "but I can tell you it was awful. Here I was planning my wedding and she was dismantling hers. Oh, the money she was going to spend on that wedding!" Laura shook her head at the memory. "There was no budget whatsoever. Even Marty was starting to get worried. He asked me at one point to see if I could talk to her about incorporating a little moderation into the planning, but you would have thought I told her to have a barbecue in the backyard from the way she reacted. I remember she said that she might as well get married at City Hall." Laura rolled her eyes. "No, she was going to have the wedding of her dreams. She had planned every detail. The menu, the dresses, the decorations, that custom-made arch, the shape of the pool . . ." Laura broke off as we all thought how the pool had played its part.

"Oh, God, I remember that arch thing," Miles said quickly, to change the morbid direction of our thoughts. "I think she must have attended a Jewish ceremony, because it was basically a chuppah. A really, really tacky chuppah," he added with a smile.

Laura sprang to Reggie's defense. "No, it wasn't! It was lovely. You saw it, didn't you, Ann?"

Ann shook her head. "No. What did it look like?"

Laura opened her mouth, but it was Miles who spoke. "It looked like a wooden arch upon which every conceivable aspect of wildlife had landed and remained stuck. Roses, bees, birds, small woodland creatures; hell, I think even Old Nessie may have been carved into that thing."

"Okay, it may have been a bit over the top, but I assure you it wasn't *that* bad," Laura insisted.

Miles shot her a challenging look. "Well, in any case, I'm almost positive that Nessie was featured."

"For a girl whose idea of roughing it is to go to a four-star hotel, I don't know why Reggie ever picked the whole 'nature' theme for her wedding," Miles said, laughing.

"Maybe like your client, she'd recently been to Versailles and was inspired by Marie Antoinette," I suggested with mock seriousness.

"She made up for it with her next wedding," Ann said. "Remember that one?"

I rolled my eyes. "How could I ever forget? The Little Bo-Peep wedding." For that one, Reggie had gone with the shepherdess theme. Wide puffy dresses, satin sashes, and lacy hats ruled the day. At the reception, real sheep wandered about the lawn. Real sheep that had apparently eaten quite well the night before. Nothing says wedding fun like stepping around mounds of sheep poop.

"Wait," said Miles. "I thought Little Boy Peep was Reggie's *second* wedding. Wasn't the one with the Indian priestess her first?"

"No, that was her third," corrected Ann. "Her second was the one where we all wore pink. Remember, it was on Valentine's Day?"

Miles gave a slight shudder. "Ah, yes. The blushing bride wore a corset of sorts, if I remember correctly."

"Now, don't make fun. Reggie's been through a lot," admonished Laura.

Miles and Ann ruined the sentiment by adding "of men" in unison to Laura's statement and then bursting into laughter. Laura appeared scandalized, but after a moment even she laughed.

CHAPTER 16

*One does not love a place the less for having
suffered in it, unless it has been all suffering,
nothing but suffering.*

—PERSUASION

*S*UNDAY DAWNED another glorious fall day. Well, I assumed it dawned that way, as I wasn't awake for the actual occurrence. Over the years, I've found the whole "crack of dawn" experience to be wholly overrated. Besides, given the week we'd had, Ann and I agreed that sleeping in was a priority. Of course, truth be told, I'd be hard-pressed to name a time when sleeping in *isn't* a priority for me.

We had planned a leisurely morning of drinking coffee on the back patio and tackling nothing more strenuous than the crossword puzzle (in *People,* not *The New York Times*) before heading out for St. Michaels. Ann had called Nana the night before to make sure our visit wasn't inconvenient. Nana had been thrilled and had insisted on us coming for lunch. Kit, of course, had been just as thrilled when we called her with the plan. Out of politeness, I won't mention my reaction to hearing that Kit was joining us, but I can tell you that "thrilled" wasn't it.

Which is why, I suppose, I was irritated to awake to a ringing doorbell at the ungodly hour of eight thirty. I was even more irritated upon opening the door to discover that it was Kit who was doing the ringing. Her blond hair was shinning, her face was dewy fresh, and her linen jumper actually looked like it had been ironed. She could have been the cover girl for *Fit Pregnancy*. Scarlett yipped at her in apparent annoyance. I didn't stop her.

"Goodness, you certainly aren't a sight for sore eyes," Kit said, her expression disdainful as her eyes traveled from my bed head to my oversized T-shirt and boxers to the pièce de résistance—my well-worn bunny slippers. "I hope you never let Peter see you like this—he'll run screaming. Don't tell me that you're still in bed at this hour!"

"Clearly not, Kit," I said. "I am standing here. Answering the door. For you."

"Well, aren't you Miss Grumpy today!" she said as I turned and headed for the kitchen like a lion stalking a gazelle to make myself some much-needed coffee. Kit trailed after me, still talking. "I can't believe you're not up yet!" she said. "For goodness' sake, I've been up for hours. I even worked out already. I've been doing this great pregnancy yoga workout. You know, you should try it."

"Thank you, but I am not pregnant," I pointed out.

"Well, I know *that*! God forbid! Mom would *freak* if you showed up *pregnant*. That would be the straw that broke the camel's back!" She said this in such a horrified tone it was almost as if she thought I actually *was* pregnant.

"Kit!" I said, a warning note in my voice.

For once she got the point. "All I'm saying is that if you ever finally *do* get married and start a family, you are going to be the quintessential grouchy expectant mother." She giggled, apparently tickled at the thought. "I can just see you, lying on the couch, moaning, and still wearing those awful bunny slippers."

"Remind me why you're here again? At eight thirty in the morning?" I asked, as I loaded the coffeemaker.

"I thought we should get an early start."

"Why on earth would we need an early start?" I asked. "We aren't expected at Nana's until noon, and it's only a forty-five-minute drive. Besides, premature arrival is a most untoward event." Before Kit could reply, I went on, "Maybe you should go spread your sunshine around someone else. I've not had my coffee yet and without it, I really can't ensure your safety."

Ann stumbled into the kitchen just then, still wiping sleep from her eyes. "Oh, hello, Kit," she said. "I'm sorry, I didn't realize you were here."

"No earthly reason why you should have," I said, before hitting Start on the coffeemaker.

"Elizabeth is grouchy," Kit announced to Ann as if I were a five-year-old.

"You know what else Elizabeth is?" I snapped, spinning around to let Kit have a piece of my mind. Granted, at this hour of the morning without the benefit of caffeine, my mind, let alone a piece of it, was apt to be pathetic. But I was determined.

Ann, who clearly knew me better than my own sister, took one look at me and saw that words were about to be said. Lovely, insulting, vulgar words. I didn't go to an all-girls Catholic school for nothing. Those girls know how to curse. Some even minored in it. I opened my mouth ready to give Kit an earful.

Quickly cutting in, Ann said, "She's a wonderful friend and cousin who has had a long week. Now, Kit, why don't you come outside with me and sit on the back patio? It's really lovely in the morning." With a friendly wink at me, Ann steered Kit outside to safety.

By the time I finished getting the coffee and the bagels ready, I was in a much calmer mood. Loading everything onto a tray, I headed out to join Ann and Kit. It was another glorious day. The sky was a clear blue with a soft cool breeze coming out of the north. Or the south. I really couldn't tell. My sense of direction is pretty lousy.

"So explain to me again why do you think Nana will be able to shed some light on this business," Kit was saying to Ann. I put the tray down on the table between them and handed Ann her coffee. She gave me a grateful smile and took a large sip before answering.

"It's nothing specific," she said slowly. "Like I said yesterday, it's just that Nana had a way of knowing everything that was going on. Part of her job was heading off trouble before it occurred—not an easy job with any of us, but especially Reggie. Let's just say she was very good at her job. She had a kind of sixth sense with us."

"I do remember that she never liked Michael," I added as I dropped into a chair and helped myself to a warm bagel. "She was right about him."

"Yes, but that doesn't mean she knows what happened to him," Kit pointed out.

"Of course not," I said, "but she might have some information that could shed a little light on the situation."

Ann stared into her coffee cup. "I just hope it's a good light," she said quietly.

As planned, we arrived in St. Michaels a little before noon. A quaint waterfront town on the Eastern Shore of Maryland, St. Michaels is known for its striking churches, elegant homes, and fashionable shopping. Nana lived in a picturesque two-story white colonial not far from the center of town. Ancient trees graced the front yard, their leafy branches looping low across the manicured lawn. Sunlight bounced off the calm blue water out back.

"Wow!" Kit exclaimed upon seeing the house as we pulled into the curved driveway. "Her house is gorgeous! It must be worth at least a million dollars! Just what kind of salary did Uncle Marty pay her?"

"Actually, I think her brother left her some money. She bought the house right after she stopped working for Dad. Right after I left for London," Ann said.

Nana opened the door and waved happily to Ann. She looked just like you'd expect someone nicknamed Nana to look. A petite woman, with a round face, sharp blue eyes, and shoulder-length hair pulled back with a black velvet ribbon. Granted she had changed somewhat since the days she managed the Reynolds children. Now in her late sixties, her hair, once a rich shade of chestnut, had faded to a silvery white, and faint wrinkles lined her checks and forehead. Her carriage, however, had not succumbed to age; she still moved with the same assured ramrod posture that instilled both fear and respect.

Ann bounded out of the car and ran to Nana on the doorstep and enveloped her in a giant hug. It wasn't the friendly hug you give an old acquaintance—this was the needy hug of a child seeking comfort. Ann seemed to sag into Nana.

"How are you holding up, honey? Are you okay?" Nana asked softly as she gently stroked Ann's back.

Ann's reply was muffled and she kept her head buried in Nana's shoulder. After a moment she stepped back. Her eyes were a tad red, but she seemed in control.

Nana glanced my way. "Hello, Elizabeth," she said. "How have you been?"

"I've been fine, Nana," I replied. "It's good to see you." Gesturing to Kit, I added, "Have you met my sister, Kit?"

Nana politely shook Kit's hand before turning back to me. "I have to admit, Elizabeth, I hardly recognized you at the funeral. I must say, you've certainly changed since I last saw you. You're so tall and slim!"

I may have neglected to mention before now that as a child I ate my feelings, feelings that usually manifested themselves as chocolate doughnuts and sausage pizza (it's been my experience that feelings rarely take the form of, say, carrots or celery). So what I'm saying is that I was on the heavy side. Still, there was no call for Kit to snigger (yes, *snigger*!) and say, "Yes, Elizabeth was something of a porker when she was younger."

Repressing the urge to deck Kit right there on the front lawn, I instead sweetly said, "Yes, but these days it's Kit who has the extra weight, but, of course, that's because she's expecting. We're all so excited."

Distracted by Nana's coos of congratulation, Kit didn't have time to decipher if my comment was intentionally snarky (it was). Once she finished congratulating Kit, Nana invited us into her house. Although it was large and spacious, it had a cozy, snug feel to it. The foyer was simple, with a wide-planked wood floor and a high ceiling. Nana led us into a cheerful sitting room that boasted a vaulted ceiling with exposed beams and a wall of windows that afforded a stunning view of the water.

Nana directed us to take seats, before asking in a serious voice, "So, how are you doing, Ann? The truth." Kit and I sat down on a canary yellow couch, while Ann took a seat on a club chair upholstered in red gingham. Nana sat down in its twin and studied her old charge with a concerned expression.

Ann shrugged before answering. "I'm not going to lie to you, Nana. The past few days have been terrible. It's been bad enough dealing with Dad's death and all the aftermath, but I've had to relive some really painful memories."

Ann fell silent. Nana said nothing. She knew Ann well enough to let her talk at her own pace. After a moment, Ann told Nana of Michael's attack. Nana's blue eyes grew dark with anger. "That son of a bitch," she muttered. Ann nodded in full agreement and then said, "But, honestly, the worst of it is that Joe is in charge of the investigation."

A knowing expression crept into Nana's eyes. Even after all these years, she didn't need to be reminded who Joe was. "Ah, so Joe is back in the picture, is he?" she said thoughtfully.

Ann flushed. "He's not back in *that* way."

Nana looked unconvinced but did not press the topic. "Well, tell me then, what's happened so far with the investigation?"

Ann quickly and succinctly brought Nana up to date with

everything that had happened so far. Nana sighed and shook her head. "I always thought that Michael would come to a bad end, but I never envisioned this."

"Did you never like him?" Ann asked.

"I have to admit that at first I thought he was charming. He knew how to work people. But after a while I sensed that his charm was all an act. There was an aspect of him that was closed off. I don't know how to explain this, but there was something artificial about him that bothered me." Nana looked at us as if at a loss for words. "You never got the impression of a true burst of feeling," she finally said. "I tried to talk to Reggie about it, but she was beyond reason when it came to him. She was head over heels about that boy."

"But she nevertheless ended it," I pointed out.

Nana nodded. "True, but I always thought there was more to it. I sometimes wondered if they didn't just have a minor tiff and Reggie overreacted and ended things. I don't have to remind you about her temper. She may have assumed that he would come back, hat in hand, and that they would work it out."

"That's exactly what I thought!" Kit exclaimed excitedly. "I told Elizabeth almost the same thing! When my husband and I were engaged, we had several big fights. It's just such a stressful time. I don't think most people realize that."

"Did Reggie ever talk to you about the breakup?" I asked Nana, ignoring Kit.

Nana shook her head. "No. She pretended not to care, but I remember the day the workman came and took back her wedding arch. At that point we'd learned about the embezzlement, but she still burst into tears when it was loaded onto the truck. Her pride may not have allowed her to ever take him back, but that didn't mean her heart wasn't hurt."

"I have to admit to you, Nana," said Ann, "I'm worried that the police aren't going to focus on anyone besides me. I wondered if *you* remember anything about the weekend of Dad's Fourth of July party—that's the last time any of us saw him."

Nana considered for a moment. "Hang on," she said and rose from her chair. She went to a built-in bookshelf on the far wall. "I still have my journals from back then."

"You kept your journals? This long?" Ann asked in surprise. "Why?"

Nana shoulders lifted in a shrug. "Hard to say, really. But every time I try to get rid of them, I end up feeling like I'm throwing away those years. But maybe it'll help us out today. Maybe I wrote something that could be useful." I was impressed. The extent of my record keeping is what I throw into my purse. Meaning at any given time you can find scraps of paper with phone numbers scribbled on them but no helpful accompanying name and crumpled Starbucks receipts from two years ago.

After studying the shelves for a few minutes, Nana pulled out a thick leather volume and returned to her chair. Opening the book, she flipped to the week in question and read over her notes. "Hmmm . . ." she said, tapping a slender finger on the page, "I have here that after the party on the fourth, the family returned to the house in Georgetown on the fifth, as construction on the pool was scheduled to begin later that day. Oh, apparently though, your father and Bonnie had a fight on the night of the fifth because I have here that Bonnie returned to St. Michaels that night."

"She left? The fight was that bad? Do you remember what the fight was about?" Ann asked.

"No. I'm sorry to say that fights between them were not uncommon. Depending on how bad they were, Bonnie usually took off for St. Michaels to pout for a day or so." Nana looked back to the journal and read some more. As she did, her lips pulled into a frown and her brows pulled together.

"What is it?" asked Ann.

Nana didn't answer right away; she seemed to be internally debating something. "I don't know if I should say this," she finally said. "Normally I wouldn't, but given the circumstances . . ."

"What?" Ann asked impatiently.

"Well, I have a note here that when I went back to the St. Michaels house on the fifteenth to supervise the pickup of Reggie's wedding arch, I found that Bonnie had had company. She'd left two wineglasses and an empty bottle of wine out on the back porch. Of course, it would never occur to her to clean up after herself."

No one spoke at first. I knew what I was thinking: Bonnie had entertained a male visitor while away from Uncle Marty. I wondered if anyone else shared my view. "Do you think . . ." I began.

Nana tipped her white head in acknowledgment at my unfinished question. "I'm sorry to say that it wouldn't surprise me. Neither of them was happy in that marriage. Your father had a mistress of sorts with his business. Bonnie was left largely bored and with a lot of free time. That's never a good combination."

Ann sat with a bewildered expression on her face. "Bonnie with another man? I guess it doesn't surprise me, given her selfish personality, but she always made such a big production of adoring my dad."

"That she did," Nana said noncommittally.

Ann glanced up. "You think it was just that, don't you? A production—an act."

"I think that she was a foolish young woman who could be easily led astray," Nana said. "I also think she was very lonely."

Ann slumped against the chair's cushioned backing. "Wow. Bonnie and another man. But who? Do you have any idea who it might have been?"

Nana shook her head. "No. And before you go off half-cocked, my dear, remember this is all rank speculation," she said with an admonishing wag of her finger. "We have no proof of anything. Two wineglasses and an empty bottle doesn't necessarily add up to an affair."

"No, but it means she had company," Ann replied.

"Which is not a crime in your own home," Nana pointed out reasonably. And giving Ann and me a pointed look, she added, "I daresay you young ladies have been known to finish a bottle yourselves." Ann and I studiously looked at each other as if we had no idea what Nana could possibly mean. She laughed and changed the subject. "Now why don't we move out to the back patio? It's still warm out. I thought we could eat lunch out there."

We all moved to the kitchen to help Nana with lunch. By unspoken agreement, the subjects of Bonnie and Michael's murder were dropped. Unfortunately, they were replaced by the subject of Kit's pregnancy (two guesses who brought *that* up). As we helped to bring the Cobb salad out to the porch, Kit began to discuss in detail her preferred birthing method (natural) and her reasons for it (immediate bonding with the baby). Perhaps to tune out a monologue that I already knew by heart, I found my brain focusing on something else: could Bonnie's visitor have been Michael?

CHAPTER 17

We have all a better guide in ourselves, if we would
attend to it, than any other person can be.

—MANSFIELD PARK

FTER OUR VISIT with Nana, Ann, Kit, and I headed
back to Uncle Marty's house. Kit wanted to hang
out, but she had to get home to Pauly. Even though I was going
to stay with Ann, Kit nevertheless left in a good mood. "Let's
plan to get together later this week for lunch and compare notes
on the case," she called out cheerily as she left. "I'll come by later
with my ideas."

With her departure, Ann and I headed for the living room
and flopped down on the couch. Scarlett, who had been sleeping on the middle cushion, leaped off the couch and stalked off
in an apparent huff. Neither of us spoke for several minutes; it
had been a long day.

"You know?" Ann said after a few minutes. "Even though I
recognized that Bonnie and Dad didn't have a happy marriage,
I never suspected her of actually seeing someone else. I mean,
she flirted and everything, but I thought it was more to make
Dad notice her. I never thought she'd actually have an affair."

"But what about Miles?" I asked. "Didn't you tell me that you thought Bonnie had a crush on him?"

"Yes, but that was different somehow. I don't know how to explain it, but with Miles I always got the impression that her feelings were ultimately harmless." Her hands fluttered in front of her as she struggled to explain. "I think she liked him, yes, but I also think she knew that nothing could ever happen because of my dad. I think she also wanted to make my dad jealous."

"Really?"

"I don't know," she amended. "Maybe I'm just being a revisionist. Thinking something and knowing something are two different things."

"Well, to be fair, we don't know that she actually did anything. Nana is right that an empty bottle of wine and two glasses don't mean anything more than she had company," I said.

"But you don't believe that, do you?"

I sighed. "No, not really."

"Neither do I. Well, I guess it doesn't matter anyway. I can't see that it has any bearing on Michael's murder."

When I didn't respond, Ann turned and studied me closely. "What are you thinking? Do you think Bonnie might have seen something? Do you think she might actually *know* something?"

I wasn't sure how to answer. "I'm not sure," I said slowly. "I guess I wondered if *Michael* could have been her visitor."

Ann sputtered in astonishment. "Michael! You think *Michael* was Bonnie's visitor? Why?"

I held up my hands, palms up. "Whoa! I said I wondered *if* he could have been her visitor. I don't know anything for sure. I just thought that Bonnie may have been at the house around the time that Michael died and . . ." I trailed off, not sure how to finish.

Ann considered what I'd said. "Do you mean you think Bonnie might have had something to do with Michael's death?"

I shook my head. "Again, I don't know. I'm just thinking out loud. It could be that Michael visited her or it could be that when Bonnie was at the house she saw something. Or it could be nothing at all."

Ann closed her eyes in concentration. "So wait. Let's say it was Michael. He leaves the party on the morning of the fifth—that fits in with his car being gone. Then he comes back later that night and meets with Bonnie. They have wine—why? I can't see them as lovers. Michael was a pig, but Bonnie was twenty years older than him."

"Maybe as a form of celebration?" I ventured.

Ann's eyes flew open. "Celebration? For what?" My meaning sunk in. "You mean Bonnie might have been Michael's accomplice in the embezzlement?"

"It's only a theory."

"But why steal from my dad in the first place?" Ann asked. "She had everything she could want—clothes, cars, jewelry. Dad gave her a generous allowance."

"Some people always want more," I said. "She might have wanted more freedom than her allowance provided. She might have also looked at it as a kind of revenge on your father—Nana said it wasn't a very happy marriage. Maybe Bonnie was tired of being put down and ignored."

Ann thought about this. "Okay, I see what you're saying. But even if Bonnie was Michael's accomplice, do you really think she could have killed him? How could she overpower Michael? He wasn't a small man."

"According to the police, he was killed with a blunt instrument. That's not hard to do if you catch someone by surprise," I said, adding, "or drug his wine first. But we're getting way ahead of ourselves. They might have been accomplices—they might not have. Bonnie could have been in on the embezzlement and still not have killed Michael. Bonnie could also have done nothing more sinister than have a glass of wine with a sympathetic friend after a fight with her husband."

Ann sank back against the couch's cushions. "Jesus. I don't know what to think. This is all becoming surreal. I don't know what to do."

"You don't have to *do* anything. Just call Joe and tell him what Nana told us. After all, it's *their* investigation."

"You're right," Ann said, brightening. "I'll call Joe."

Ann's call to Joe lasted much longer than one would expect a simple exchange of information to take. I took that as a good sign. From the smile that played on her lips as they talked, I took it as a really good sign. Leaving her to finish her conversation in private, I headed for my room to call Peter. Unfortunately, he was in a meeting and couldn't talk. I had just hung up when my phone rang again. It was Aunt Winnie.

"What's this I hear about you and Kit teaming up to solve Michael's murder?" she asked as soon as I answered.

"What . . . ?" I sputtered, confused. Then the light dawned. "Oh, wait, let me guess. Kit called you, didn't she?"

"Bingo. Apparently you two are doing a little investigating?" I could hear the amusement in her voice.

"It's not like that," I said with a groan. "Ann wanted to check out a few ideas and asked me to tag along. When Kit found out—"

"She decided to tag along as well," Aunt Winnie finished.

"Exactly."

"Elizabeth, I'm forever grateful to you for your help last New Year's, but please be careful," she said, the amusement now gone from her voice. "You are not a trained detective. You have a sharp mind and a good sense of people, but there's something you don't have."

"What's that?"

"A detective's license and a gun," she said bluntly. "As you are already well aware from experience, someone who has killed once might do so again, especially if they think they are going to get caught."

"I promise you, Aunt Winnie, I'm not in any danger. I am just helping Ann. I think she's conducting her own limited investigation partly to prove that she had nothing to do with it but mainly as a reason to keep in touch with Joe. I'm pretty sure that he still has feelings for her. My only real goal here is to help get them back together."

Aunt Winnie laughed. "One word, honey: bullshit. I know you too well. If you really think that's your only motive, you are kidding yourself. You're bored and looking for some excitement. Please, for my sake, go take up bungee jumping or hang gliding. They're safer."

"I'm not—" I began to argue, but she cut me off.

"Yes. You. Are."

I was silent as I thought about what she was saying. I *was* bored. I knew it and apparently so did she.

"What's the matter with me?" I asked wearily.

"Nothing at all, honey," she said gently. "Twenty years ago, you would have been told to settle down and raise a family. God knows, I heard that enough times. It's utter crap, of course. You need to start doing what you love, that's all. You hate your job and Peter is gone a lot. You're just trying to fill the void. But for my sake, don't fill it with dead bodies."

I laughed. "Okay, point taken. Maybe I'll check the want ads tomorrow."

"An excellent idea. I'm not saying you shouldn't help Ann. I just want you in one piece. Remember, I need you this fall."

"So this isn't about my safety, then, it's just about you getting some free labor out of me, isn't it?" I joked.

"Damn skippy it is," she said.

Over the next few days, Ann and I spent hours hunting down and cataloging all the items listed in Uncle Marty's will. Many of the pieces were easy to find, such as jewelry, paintings, glassware, place settings, and flatware. Other objects, such as letters, cards, and artwork the girls did as children, were more difficult to locate and necessitated searches of both Uncle Marty's office and the attic.

The attic was jam-packed with boxes, trunks, and discarded furniture; among which there were a fair number of mirrors. Ann and I rearranged the space somewhat, pushing back boxes and dragging a few chairs together to create a kind of work area. From there we could sit and sort through some forty years of mementos. Uncle Marty had saved everything. Every report card, finger painting, and Father's Day card was tucked into labeled envelopes. There were some boxes that coordinated with years, others with vacations or holidays. We went through it all.

I noticed at one point that Ann had pulled a small shoe box onto her lap and was digging through the contents with a wistful smile on her face. "Anything interesting?" I asked.

Ann looked up as if surprised to find me there. She seemed a million miles away. "Oh, no," she said. "Just some old letters from Joe."

"I'm sorry. Are you okay?"

She nodded. "I will be. Let's keep going."

I grabbed the next box nearest to me. It was simply labeled REGGIE/WEDDING/M. "Hey, here's a box full of plans for Reggie and Michael's wedding," I said.

Ann looked up. "Do you think there would be anything in there that could help us?"

I shrugged. "I don't know. There might be."

Although I looked carefully through the contents of that box, hoping for some clue about Michael's murder, there was nothing. All I discovered were detailed plans for Reggie's scrapped wedding to Michael. I found invitation mock-ups, guest lists, catering menus, music selections, flower choices, and a photo of the arch (there were indeed woodland creatures but, alas, no Nessie), but no clues as to why the bridegroom had been murdered.

After the attic, we tackled the office. Here, too, we found a complete and organized cataloging of the past forty years. Each year was captured into a leather-bound volume, much like the kind that Nana employed. I pulled out the year that Reggie's wedding was to have taken place and opened it to July. I don't know what I was looking for, but there were no telling notations about Michael. There were notes about business transactions, including Miles's trip to New York City, with a meticulous account of his receipts. Not only were the airfare, hotel bill, and several restaurant meals itemized, but also were all the miscellaneous tips to the hotel staff. Lord, what was it with some people and their organizational skills? I felt more ashamed than ever of the contents of my purse. However, the meeting apparently went well because there was a notation underneath it all that read: "Mtg. success/signed on 7/6!!"

There were also several notes about the bills coming in for the wedding. Although Reggie was obviously working under the premise that the sky was the limit for spending, it appeared that Uncle Marty was growing concerned at the spiraling costs. The fabled arch alone cost $20,000, and there was a note reading "talk to Reg re: $wans." From the scribble that followed this entry, I realized that Reggie apparently not only planned on renting real swans for the reception, she also was having someone called a "marzipan master" create individual swans for the guests' dessert.

"It looks like Laura was right about Reggie's budget for the wedding," I said to Ann. "The bills were out of control! Take a look at these." I handed her the journal. Ann shook her head in disbelief as she read. "Lord, it's all so silly. Seventy thousand for flowers! My mother would never have allowed this."

I smiled at her. "Was there method, moderation, and economy employed when she was alive?"

Ann laughed, handing me back the book. "Something like that. There sure as hell weren't baby swans frolicking about the back lawn."

I read more. After the notations about the bills, there were several angry entries of the various meetings with the Board of Directors that took place after Michael's embezzlement came to light. From the venom that laced Uncle Marty's entries, if Michael weren't already dead, Uncle Marty would be my top suspect.

It was all very interesting, but other than an odd fact or two, it didn't bring me any closer to finding out who killed Michael.

The rest of the week progressed slowly, and the only thing I was able to make progress on was my promise to Aunt Winnie. I scoured the want ads, contacted a headhunter, and updated my résumé. I kept my promise to Kit and babysat little Pauly while she and Paul went out to dinner, during which I incurred only minor injuries. Peter's work crisis seemed finally to be coming under control and he expected to be home by the end of the week. Joe and Ann continued to talk—ostensibly about progress on the case (of which there was absolutely none, of course), and Ann seemed happier than I'd seen her in years. While life hadn't gone back to normal per se, it was definitely heading in the right direction.

And then Bonnie called and it all went to hell in a handbasket.

CHAPTER 18

It was a struggle between propriety and vanity;
but vanity got the better.

—PERSUASION

*S*HE'S MET SOMEBODY!" Ann shrieked into the phone.
I pulled the receiver away from my ear and said,
"Who's met somebody?"

"Bonnie!" came the hysterical answer. "Apparently he's her
'soul mate' and she's bringing him home with her! Can you believe it?"

I stared unseeingly at the article on my desk. "Wait. Bonnie
is bringing home a guy? Who is he?"

"His name is Julian. Can you believe it? And not just Julian—
Julian St. Clair, if you please! Dad's funeral was only last week!
Not only does she run off to a spa the day after the funeral, but
now she's coming back with her soul mate!"

"Whose name is Julian St. Clair," I added. I admit I was
somewhat at a loss for words. Granted, Bonnie certainly had
outdone herself this time, but I didn't quite understand Ann's
extreme reaction to it. "Ann, I'm sure it's harmless. Bonnie has
always been daffy. And besides, so what if she's met someone? I

mean the name does sound like a character out of a Harlequin romance novel, but where's the harm?"

"Where's the harm?" Ann repeated in astonishment, her voice growing shrill. "Where's the *harm?* Well, aside from the general horrible *tackiness* of it all, there's the potential for a great deal of harm! I haven't gotten to the worst part yet. Julian is not only her soul mate, but her new financial adviser! Apparently he's, and I'm quoting here, 'an absolute genius with money.'"

"Oh," I said. "Oh, God."

"Oh, *shit* is more like it! What am I going to do? They're coming home today!"

"Okay. Don't panic," I said, hoping to calm her down. "Nothing has happened. Yet. Maybe Julian is actually a nice, stable accountant. Maybe he *is* her soul mate."

Of course, neither of us believed that. Nevertheless, we weren't prepared for the horrible reality that was Julian.

After work I went straight to Uncle Marty's house. Ann looked terrible. Her eyes appeared dazed and her color pale. Her hair stood out in various directions in a manner that suggested she'd been pulling at it. A lot. In lieu of a greeting, she handed me a large glass of white wine. "Here. You're going to need this," she said.

I took the glass. "He's that bad?"

"Worse."

I trusted Ann's judgment. I took a sip. "Where is he?" I asked.

"They're both out on the back patio. Come on," she said wearily, turning and heading that way.

With some trepidation, I followed her. I caught sight of Bonnie first. Wearing cream linen pants and a coral silk blouse, she was reclining on the chaise longue with Scarlett curled up at her feet. Oversized sunglasses hid most of her face. In her right hand, she held a martini glass; in her left, a cigarette. Seeing me, she smiled and sat up a little straighter. "Elizabeth, darling! How are you? Annabel tells me you've been just a wonderful help to her this past week. She certainly looks better than she has in years! Her face has gotten some color in it." To Ann, she asked, "Ann, dear, did you start using that new moisturizer I gave you? It's supposed to work wonders."

"No."

"Oh, well. You should, you know. You know what they say about the face. It's the gateway to the soul."

"That would be the eyes, actually," said Ann.

Bonnie crinkled her nose and considered this. "Well, the moisturizer is supposed to help with crow's-feet, too." Shifting her gaze to my direction, she said, "Anyway, thank you, Elizabeth, for all your help to Ann. It's all such a ghastly mess. I know I could never stomach it. I'd be hopeless at it."

It was unclear if she was referring to the murder investigation or the cataloging of Uncle Marty's things. Not that it really mattered. Either way she was right—she would have been hopeless at both.

Bonnie continued, "Now, I'd like to introduce you to someone very special. Elizabeth, this is my friend Julian St. Clair." With a smoky flourish, she gestured to the man sitting languidly at the table.

I now understood the reason for Ann's distress. I'd heard the term *lounge lizard,* but until now I had never visualized one. Next to the definition in the dictionary, there should be a picture of Julian. I judged him to be in his early to late fifties. He was fit, deeply tan, with slicked black hair and predatory blue eyes. His mouth was full, his cheeks were artfully stubbled, and his chin was weak. He wore an expensive beige linen blazer, tight black jeans, and Italian loafers. I revised my earlier categorization of him as someone out of a Harlequin romance novel; he was more like the villain from one of the cheesier Bond movies.

As I turned his way, he politely rose to his feet. "It's such a pleasure to meet you, Elizabeth. I'm so looking forward to meeting all of Bonnie's extended family," he said in a voice that hinted at a foreign accent. From where I couldn't tell, but I would bet money that it was about as authentic as his tan. Glancing over at Bonnie, he whispered confidentially to me, "She's quite a special lady."

Oh, please. I took a quick sip of wine to hide the disgusted grimace I was quite sure was visible on my face. Bonnie simpered. Scarlett ignored us all and slept. For once, she had the right idea.

Julian continued. "Bonnie tells me that you have been helping Ann sort out this unfortunate business with the murder of the young man, Michael?"

"Well, we've been doing what we can to help the police," I answered, taking a seat at the table. I was unsure how much Ann had actually shared with Bonnie and how much Bonnie had made up.

"Such a terrible tragedy," he murmured. "Bonnie mentioned that she had concerns about her own dear husband's death."

I looked over at Bonnie in annoyance. Was she really still pushing her ridiculous theory that Marty was murdered? Bonnie met my glance with an innocent wide-eyed gaze.

"I told Julian all about it," she said breathlessly. "He agrees with me about poor Marty. Tell me, do the police think there's a connection?"

"No," I answered firmly. Changing the subject, I turned back to Julian and said, "I understand that you two met at the spa?"

"Yes," said Julian. "I noticed Bonnie one morning at the pool. I could see right away from her amazing aura that she was a singular individual. I introduced myself and our connection was instantaneous—almost cosmic." He smiled at Bonnie, his small white teeth flashing brilliantly in the sunlight. From the doorway, Ann made a noise and abruptly went back inside.

"I'm sorry," I said. "Did you say her 'aura'?"

Julian nodded and leaned toward me, his manner intimate and faintly flirtatious. "Yes, her spiritual signature is very clear and strong. As you must already know, the aura is a reflection of our true nature at any given moment." He placed his hand over mine. I wasn't surprised to see that his nails were manicured and buffed to a glossy shine and that he was wearing a gold pinkie ring. "Surely a clever young woman such as yourself must have noticed it," he said as he leaned toward me. The small movement sent a whiff of his cologne my way. My nostrils began to sting. And then burn.

I quickly slid my hand out from under his and moved it under my nose to block the odor. Unfortunately, the scent had transferred itself to my fingers. My eyes began to water. Julian continued, unaware of my distress. "Of course, not everyone has the trained eye. Bonnie's aura is bright, clean pink. It's very rare."

"Of course it is," I murmured, as I tried to pinpoint the main ingredient of the smell. Gasoline? Formaldehyde?

"The pink aura is an indication that the individual has achieved a perfect balance between spiritual awareness and the material existence." I glanced at Bonnie to gauge her reaction to this, but she was busy admiring her manicure, her satisfied expression signifying a kind of spiritual appreciation of the material, I guess.

"Well, that *is* something," I said in what I hoped was a tone of awe. Julian completely missed the sarcasm in my voice and nodded importantly. Bonnie attempted to look modest.

"The most advanced people also have a yellow halo around their head," Julian continued, as if sharing a secret.

"Like Jesus?" I cried excitedly.

This time Julian caught the sarcasm. His eyes narrowed slightly and he leaned away from me. "Did anyone ever tell you that you have a very distinctive aura, my dear? It's very dark."

"Oh, I know," I replied confidentially. "But that's because I'm Irish. To paraphrase Yeats, we Irish have an abiding sense of tragedy, which sustains us through temporary periods of joy."

Julian said nothing. Lighting one of those small, nasty-smelling European cigarettes, he leaned farther back in his chair and turned his attention back to Bonnie. He was not going to waste any more time trying to charm me, for which I was grateful. Frankly, I don't think my nose could take it.

Julian and Bonnie went out for dinner that night. Ann and I opted to eat in—not that we were asked to join them, of course, and not that we would have even if we were asked. With their departure, Ann and I settled into our routine of the past week. We cooked a simple dinner (grilled chicken, squash, brown rice) and took our plates out onto the back patio. The night was almost cool (that previously mentioned breeze from either the north or south having picked up) and the stars stood out with unusual intensity. If it weren't for the lingering scent of Julian's cologne, it might have all seemed a very bad dream. Bonnie was absolutely besotted with the man and clearly had every intention of handing over the entire contents of her bank account to him for "handling." As a grown woman (at least according to her birth certificate), she had every right to make all the idiotic decisions she wanted to. However, as she was still holding on to the proceeds from the sale of the St. Michaels house, I very much doubted that Julian's role of financial adviser would go uncontested by the rest of the family.

"Can you believe this?" Ann asked, as she angrily speared a piece of chicken. "It's bad enough that I've got to deal with a murder investigation, but then Bonnie decides to bring home some greasy boy toy who not only 'sees auras' but smells like he's been marinating in gigolo juice! Have you ever smelled anything so god-awful in your life?"

I laughed. "No, but I imagine that cologne is restricted to a very elite clientele, clientele obviously lacking in olfactory cells."

"I can't imagine the ingredients in that concoction are legal." Ann rolled her eyes in disgust. "But in any case, it's not the sort of scent you'd expect from your money investor."

"Speaking of which, what are we going to do about that?

We can't allow Bonnie to give him access to her accounts. He'll drain them dry!"

"I know. I know," Ann said with a shake of her head. "But short of having her committed, I don't know what we can do."

"Have you called Reggie and Frances and brought them up to date?"

"Yes. We're going to meet for dinner tomorrow night. I want to talk to them both before they come here. I don't think they completely understand the severity of the situation. I don't think anyone really *can* until they meet Julian in person."

I nodded. "The smell alone will tip them off."

It was late by the time Bonnie and Julian returned. Ann made a point of staying up until they got home so she could make sure that Julian at least began the night in the second guest bedroom. "I'll be damned if I'll let her take that man into her bedroom," she said. "All that oil in his hair will ruin the good sheets."

Bonnie made no objection to the arrangement, a factor I took as a good sign. Perhaps it wasn't too late to knock some sense into her silly head. Once Julian retired for the night (after making a big show of gallantly kissing Bonnie's hand), Bonnie followed Ann and me into the kitchen. Pouring herself a glass of white wine, she settled herself at the kitchen counter and said, "So how are the plans coming for Marty's party?"

Ann turned and contemplated her stepmother in horrified disbelief. "The party? Well, gee, Bonnie, I haven't really had time to do anything about that. I've been rather busy, you know?"

Bonnie's blue eyes opened in surprise. "Busy? Doing what?"

Ann let out a strangled laugh. "A great deal, actually. I've been cataloging and organizing everything Dad mentioned in his will, not to mention dealing with the police."

Bonnie shrugged. Never having had to organize anything beyond her shoes, she didn't see the problem. "Well, I would still like to have it. I think Saturday would be perfect."

Ann gaped at her. "Saturday? This Saturday?" Bonnie nodded. "But it's already Thursday! I can't possibly put together a memorial party in just two days!"

"Oh, Annabel, I'm sure Elizabeth here will help you. Besides, as I've always told you, you can do whatever you put your mind to." Bonnie lifted the wineglass in a toast to Ann and took a large sip.

Ann turned to me, her expression one of incredulous fury. While I don't confess to an ability to read minds, I nevertheless had a pretty good idea what Ann would do right now if, as Bonnie suggested, she just put her mind to it. And while it was true that Ann could always count on me, I didn't think assault and verbal battery was our best course of action right now.

"I'd be happy to help," I said quickly, hoping to forestall the outburst I saw forming in Ann's head. "Ann and I will get started on that now. Bonnie, you must be exhausted. Why don't you go to bed and let us get started with the plans? We can tell you all about it in the morning."

Bonnie slumped a little in her seat and nodded. "It *has* been an exhausting week," she admitted with a small sigh. "Julian's been wonderful, of course, but even he can't take away the dreadful shock of Marty's death."

Next to me, Ann's mouth began to twist and curl in an apparent effort to prevent herself from screaming. "Exactly," I said.

"You should get to bed. Ann and I can handle this. You'll feel better after a good night's sleep."

Bonnie took another sip of her wine before setting the glass on the counter. "You're probably right. Let me know what I can do to help," she said to Ann, as she slid out of her chair and scooped up Scarlett. "Julian and I have lunch plans and after that I'm taking him sightseeing. But I should be around later. I think. It really depends on what Julian wants to do."

"I'll keep that in mind," Ann said through clenched teeth.

With a backward wave of her hand, Bonnie floated out of the kitchen, Scarlett tucked under her arm.

"She's—" Ann began, but I cut her off.

"Yes, she is. And more. But there's no point wasting your breath about it. She is what she is. We'll call everyone and tell them to be here at five on Saturday. We'll get some steaks and wine and do a cookout. That will be the easy part. The hard part will be convincing her not to hand over all the money to Julian."

"Is there anything we can do legally?" Ann asked.

"Short of having her ruled incompetent by the courts, I'm not sure."

"Well, I'm sure as hell going to find out. I'll be damned if I'm going to sit by and let her drain everything my father worked for just so she can hand it over to that gigolo."

"Don't worry. That won't happen. I promise," I said.

CHAPTER 19

*You ought certainly to forgive them as a Christian, but
never to admit them in your sight, or allow their names
to be mentioned in your hearing.*

—PRIDE AND PREJUDICE

FTER ANN WENT TO BED, I called Aunt Winnie
and brought her up to date on the latest events. When
I got to the part about Julian and the money, she began to curse.
Spectacularly. Brilliantly. Like the dad in *A Christmas Story,* she
worked in profanity the way other artists worked with oil or
clay. It was her true medium. When she finished, I said, "Yes,
yes. But what are we going to *do?*"

"I don't know yet. But I'm coming down tomorrow. Let me
book a flight. I'll call you later with the details."

My next call was to Peter. While the essence of his reaction
to hearing about Bonnie was essentially the same as Aunt Winnie's (shock, disgust, concern), it was not nearly as vulgar. "Well,
my flight gets in Saturday afternoon," he said. "I don't know
what I can do, but I'll be there for you."

"That's all I need."

We talked for several minutes more, but the points of *that*
conversation didn't have any relevance on either Michael's death

or Bonnie's grifter boy toy. As such, it was the nicest conversation I'd had all week.

Work the next day was a mess, of course, but thankfully it passed quickly. Ann called Frances and Reggie and got us a reservation at one of our favorite restaurants, 1789. Aunt Winnie's flight got in at four, and she was going to join us.

Ann and I picked up Aunt Winnie at the airport. As I mentioned, Aunt Winnie and her boyfriend, Randy, were renovating a house on Nantucket to serve as a B and B. From the looks of her outfit, apparently her time on the island hadn't been spent in isolated concentration on the house. Normally she gravitated toward slightly edgy ensembles, especially those that emphasized her ample curves and deep cleavage. Today she was wearing an orange poplin A-line skirt emblazoned with dark blue lilies, topped with a bright red cardigan over a light blue blouse. Tan espadrilles completed the look.

Seeing me, she thrust out her left hip and struck a pose. "I've gone native," she said. "What do you think?"

"I know that dress is your passion, but in this case, rather than indulging in a most harmless delight in looking fine, you look like you were attacked by Lilly Pulitzer," I said slowly.

"Well, you would be wrong, missy," she said, putting her hands on her hips. "This look is all the rage." Eyeing my own comparatively drab ensemble of a navy skirt and short-sleeve blue-and-white-striped oxford, she added, "I think you could do with a wardrobe update yourself, missy."

"Well, I think you look wonderful," Ann said with a laugh. Giving her a hug, she added, "Thank you so much for coming, Aunt Winnie. As you've probably heard, things are a real mess."

"Yes, well, that's usually what happens when Bonnie gets involved. It's a particular talent she has," said Aunt Winnie, after giving me a hug. "So what's the plan?"

"We don't have one yet. We're meeting Frances and Reggie for dinner. We thought we could discuss our options then."

"Well, I'm here as long as you need me," Aunt Winnie said. Handing me her suitcase, she slid into Ann's car. "Let's go."

"How's the house?" I asked Aunt Winnie as we pulled out into traffic.

There was a brief pause before she answered. "Would you believe me if I told you it was haunted?"

I laughed. "Are you trying to prepare me for what horrors I will encounter this fall? Are there sliding panels, tapestries, and dimly lit halls?"

For once Aunt Winnie didn't respond in kind. "I'm serious," she said. "There's something weird going on there. I don't know what it is yet, but it's *something*."

"Wait—you're not kidding? What's going on?"

"I'm not sure," she said. I glanced at her purse lying on the seat next to her. A well-worn copy of *The Monk* was visible. I looked from it to her. She caught my meaning. "Don't . . ." she began.

"Don't what?" I answered.

"Don't try and blame my suspicions on my reading material. I read *Dracula* and I didn't go around thinking that the undead were real," she said. "Though it would be something if that vamp Eric from *True Blood* was real."

"Um. Okay. Well, what does Randy think?" I asked.

"He thinks it's nothing," came the disgruntled reply. I have to admit, that made me feel better. Randy was level-headed and sensible. Not that Aunt Winnie wasn't exactly, but if Randy wasn't concerned, then I could relax a bit. Aunt Winnie seemed to sense my doubt and dropped the subject.

Forty-five minutes later, we arrived at 1789. A Georgetown tradition for dining, the renovated Federal house is decorated with American antiques, equestrian and historical prints, and Limoges china. If the Great House at Upper Cross had an American counterpart, it would be 1789.

Frances and Scott were waiting for us when we arrived. Scott was once again wearing an expensive suit and looking like he'd rather not be. Frances was neatly turned out in a Burberry print sheath. After greeting Aunt Winnie, Frances said, "Reggie is running late. Some bridezilla gone amok or something. She said she'd be here soon, though."

Once seated and drinks ordered, Aunt Winnie looked around the table. "Okay. So I gather that Bonnie is not only holding on to the proceeds from the sale of the house, but she's planning on giving this Julian character those proceeds plus God knows what else for him to 'invest.' Now, I imagine that any decent lawyer will be able to clear up Bonnie's . . . shall we say *misunderstanding* about the proceeds on the house. The bigger problem is, how do we stop her from handing over the rest of her assets?"

"Frankly, I don't care how she handles her *own* money," said Frances. "She's a grown woman and I don't see what we can do to stop her. I've spoken to Stephen Guilford about the problems of the house, and from what I gather, we can get a court order to freeze the assets, but that, of course, takes time. For all we know, Bonnie may have already written this Julian a check."

Scott nodded. "And I don't know about the rest of you, but Frances and I need that money."

"Scott!" Frances admonished.

Scott's cheeks flushed and he glanced apologetically at his wife. "Sorry, Frances."

Frances briefly closed her eyes. "It's fine. There's no point trying to hide it. Go ahead and tell them."

"When Marty took a turn for the worse and officially tapped me for his successor, there were a few hiccups," Scott said. "We lost a couple of bids and a few employees tried to take advantage of the change. I took full responsibility for the gaffes and used my own money to cover the losses because I knew we were due the money from the St. Michaels house. But if Bonnie gives that money away—"

"We could lose everything," interjected Frances, her face pinched with worry. "The house, the cars, *everything*!"

"Well, we'll just have to make sure that we get that money back, then," said Aunt Winnie with determination.

"What money?" said a voice to my left. Turning, I saw that it was Reggie. Her normally perfect face was almost haggard. Her black dress was uncharacteristically wrinkled and her posture sagged. She sank wearily into an empty chair and gazed questioningly at us.

"The money from the sale of the house," explained Frances. "Bonnie plans on giving it all to that horrible man she brought home."

"Perfect. Just perfect," Reggie said. "That's the cherry on the top of my week. Where's the waitress? I need a drink." Seeing our server returning to the table with our drinks, Reggie ordered herself a martini. "Make it a double," she added.

"What's wrong with you?" asked Ann.

"What isn't wrong?" Reggie replied testily. "I've spent the past three hours dealing with a young woman who makes Leona Helmsley look like a pussycat. She's forced her bridesmaids to submit to a weigh-in and screamed at one poor girl for not hitting her weekly goal. I swear to God, I think she's going to make her own mother step on the scales before the end of next week. She's also planning on singing her vows—in Italian, no less—and is constantly belting them out. My phone has been ringing off the hook from reporters asking about Michael, and now Bonnie is planning on giving away all of Dad's money to some spa-trolling lothario." Reggie looked pointedly at the empty spot in front of her. "And I don't have a drink."

The waitress arrived with Reggie's martini and Reggie gratefully accepted it. Taking a large gulp she said, "That's better. Now, what did I miss?"

Frances said, "We were discussing what to do about Bonnie. Scott and I will do what we can between now and tomorrow to find out our legal options. Should we try to talk to Bonnie at the party tomorrow?"

"I don't know if it'll do any good," replied Scott. "You know how she gets."

"I'll talk to her," said Aunt Winnie. "I think I can be a little more . . . direct with her about this than any of you can. Speaking of tomorrow, what is the plan?"

"Nothing fancy," replied Ann. "We thought we'd do a cookout for the family. I don't know what Bonnie is expecting, but frankly, with all that's going on right now, that's about all I can handle."

"I assume Julian will be there?" asked Aunt Winnie.

Ann nodded.

"Good," said Aunt Winnie with a smirk. "I can't wait to get a load of him."

CHAPTER 20

*His own enjoyment, or his own ease, was, in
every particular, his ruling principle.*

—SENSE AND SENSIBILITY

AWOKE EARLY on Saturday. Not to sound superstitious, but I took this as a bad sign; sleeping in is one of my favorite things to do. Over the years, I've noticed that an early awakening usually heralds calamity. Rather than dwell on what really motivated my early rising, I chose to attribute it to my excitement at finally seeing Peter again. I knew that wasn't it, but I nevertheless told myself that's what it was. An anticipation of excitement was a much easier explanation to deal with than an anticipation of disaster. Besides, I didn't minor in denial for no reason.

I headed downstairs and found that Ann had arisen early as well. She had already started the coffee and was buttering a bagel when I entered into the kitchen. "Good morning," she said. "You ready for today?"

"As much as I can be, I suppose," I said, pouring myself a large cup of coffee. "What do you need me to do?"

"Nothing much. I'm going shopping in a little bit. I guess

the main thing I need is your support. I have a feeling today will be a tough one."

"Yes, well, unfortunately, I doubt that prediction will get you a spot on the Psychic Friends Network. Are you going to invite Joe?" I asked as nonchalantly as I could. From the way Ann gaped at me in horror, I gathered I needed to work on my nonchalant affectations.

"Invite Joe? Are you kidding? Why would I do that?"

"I don't know," I said, after taking a sip of coffee. "I guess I think you two should give it another try."

"But to invite him to a party honoring my father? Let's face it, he wasn't his biggest fan."

"He who?" I asked. "He Joe or he your father?"

With a wry smile she said, "Both."

Peter's flight got in at one. I hadn't realized how much I'd missed him until I saw him emerge from the gate. It was all I could do to suppress my squeal of excitement. It had been so long since I'd seen him that I almost expected him to have changed. But he hadn't. He was still the six-foot-tall, brown-haired man I'd said good-bye to a few weeks earlier. I ran up to him and he enveloped me in a hug that left me with no doubt that he'd missed me just as much as I'd missed him. For the one hundredth time that week I cursed the fact that my apartment was uninhabitable.

After we said our hellos (in various different manners), we decided to grab a bite to eat while I brought him up to date on the latest developments. Although Peter was concerned about the potential of Julian draining Bonnie dry, he was more upset that Ann and I were "playing sleuth," as he called it. Because he'd just gotten back, I didn't argue the point.

"Damn it, Elizabeth," he said. "A man was killed. Your snooping around trying to find the killer could scare the killer into trying to silence you or Ann!"

I poked at my chicken salad. I didn't have a response to that. He was right, and I couldn't really argue the point as it was almost exactly what I had advised Ann.

"I know," I said. "You're right. I'll stay out of it and I'll try and convince Ann to stay out of it as well. Although to be honest, I think that will be hard to do."

"Don't tell me the sleuthing gene runs in the family," teased Peter.

"No, at least I don't think so," I said with a smile. "I think Ann's desire to get involved is so that she has a reason to stay in touch with Joe."

Peter said nothing. Taking a bite of his cheeseburger, he eyed me suspiciously.

"What?" I asked defensively.

He shook his head. "I'm not sure which is worse. You playing at sleuth or you playing at matchmaker."

"Hard to say, seeing how I'm excellent at both," I retorted as I helped myself to his fries.

"I still say it's silly. Dangerously silly," he said.

"Silly things do cease to be silly if they are done by sensible people in an impudent way."

His eyes narrowed. "*Pride and Prejudice?*"

"*Emma.*"

Peter rolled his eyes.

We finished our lunches and headed over to Kit's to pick up Aunt Winnie. She had opted to stay with Kit while in town. Although it made more sense for her to stay with Ann, she knew that Kit would view such an arrangement as a grave insult.

Aunt Winnie opened the door at our knock. After greeting Peter, she turned to me. "What the hell is with the jungle theme in your sister's guest room?" she asked in a hushed voice. "I think that damn giraffe has Graves' disease."

"I tried to warn you."

"Well, you didn't warn me hard enough. I think I slept for only four hours!"

Kit entered the foyer and greeted us in some kind of strange gesticulating pantomime. Our faces must have registered confusion because she finally gave up and whispered, "I just put Pauly down for a nap. Keep your voices down. You know how he is when he doesn't nap." I did; the kid turned into Damien on crack.

"I thought I'd drive Aunt Winnie over to Ann's," I whispered back. "She wants to have a word alone with Bonnie and meet Julian before the guests arrive."

Kit's mouth pinched in concern. "Is this Julian guy that bad?"

I nodded. "Worse. He makes George look like Gandhi."

"That *is* bad."

"Speaking of George, are he and Mom coming over?"

Kit shrugged. "I have no idea. I called but he answered. You know how he is with phone messages. There was a game on in the background, so who knows if he even heard me."

I sympathized. George loved all forms of televised sports. NASCAR, golf, fishing, football, you name it. If lawn care became a televised sport, George would watch it.

Kit promised to keep trying to get hold of our mom and said she'd see us at Uncle Marty's after Pauly woke up from his nap. We headed out to my car—a used blue Volkswagen Jetta (yes, thank you, I *am* living the dream). At the car, Aunt Winnie dug out a bag from her purse and with great flourish handed it to Peter. A knowing smile played on his lips as he took it. "Dare I ask?" he said, as he peered cautiously into the bag.

"Now, now, don't be skittish."

Aunt Winnie and Peter had had a running contest for years to see who could outdo the other with inappropriate gifts. Last month Peter had sent Aunt Winnie an enormous bouquet of tail flowers, those vaguely sexual red flowers found only in Chinese restaurants. They are kind of flat with a long red stem jutting out from the center. One in a single vase is bad enough, but two dozen of them is patently pornographic. Peter pulled the item out of the bag; it was a white T-shirt. Shaking it open, he looked at the front and burst out laughing. He held it up so that I could see. It read: I AM THE MAN FROM NANTUCKET.

Aunt Winnie giggled. "So what do you think?"

"I think," I said as I studied the shirt, "that I would venture to recommend a larger allowance of prose in your daily study."

Aunt Winnie laughed again and quipped, "I declare little faith in the efficacy of any books on gags like this."

"Don't you two ever stop?" Peter asked in mock exasperation.

"No," Aunt Winnie and I answered in emphatic unison.

As we drove to Uncle Marty's, Aunt Winnie told Peter what she and Randy had done so far on the house in Nantucket and asked his advice about some renovations. I stayed quiet as the two of them launched into some kind of builder code that was complete gibberish to me. It was a bit like that scene in *Mr. Blandings Builds His Dream House*, where the contractor asks the hapless Cary Grant, "The second-floor lintels between the lally columns, should we rabbet them?" and the camera zooms in on his utter confusion. I suspected that my face now held a similar expression of befuddlement.

Finally we arrived at Uncle Marty's. With minimal difficulty I found a parking spot and we headed to the house. Ann greeted us at the door. She was wearing a bright burgundy wrap dress, but her face was wan and pale.

"That bad?" I asked.

"You've no idea," she muttered. Turning to Peter, she hugged him. "It's good to see you again, Peter," she said. "How was your trip?"

"It was fine," he said. "I was sorry to hear about your father, Ann. Elizabeth told me a lot about him. I'm really sorry I couldn't attend the funeral."

"I completely understand," said Ann. "Thanks for the flowers, by the way. They were lovely. I gather Elizabeth's kept you abreast of the rest of the drama? About Michael's murder and Bonnie's new friend?"

"Yes. Again you have my sympathies."

Ann shook her head in disbelief. "The whole thing is so surreal. Here I am, getting ready to host a party in memory of my father, and his widow is out back parading about with some Casanova in cheap cologne."

"What can I do to help?" I asked.

"Most of the guests are coming around five. I've got everything under control. Could you just keep Bonnie away from me? Every once in a while she wanders into the kitchen trying to impress Julian with her domestic skills. The last time she almost cut off her thumb trying to peel an apple."

"I can do that," I said. "Where is she?"

"On the back patio. I warn you, she's sunning herself."

"And why are you warning me?"

"Because she's wearing a new bathing suit. It might have been a bikini before it shrunk. I don't even know how to describe Julian's attire. Obscene might be a start, though."

"Oh, dear God."

Ann paused. "Yeah, okay," she said in agreement after apparently considering the matter. "You could *try* prayer, but to be honest, I don't think His presence is here today."

Peter, Aunt Winnie, and I followed Ann into the kitchen and then headed out to the patio. It was a beautiful day, perfect for a barbecue. Autumn had not yet claimed the season. The air still held some lingering summer warmth and the sun shimmered overhead in one of those flawless blue skies dotted with white puffs of cloud. However, the setting wasn't entirely unspoiled. As Ann had warned us, Bonnie was reclining on one of the chaise longues wearing a flimsy black two-piece, a large black straw hat, and large black sunglasses. Widow's weeds for the gal on the make, I suppose. On the chaise next to her, Julian sat wearing a snug Burberry swimsuit. It was the tap pants style normally favored by small girls with no hips. I glanced away. My eyes hurt.

Bonnie gracefully rose to her feet and ambled toward us, her kitten heels tapping rhythmically on the stone patio and her newly tanned arms stretched out to greet us. When she got near us, Aunt Winnie said in a low voice, "Christ, Bonnie, what's with the suit? Where's the rest of it? On layaway?"

Bonnie's arms fell to her sides and her coral mouth pursed in annoyance. "I'll have you know this is one of this season's most popular suits," she said in a huff.

"Maybe for pubescent twelve-year-olds, but not recently widowed women in their sixties. Really, Bonnie, what's gotten into you? Marty's been dead just over a week."

"Nothing's gotten into me! If you haven't forgotten, we are gathering here today to celebrate poor Martin's memory, a celebration that was *my* idea."

"Actually it was Ann's," snapped Aunt Winnie. "But that's not the point. Who's your friend?"

Bonnie turned to where Julian sat. He watched us with a faintly uneasy expression. "That is Julian," said Bonnie. "He's been absolutely wonderful."

"Oh, I'll just bet he has," murmured Aunt Winnie.

Bonnie raised her voice. "Julian, dear? I'd like to introduce you to some people."

As bidden, Julian rose and crossed to us. It was an awkward moment, as we all attempted not to stare at the very small woodland animal that appeared to be nesting in the front of his suit.

Really, there wasn't enough alcohol in the world to get me past *that* image.

"Julian," said Bonnie, "this is Elizabeth's friend Peter Mc-Gowan, and this is Marty's younger sister, Winifred Reynolds."

From inside the house, Ann poked her head out the door and called out, "Bonnie? There's a phone call for you." Bonnie quickly excused herself and disappeared.

Julian smiled and extended his hand, first to Peter and then to Aunt Winnie. To Aunt Winnie he said, "It's a pleasure to meet you, Winifred. I'm sorry for your recent loss. Bonnie told me a lot about Marty. He sounded like a wonderful man."

"Yes," Aunt Winnie said with a small nod. She shot Julian a syrupy smile. She didn't let go of Julian's hand, instead sandwiching it with her left hand. When she wants to, Aunt Winnie can appear quite innocent. Not to those who know her well, of course, but to those people she needs to glamour—people like traffic cops or fortune-hunting grifters—she can con the best of them. Julian seemed to relax a little at her smile. Rookie mistake. Peter and I stepped back, eager to watch the show unfold.

"Bonnie's told me how attentive you've been to her," said Aunt Winnie.

Julian tried to appear modest. He failed. "Well, I don't pretend to be able to come close to a man like your brother, but I do take some small comfort in knowing that I could help out Bonnie during this very difficult time. She's a very special lady. She has a magnificent aura."

"Does she now? I never knew. You read auras?"

Julian nodded. "It is one of my passions. I don't want to appear conceited, but it's something of a gift as well. My abilities have been called unique by some."

And utter poppycock by others, I amended silently.

"Excellent," murmured Aunt Winnie. "Excellent."

"I understand that you run a bed-and-breakfast in New England," Julian continued.

"That's right, I do," agreed Aunt Winnie. "But Bonnie didn't mention what *you* do."

"Oh, my only job right now is to make Bonnie happy," Julian replied.

"Really? How fortunate for her. Tell me, do you get dental with that?" Aunt Winnie's voice lost its earlier sweet intonation. It was now hard and clear.

Too late Julian realized his mistake; so much for his ability to read people's auras. His eyes narrowed and he tried to pull his hand away. Aunt Winnie held tight and leaned in close. "Listen to me and listen well, Mr. Julian St. Clair—if that is indeed your real name," she said, dropping her voice to a low hiss. "Bonnie is not an accurate reflection of the intelligence quota of this family and by no means is she unguarded. Any designs you have on her or her money have been duly noted and protective steps have been taken. If I were you, I'd tread very carefully, or you may find yourself having more in common with my dearly departed brother than you ever imagined or wanted." Julian's eyes widened in surprise. Her message delivered, Aunt Winnie let go of his hand and took a step back.

"Well, how are we all getting on out here?" Bonnie sang out as she returned to the patio. Linking her arm through Julian's, Bonnie looked from him to us. "Isn't he just unbelievable?"

"I was just telling him the same thing, actually," Aunt Winnie agreed serenely.

Julian said nothing. However, I noticed there was a fine sheen of perspiration across his forehead. There might have been a fine sheen of perspiration elsewhere as well, but there was no way in hell I was going to look for it.

CHAPTER 21

There is nothing like staying at home for real comfort.

—EMMA

Y FIVE O'CLOCK the rest of the guests had arrived and the tribute to Uncle Marty was in full swing. The weather had held; it was still a beautiful day only now a shade cooler. Soft music played from hidden speakers: Frank Sinatra was singing about a love affair gone wrong or one gone right; sometimes it's hard to tell with him. The pool was open, heated, and inviting, but no one was swimming.

Miles and Laura sat with Nana under the poolside umbrella chatting amiably. Every once in a while Nana would look around, her expression almost wistful. It had been several years since she'd been to the house. My mother stood on the patio talking with Kit. Neither George nor Pauly came. One had a previous engagement and one didn't do well in large social settings at the end of the day. To be honest, the excuse worked both ways. Frances and Scott sat on chairs they'd pulled up to the pool's edge. Frances's twins, the aforementioned Thing One and Thing Two, ran around in an unsupervised sugar high, having just finished stuffing themselves with cookies. Every few minutes or so, Frances would halfheartedly tell one or the other to "settle down, now!" This command was usually followed by a comment such as, "Oh, those boys!" or (even better) "My goodness, they are such typical boys! They have so much energy!"

The boys, who were only typical examples of poor parenting, ignored her and continued their game, the point of which seemed to be to zoom around the yard coming as close as possible to knocking one of the guests into the pool. They hadn't succeeded yet, but the night was still early.

As I looked around, I realized that the group assembled today was almost identical to the group that assembled all those years ago for the Fourth of July. I just hoped that this time nothing untoward happened.

I can be really naïve sometimes.

Aunt Winnie, Ann, and I focused on keeping drinks refreshed and the hors d'oeuvres coming. Peter opted to man the grill, saying it was by far the safest place to be. The biggest surprise of the evening (so far) went to Reggie. She showed up with none other than Donny Mancuso. While he was wearing a light blue oxford shirt instead of a too-tight work polo, he still managed to give the impression of a midway transformation from Bruce Banner into the Hulk. Reggie, clinging to his massive arm, looked more like a Barbie doll than ever. Well, the kind of Barbie that would result if Mattel ever decided to create a line of sultry brunette dolls wearing a lusty come-hither expression.

"Hello, everyone!" Reggie called out when they arrived. "I'm sure you all remember Donny."

We all did and various greetings were offered. Reggie smiled up at him. "Donny's been an absolute dear the past few days. I don't know what I would have done without him."

Well, that was something to chew on, I thought. What exactly had old Donny been doing to help? Or was it something that Donny had done years ago—namely, get rid of Michael? Donny gave no indication. He merely smiled and said hello and kept his arm out for Reggie.

Bonnie and Julian, thankfully having changed out of their unsuitable cruise wear, now wandered from guest to guest, never staying too long with any one person. Bonnie wore a slinky white dress, while Julian had opted for a cream linen suit. Bonnie carried Scarlett with her like she was an accessory. At various intervals, Bonnie would talk about her "dear Marty" and then let out a little melancholy sigh. With a sad shake of her blond head, she'd then give Julian a significant glance and murmur about his having been taken "too soon." Julian would nod sympathetically and stroke her hand. Not surprisingly, the tension they left in their wake was palpable, and I began to wish that one of the Things would push one of *them* into the pool.

After a while Bonnie and Julian sat down—alone—at the table. Bonnie sipped from a martini glass while Julian stared at the pool, idly smoking his foul-smelling European cigarette. Although most of the other guests stood nearby, no one seemed inclined to join them. Thing One and Thing Two continued to zoom about, blissfully ignoring Frances's empty threats to "take you two home right now!" As I circulated with the cheese tray, cautiously staying out of the twins' path, Bonnie glanced up at me. "Well, great balls of fire, don't you look serious!" she chirped. Her gaze moving to Frances and Aunt Winnie, she added, "Why the long faces?"

Aunt Winnie rolled her eyes in annoyance before answering.

"Let's see, Bonnie. Where should I start?" She pretended to ponder the question. "Well, one reason might be that we are gathered here today to pay tribute to my dear departed brother. As it's been only a little more than a week since his funeral, *some* of us might still be mourning his passing." She deliberately paused to glance meaningfully first at Bonnie's white dress and then at Julian. A faint stain of crimson appeared on Bonnie's tanned cheeks. Aunt Winnie went on. "A second reason might be that during your absence, the family has been thrust into a rather unpleasant murder investigation involving someone who was once very close to many of us." Aunt Winnie sat down in one of the empty seats at the table and assumed an exaggerated attitude of naïveté. Clasping her hands in her lap and opening her green eyes very wide, she said, "So, gee, now that I think about it, I guess *some* of us might not be in a celebratory mood today."

Bonnie's eyes narrowed. I don't know what, if anything, she was going to say because it was Julian who spoke. "So true. 'Cowards die many times before their deaths,'" he began and then soulfully continued, "'The valiant never taste of death but once.'" He looked around expecting us to be impressed by his quotation. We weren't. "Words from the great Sir Walter Raleigh," he added.

"Actually, they're words from the great William Shakespeare," said Ann.

Julian blinked, then gave her an oily smile. "But of course, my dear. If you say so. Far be it from me to contradict someone as lovely as yourself."

Oh, puke. I glanced at Ann. Her mouth curled in irritation. Through gritted teeth she added, "*Julius Caesar,* Act 2, scene 2."

Julian smiled brightly. "But of course it is, my dear. Shakespeare wrote some wonderful tragedies, did he not? And speaking of tragedies, this business with that young fellow Michael is quite tragic. However, I understand that in the end, it was discovered that he was not, shall we say, a gentleman."

"Amen to that," sniffed Bonnie.

"But do the police really believe that a family as illustrious as yours could be involved in such a sordid crime?" asked Julian after taking a deep drag from his cigarette.

"That's exactly what I say," said Bonnie. "It's preposterous. I've never heard of such bad taste."

"I didn't realize that 'illustrious' families, as you call them, are immune from baser human instincts," snapped Aunt Winnie.

Ann sighed. "Bonnie, the fact remains that Michael was found on our property. From what the police have been able to piece together, he was either killed at the party or the next day. That puts us all in an uncomfortable spotlight."

"Well, fiddle-dee-dee," Bonnie persisted. "We all loved him—we didn't know then that he was embezzling! Everyone loved him . . . well, except for Scott, of course."

What? I looked over to see Scott's reaction to this, but he'd gone inside. Frances, however, was here so I saw her reaction. Her body went rigid. "What do you mean, except for Scott?"

Bonnie looked up at Frances with innocent eyes. "Well, they fought, of course. Don't you remember? Michael and Scott got into a terrible fight at the party."

Frances kept her eyes trained on Bonnie. "You must be mistaken, Bonnie. There was no fight. Why on earth would Scott fight with Michael?"

Bonnie shook her head like a stubborn child. "No, they were fighting. It was about the business." I glanced at Frances. Her face was devoid of color, her cheeks were almost white, and her lips were pressed into a hard, thin beige line. Bonnie continued with her tale. "Michael was taunting Scott. He was saying that Marty wouldn't have picked Scott to take over the business under any circumstances. Michael said something to the effect that he was better than Scott and everyone knew it. Scott was pretty angry."

Frances said nothing. Fury radiated from her.

"Don't get me wrong. I don't blame Scott for arguing with him," Bonnie said. "I mean, Michael was being nasty. It's just that . . ." She trailed off as if unsure what to say.

It's just what? I wondered. That it could look bad? That Scott was pretty drunk and clearly angry? That Scott has either blanked out the fight or is lying about it? None were particularly attractive options.

Frances's eyes narrowed and she leaned toward Bonnie. "That never happened," she said, tapping out each syllable on the tabletop with her finger for emphasis.

"Frances, what are you saying?" Bonnie asked.

"I think it's pretty clear what I am saying. I don't know what you *think* you remember from that night, but Scott and I came upstairs together. I was with him all night and there was no fight with Michael. You are mistaken."

A chill settled over me as Bonnie protested this. "But Frances, that's simply not true. You can't lie about this. It'll only make it worse."

"Do not tell me what to do," she said. "And if you repeat that ridiculous story to anyone, you could ruin everything Scott and I have worked for. I won't let you do that."

Over the years, the family had joked about Frances's resemblance to Lady Macbeth where Scott's career was concerned. Never had it been more apparent than now.

"What's going on here?" asked a voice. It was Scott. He was standing in the doorway, staring at Frances in confusion.

Frances whirled around. "Nothing. Nothing at all. Bonnie and I were just having a disagreement. But it's fine now."

"A disagreement about what?" he asked.

"Bonnie claims to have heard you and Michael fighting at Dad's Fourth of July party," she said. "I merely told her that she is mistaken and . . . *encouraged* her not to repeat the story."

Scott's brows drew together. He glanced doubtfully at Bonnie. "You heard me fight with Michael?"

"She *thinks* she did, Scott," Frances said. "But she's wrong. You were with me all night. I will swear to that in court if I have to."

"Frances, just stop for a minute." Scott held up a large hand. Turning back to Bonnie, he said, "Bonnie, I don't have any memory of fighting with Michael, but considering that I was drinking back then that's not too surprising. Sadly, there are a lot of evenings I don't remember. What did you hear?" Scott's face held an expression of sincere befuddlement. If he did remember the fight with Michael, he was doing an excellent job of hiding it.

Finally, Bonnie said, "You and Michael were on the patio at the end of the night. Michael was saying terrible things to you about his being chosen over you to run the company. You were pretty angry."

Scott's forehead bunched in concentration as he tried to search his brain for the memory. Eventually he shook his head in defeat. "I vaguely remember talking to him, but that's all. I didn't like him—well, to be perfectly blunt, I thought he was an asshole. But I don't remember the fight."

"That's because it *didn't* happen," interjected Frances. "If I remember correctly, Bonnie, you were drinking wine that night. I wasn't, because I was still nursing the twins. Who's to say that you didn't imagine it, dream it, or that your memory is just faulty?"

"Frances! This is absurd. I am not making this up and I certainly wasn't drunk. I saw them fighting and overheard what they said. I'm not saying it means anything; it's just a simple statement of fact," Bonnie cried.

"A fact that is *wrong*. Scott came upstairs with me that night. He was never alone with Michael."

"Frances, that's not true," said Scott. "You did go up before me. I did sit outside with Michael and talk. I do remember that much."

Frances smiled—not very nicely—and said, "No, Scott. You are forgetting that I was there when you talked to Michael. And then we went to bed. Together. You were with me for the rest of the night. You had been drinking too much, which was why I insisted that you go to bed."

Suddenly Scott looked down at his right hand in remembrance. "My hand," he said quietly. Looking up at Frances, he repeated, "My hand. The next morning there was a cut on it. You told me that I cut it on a glass I dropped. Is that true?"

Frances flushed slightly but gave a curt nod. "Of course it's true. You dropped a glass in the bathroom. You cut yourself when you tried to clean it up."

No one spoke. Scott looked from Frances to Bonnie, clearly upset and confused. "I don't know what I'm supposed to do here," Scott said. "I don't remember fighting with Michael—that's the truth. But I don't see how Bonnie has any reason to lie about it either. However, no matter what happened, I can't believe that I could have been involved in Michael's disappearance."

"That's because you weren't," Frances said firmly. Turning to Bonnie, she said, "And if anyone else suggests otherwise, they are not only wrong but skating on very thin ice."

The rest of us stood very still. My mind was racing. Obviously Frances was lying to cover for Scott. The question was, was she lying because she knew Scott hadn't done anything, or because she knew he had? No one spoke for a minute, all of us lost in the same unspoken thought. As Lady Macbeth might opine, Scott was too full of the milk of human kindness to kill Michael. Conversely, Frances would be the type to screw her courage to the sticking place and do the dirty deed.

Rather than dredging up additional pithy Shakespeare quotes (you're welcome), I focused on a new thought: in giving Scott a solid alibi for that night, she was also giving herself one. That thought triggered a far-flung memory, but before I could catch it, it faded away.

"What do you take me for?" Bonnie now asked Frances with a faint smile. "I'm not going to mention it to the police. But even if I did, I don't see what the harm would be. So what if Scott fought with Michael? I don't how see how that affects the family."

"It's a problem because his body was buried underneath the pool's foundation, Bonnie! And construction on the pool began the day after the Fourth of July party, on the fifth," Ann added unnecessarily. But then again, maybe it was necessary; after all, she was talking to Bonnie. "Michael had to have been buried a day or so after the party."

"But we'd all left the house by then and we didn't go back . . ." Bonnie abruptly stopped. Somewhere in the deep recesses of her mind, something clicked. She'd remembered the fight with Uncle Marty and her self-imposed exile to St. Michaels. Honestly, you couldn't ask for a more obvious example of someone Remembering Something Important than the procession of expressions that moved across Bonnie's face. First her brows pulled together in deep concentration. Then they cleared, leading the way to a widening of the eyes. This was followed by lips forming a small "o." Finally, her eyes narrowed, first into an angry slant and then shifting into more of a sly gaze. Yes, people, Bonnie knew something! The question was (as was usually the question with matters concerning Bonnie's intellect): exactly *what* did she know?

"Bonnie?" I asked. "What is it? Have you remembered something?"

She did not answer right away. Finally she said, "No, but I just remembered that I went back out to the house after the party. I was there for a day or so. I must have been there when . . ." She fell silent, pressing a delicate hand to her mouth in apparent anguish. She turned large blue eyes to Julian. "Why, to think that I might have been there when he was killed! Oh, how terrible! Just to think that I might have been killed, *too,* if I'd seen anything! Why, it makes me almost dizzy!"

Julian extended his perfectly manicured hand to hers and made soft noises, which I gathered were supposed to soothe the distraught Bonnie. I don't know what it did for her; all it did for me was set my teeth on edge. Finally he murmured, "You poor, poor dear. How much more can a person take? It's quite unbelievable. But you're safe now."

Bonnie granted him a misty smile. "But still, if I *had* seen something, how different things might be now. There'd be none of this confusion and uncertainty. The police would know who the killer was and we'd be fine. Oh, I don't know how I can ever forgive myself. It's going to take a lot, I can tell you that. I feel as if I've let everyone down! But most of all I feel as if I've let down my poor Marty!"

Aunt Winnie studied Bonnie, a curious expression on her face. "Bonnie, what the hell are you talking about? If you didn't see anything while you were at the house, then you didn't see anything. However, if you did, then you need to tell the police."

Bonnie shook her blond head vigorously. "But that's just the problem. I *didn't* see anything. And I feel just terrible about it because I *should* have."

"There's no use regretting the past, my dear," said Julian. "What matters now is the future. And I can see from your aura that your future is bright. As I promised you earlier, I'm going to help you make sure of it."

"And how do you plan on doing that, may I ask?" asked Laura. Miles stood next to her, his face etched with disgust.

Although the twins were playing a game of tag around his legs, I doubted this was the reason for his dour expression.

Julian turned her way. Again, he appeared to try to look modest. Again, he failed. To be fair, it is hard to appear modest while ensconced from head to toe in expensive and deliberately wrinkled linen and smoking a preposterously tiny cigarette. "I don't know if Bonnie mentioned to you that I am something of a whiz with investments," he said. "I am going to make sure that your charming mother—"

"Stepmother," interjected Reggie.

"Charming *step*mother," Julian amended with a discreet nod, "is set for life. She shall never want for money or my friendship." Taking Bonnie's hand in his, he bestowed it with a small kiss.

Behind me someone gagged. I didn't need to turn around to know who it was. Aunt Winnie has a distinctive gag.

"Speaking of this plan for investment," said Reggie, "there are a few things I think that we need to discuss. First and foremost, exactly what money are you investing? There's a rather large sum from the sale of the house on St. Michaels that is due to us. Some of us are counting on that income."

Bonnie waved aside Reggie's words. "Darling, you don't need to worry about that. I was going to surprise you with this later, but I suppose now is as good a time as any."

"Surprise us with what?" Reggie asked, her voice hard.

"With your present. Julian is going to invest it all for us— everything! He promises that he can practically double it, maybe even triple it! Isn't that too marvelous?"

From the horrified faces around me, it was clear that "marvelous" wasn't their word of choice. But before the inevitable explosion of anger and disbelief erupted, there was another explosion of sorts—a tremendous splash.

We all looked to the pool to see Miles sputtering in the water. His glasses were askew and his blue blazer and khaki trousers were completely soaked. On the ledge in front of him, grinning evilly like twin Damiens, stood Thing One and Thing Two.

CHAPTER 22

We must not be so ready to fancy ourselves
intentionally injured.

—PRIDE AND PREJUDICE

F COURSE, the first words heard were Frances's. "Caden and Cameron!" she cried in obvious distress. Any hope that she was going to finally follow through with a much-deserved punishment on the twins was dashed with her follow-up of, "Are you all right? I told you not to run near the pool's edge! Neither of you have passed your swim test! You might have drowned!"

Laura ran over to help Miles, who was still spitting out pool water. Ann dashed inside to grab a towel.

Scott, thankfully, saw things a little more realistically than Frances. Truth be told, Scott was better with the boys than Frances was. He just seldom exerted himself to contradict Frances. Marching over to the twins, he grabbed each by the hand and yanked them away from the pool's edge. "Now look what you've done!" he admonished sternly, bending low so as to make eye contact with their sullen faces. "How many times were you warned not to run about? Now you've pushed Uncle Miles into the pool. Apologize immediately!"

"But Daddy!" cried Cameron/Thing One. "I didn't push him! He just fell."

"Cameron! Apologize!"

"But I didn't push him!" came the screeching reply.

"Don't blame it on me!" cried his brother Caden/Thing Two.

Frances moved to where Scott stood. "Scott, don't yell at them!" she screamed angrily and with unintentional irony. "Yelling doesn't solve anything!"

As she unclasped the boys' hands from Scott's, she said to the boys, "No one is blaming anyone. You both just need to settle down, that's all. I suspect you've had too much sugar." She glared at Scott as if this was somehow his fault. Then turning to Miles, she said, "I am sorry, Miles. I hope you're all right."

Shaking beads of water from his body like a wet dog, Miles nodded. "I'll be fine." Turning to Laura, he said, "I'm going to run home and change. I'll just be a few minutes." Ann returned with a towel. Taking it with a grateful smile, Miles wiped his face and then his glasses dry.

"Do you want me to come with you?" offered Laura.

"No, you stay here," replied Miles as he headed out the door. "I'll only be a few minutes."

Sensing that the sentiment of the group was against her and the twins, Frances said, "You two need to apologize to Uncle Miles when he gets back."

"But I didn't do anything!" they cried in unison. Frances rolled her eyes heavenward and smiled wanly at the rest of us. "Lord," she said, "but I can't wait until this phase of 'I'm Always Innocent' is over. But you know how boys are."

No one replied and I wondered what came after the "I'm

Always Innocent" phase. Not having read Dr. Spock, I didn't know. Was there a subsequent "I Was Framed" phase? Perhaps followed by the "Petty Crimes and Misdemeanors" phase? Was there a "Felony" phase? If there was, the twins were certainly going to excel.

The silence grew awkward. Finally, in a clear attempt to break the tension, Peter said, "Why don't I get the steaks started?"

"Perfect idea," agreed Ann. "I'll go get them for you," she added as she ducked back into the kitchen. Scott advanced on his children, for once appearing not to care what Frances thought of his disciplinary philosophy. Grabbing both of them by the hand again, he said, "Both of you are coming inside with me for a well-deserved time-out!"

Although the boys (not to mention Frances) protested against this outrage (Frances loudest of all), Scott remained firm and dragged them into the house. Frances followed, protesting that children need firm yet gentle handling and that time-outs weren't always effective.

With their retreat, the atmosphere calmed a little but not completely. There still was the matter of Bonnie's announcement hanging in the air.

Reggie was the first to reopen the subject. "Listen here, Bonnie. You can do what you want with *your* money, but I will not let you throw away mine."

Bonnie affected a look of confusion. "Darling, why are you so upset? Julian is a whiz at investing. I'm doing this for you!"

Reggie clenched her hands at her sides. "I don't want him to."

Bonnie shrugged and gave a light laugh. "Oh, but then, even as a child, you never wanted to do what was best for you. If I remember correctly, you didn't want to take swimming lessons either. My how you fussed and kicked, but aren't you glad you took them now?"

In addition to clenching her hands, Reggie's jaw now bunched. "That is not the same as investing! You are playing with people's futures here!"

"Actually, I'm *helping* your futures."

Reggie's eyes clenched shut in frustration. Soon her entire body would be one big clench. "I can't take this anymore," she muttered. "I'm getting a massive headache. I need an aspirin. And a martini. And not necessarily in that order. Excuse me." She turned and stalked angrily into the house. Donny looked at us in hulkish silence for a moment before lumbering after her.

From her chair, Aunt Winnie eyed Bonnie suspiciously. "What are you doing here, Bonnie? The truth."

Bonnie gave an innocent shrug. Offering Aunt Winnie an almost feline smile, she said, "I have no idea what you mean, Winifred. We're here to celebrate Marty's memory, and as a special surprise, I've arranged for the children to receive a lovely return on their inheritance. It's the least I can do for them." Picking up her martini glass, she delicately swallowed the last sip like a cat finishing its cream.

Suddenly I understood exactly what Bonnie was doing. It was revenge pure and simple. Revenge for years of being dismissed as a bubblehead. Revenge for being called "McClueless." Revenge for an unhappy marriage to a man whose children despised her. We had it all upside down.

Julian wasn't using Bonnie.

Bonnie was using him.

CHAPTER 23

Stupid men are the only ones worth knowing, after all.

—PRIDE AND PREJUDICE

Y EYES FLEW to Aunt Winnie's, wondering if she'd had the same idea. From the way *her* eyes were widening with appalled shock as she stared at Bonnie, I was pretty confident that she had.

"I think I'm in need of another martini," Bonnie said, setting her empty glass on the table. "Julian, how about you? Would you like one?"

Julian made a show of checking his watch. "Why not? After all, it is past five o'clock!" He chuckled appreciatively as this apparent witticism.

Bonnie smiled at him. Picking her glass back up, she looked my way. "Elizabeth? Would you be a dear and ask Reggie to make me another drink and to make one for Julian as well?" Bonnie turned to Julian, saying, "Reggie makes the best martinis."

I was happy to run that errand. It gave me an excuse to go into the house and tell Ann my theory about the real reason behind Bonnie's relationship with Julian. I took the offered glass and headed inside, where I found Ann basting a platter full of thick steaks with some kind of sweet-smelling marinade. Reggie, Donny, and Frances sat on stools at the counter. Reggie was holding her head in her hands. Donny was gently rubbing her back. From the hard line of Frances's mouth and her ramrod posture, she appeared to still be angry at Scott . . . or Bonnie . . . or the world. From upstairs I could hear the twins' howls of indignation as Scott enforced the time-out.

Holding up Bonnie's empty glass, I said, "Bonnie has requested a refill on her martini and one for Julian. She asked that Reggie make them."

Reggie sighed and rolled her eyes. "I can make them," I offered hastily. "Just point me in the right direction . . . and remind me what's in a martini."

Reggie pushed her stool back and stood up. "No, better let me do it. I need one anyway. Besides, she's pretty particular about how she likes them. God forbid we anger the little diva. After all, she holds all the cards." Taking the glass from me, she headed to the dining room where the liquor cart was located.

"What can I do to help?" I asked Ann.

Ann looked around and said, "Would you mind starting the tomato and mozzarella? The tomatoes are in the bowl on the table and the mozzarella is in the refrigerator."

I grabbed a cutting board, a knife, and the tomatoes and mozzarella, and began slicing them. Taking a plate down from the cabinet, I began to arrange the tomatoes and mozzarella in what I hoped would result in a spiral pattern. "I had an idea outside," I said, then stopped, unsure exactly how my idea would be received. I was basically about to tell them that I thought their stepmother was trying to avenge herself of years of familial abuse. That might be a tough pill to swallow.

"Does your idea involve committing Bonnie?" Reggie called from the other room. "Or better yet, just killing her?"

"Reggie!" admonished Frances. "That's not funny!"

"Who said I was trying to be funny?"

Reggie returned with the drinks in her hands. Setting two on the counter she said, "What was your idea, Elizabeth?"

I looked down at my plate before answering. It looked like a close-up of an Impressionist painting. All spots and swirls. I sighed. Like this day, my cheese/tomato pattern had spiraled out of control. I wonder if somewhere in the Hamptons, and for no apparent reason, Martha Stewart was overcome by a shudder of domestic horror. "Well," I said, "what if Bonnie *knows* Julian is a fake? What if she *wants* you all to lose that money?"

"I don't follow you," said Reggie, taking a sip of her drink.

"I do," Frances said slowly. "You think she wants to screw us, don't you? But why? Why would she do that?"

"Because she hates us," Ann said, putting down the marinating brush, her expression thoughtful. "Now that Dad's gone, she can do what she likes. Under the terms of the will, Bonnie has the use of this house until her death. When she dies, the house comes to us. In addition, she received a small inheritance. It really wasn't much. She might see this as an opportunity to make some more money. She takes the money from the sale of the house and purposely gives it to a con artist—in this case, Julian. Julian pockets the money and claims that he's lost it in a bad investment. None of us would be surprised—that's what we think is going to happen anyway. But do you really think she wants Julian to take all the money, or do you think she's in on it with him?" she said, turning to me.

"What? Do you mean like a fifty-fifty split?" asked Reggie, her drink frozen halfway to her mouth.

I looked at Reggie and nodded. "It's a possibility."

"That bitch!" expostulated Reggie, putting down her drink and angrily slapping the counter with her hand.

"I bet I don't need to guess who we're talking about," said a voice from the doorway. It was Miles, dried and in new clothes. "I gather it's about Bonnie. What's happened?"

Ann looked at me questioningly. I signaled for her to tell Miles. I saw no reason to keep my theory a secret. "Elizabeth was wondering if Bonnie could be giving Julian that money as a form of revenge on us," Ann said. "I mean, let's face it, we've never gotten along with her. Now that Dad's gone . . ."

"I see what you mean," Miles said thoughtfully. "She could give the money to Julian and then somehow split it with him. Yes, it's not completely out of the question."

"Well, if that's the case—and even if it's not the case—what do we do to stop her?" asked Frances.

We all looked to Miles for the answer, but for once he had none. The patio door opened and Laura walked in. "Goodness, so this is where the party's got to. What are you all doing in here?" Seeing our dour expressions, her voice dropped and she added, "What's happened?"

"Nothing," said Miles. "Just a theory on the true relationship between Bonnie and Julian." The ringing of the doorbell prevented Miles from expanding on this theory.

Ann went to answer the door. I heard her give an exclamation of surprise, an exclamation of happy surprise. Seconds later she reappeared with Joe in tow.

"Hey, everybody," Ann said, her face more flushed than it had been moments before. "Um, Joe stopped by to bring me up to date on the case with Michael."

"Really?" said Miles. "Have there been any developments?"

Joe cleared his throat before answering. "Unfortunately, no. But I was in the area, so I thought I'd stop by. I'm sorry, I didn't realize you were having a party. I don't want to intrude. I'll just see myself out."

As it was clear to me that Joe had used the pretext of the case as an excuse to see Ann, I said, "You're not intruding, Joe. It's just a simple cookout. Please stay."

Joe glanced at Ann. "You're more than welcome to join us," she added with a shy smile.

"Well, if you're sure," he said quietly, his eyes fixed on Ann's.

Everyone voiced agreement that Joe should stay. Well, everyone except Laura. Her lips pulled down into a faint frown and she folded her arms across her chest. From the doubtful glance she shot Miles, it was clear that she still harbored doubts about the wisdom of Ann's involvement with Joe.

Miles shrugged away her unspoken message of concern. "You're always welcome here, Joe," he said. "Come on outside and join the party. You can meet Bonnie's new friend, Julian. In fact, I would love to hear your opinion of the man."

As Ann led Joe outside, I grabbed the platter of steaks. "Miles, can you get those drinks on the counter?" called Reggie. "They're for Bonnie and Julian." Miles did so and deposited them at the table. Bonnie and Julian thanked Reggie for making the drinks. Joe was introduced to Julian, and his reaction was studied by most everyone else. From the way Joe's face became almost studiously blank, it was clear (to me, anyway) that Joe held the same low opinion of Julian that most everyone else did.

However, if Bonnie and Julian picked up on Joe's negative opinion, they hid it well. They chatted in contented oblivion and sipped their drinks. Within a few minutes, however, Bonnie's bubbly mood changed. "Julian, do you think you could put that thing out?" she snapped, indicating his cigarette. "It's very bothersome."

Julian appeared startled at her annoyed tone but graciously put out the offending embers. "But of course, my dear. I am terribly sorry," he said as he ground down the tip.

Bonnie pressed her fingertips to her temples. "I'm sorry, Julian. It's just that I have a sudden headache. I think this sun is getting to me." She squinted sullenly at the offending orb in the sky.

Julian was quick to react. "Would you like me to get you some aspirin?"

Bonnie shook her head. "No, I'll be fine, but thank you."

Julian glanced at the rest of us, his face pulled down in an expression that indicated his grave concern. I'm sorry to say he did not find a similar sentiment on ours. Bonnie was no stranger to issuing complaints. "My dear, why don't you trade places with me? I am in the shade, while you are in the sun. I have been very thoughtless. Come, I insist," he said, getting to his feet. He moved behind her chair. "Let me help you."

Bonnie allowed herself to be gently moved to the shady chair.

Julian took his new seat and peered anxiously at her. "Better?" he asked.

"Yes, thank you."

But it wasn't. Minutes later, Bonnie began to complain that her stomach hurt. "You must be hungry." Julian said. "Perhaps the steaks are almost ready?"

"Just another minute," Peter called from his post at the grill.

"Perhaps you should go inside and rest until the steaks are ready," suggested Julian. "I will bring one in to you once they are done."

"No," replied Bonnie, pulling her lips into an obstinate line. "I'm fine." However, no sooner had she said this than she let out a low groan and clutched at her stomach. "This is silly," said Julian. "I insist that you go inside and rest."

Bonnie stubbornly rejected this idea, adamantly shaking her head in refusal. "This day is for Marty," she said. "I can't forget that. In fact, why don't we have a toast? I propose a toast to Marty's memory." She raised the glass in front of her. When the rest of us had done likewise with ours, she stretched out her arm a bit straighter. Then in a voice low from either emotion or stomach cramps, she said, "To Martin Reynolds—a man like no other!"

As toasts go, it wasn't a particularly memorable line. No, what made it memorable was the fact that seconds after she said it, Bonnie collapsed to the ground, her glass shattering into thousands of pieces beside her.

CHAPTER 24

Well! Evil to some is always good to others.

—EMMA

IN ALL THE CONFUSION, it's hard to remember exactly what happened next. There were screams, of course, and people running and one small dog barking incessantly. Someone called 911. I think it was Joe. Ann ran over to Bonnie and tried to revive her. She wasn't dead, but she sure as hell wasn't very responsive either. Her skin was gray beneath her tan, and her face was slack.

Finally the paramedics came bursting onto the patio and we all stood back and let them do their job. They were able to get a pulse on her and rapidly loaded her onto a gurney and out to the waiting ambulance. Julian tried to go with Bonnie but was firmly, albeit politely, denied access. Peter, Aunt Winnie, and I drove to the hospital in my car. Joe drove Ann. Everyone else formed various car pools as well. Julian also went to the hospital, but I think he went by cab.

We arrived at the hospital and quickly made our way to the reception desk. A large woman with an expression that suggested a genetic link with the subfamily Bovinae listened apathetically to our story and then told us to take seats in the waiting room. We were duly informed that someone would be with us "shortly." Someone wasn't. Miles joined us, as did Reggie and Frances. Kit also came. I was surprised at first but then realized Kit would sooner cut off her left foot than miss out on any potential drama. Scott had taken the twins home, and Donny apparently had better things to do than hang out at a hospital. Laura drove Nana back to her house in St. Michaels and my mother returned to her house.

As the ten of us sat huddled together in the drab waiting room, ignorant of Bonnie's condition, we offered various explanations of what had happened. Heart attack seemed the most popular guess, with stroke being a close second. It wasn't until I saw the grim-faced doctor coming our way accompanied by a policeman that I began to suspect the truth.

"Hello," the doctor said stiffly when he got to us, "I'm Dr. Moser. I'm taking care of Mrs. Reynolds." Dr. Moser was about six two with wire-rimmed glasses and a scattering of gray hair. He studied our little group with a guarded expression. Gesturing to the officer next to him, he added, "This is Officer Daschle." Officer Daschle was about five ten, with a stocky build and a blond crew cut. Unlike Dr. Moser, Officer Daschle watched us with an expression that was much easier to interpret. Angry suspicion radiated from his dark brown eyes.

"How is she?" asked Ann. "How's Bonnie?"

Officer Daschle turned to Ann. "May I ask who *you* are?" he asked brusquely.

Joe's jaw tightened at Officer Daschle's tone with Ann. Stepping forward he said, "This is Ann Reynolds. She's Mrs. Reynolds's stepdaughter."

Officer Daschle cast a suspicious eye at Joe. "And who are you?"

"Detective Joe Muldoon. I'm a . . . friend of Miss Reynolds."

Officer Daschle nodded. "Pleased to meet you, Detective. I think I'll need to talk with you later." To Ann he said, "Well, Miss Reynolds, I'm sorry to say but your stepmother is in serious condition."

"Was it a heart attack?" Reggie asked Dr. Moser.

Dr. Moser paused ominously before answering. "No, I'm afraid it wasn't a heart attack."

"A stroke, then?" Kit asked confidently. Earlier Kit had predicted that Bonnie had had a stroke.

Dr. Moser shook his head. "No. She was poisoned."

"Poisoned!" cried several voices. Joe's face hardened and he glanced suspiciously at Julian.

"Do you mean food poisoning?" asked Kit. "Are the rest of us in any danger? I'm pregnant—should I call my OB-GYN?" She clutched her belly protectively.

"It was not food poisoning," said Dr. Moser. "We believe it was *Convallaria majalis* or, as it is more commonly known, lily of the valley."

"You mean the flower?" asked Ann, perplexed.

"Yes. It is very common and very toxic. If ingested it generally leads to heart failure."

"Is Bonnie going to be okay?" asked Aunt Winnie.

"I sincerely hope so," Dr. Moser replied. "She's in excellent physical condition for a woman her age; however, it's too soon to tell. We've had to pump her stomach and she's been given cardiac depressants to control her cardiac rhythm. Sometimes lily of the valley is mistaken for garlic. Do you by chance have a home garden?"

Ann shook her head. "No. Nothing at all like that."

"May I ask what you were eating and drinking?"

"We all had some cheese and crackers," said Ann. For some reason, everyone turned to look at me.

"It couldn't have been that," said Dr. Moser with a shake of his head. To my relief everyone stopped looking at me.

"We had just put the steaks on the grill," Ann continued. "Bonnie was drinking a martini—"

Dr. Moser interrupted. "A martini? Who made the drink?"

No one answered right away, but we all looked at Reggie. "I did," she finally answered. "Why?"

"As I said," continued Dr. Moser, "lily of the valley is very toxic. Even putting the flowers into a glass of water would turn the water toxic. If that water was then added to a drink, it would poison the drink."

"But I didn't poison her drink!" exclaimed Reggie. "I made one for me and Julian! I made it the way I usually do—with gin, vermouth, and three olives!"

Officer Daschle took out his notebook and wrote something down. I doubted it was the recipe.

"I only made the drink—I didn't even bring it to her!" Reggie added.

Officer Daschle looked up from his scribbling. "Who did bring out the drinks?" he asked.

Miles spoke up immediately. "I brought them out."

"Interesting," he murmured, his head bent low again over his notebook.

Miles flushed and began to protest. "I only brought them out! I certainly didn't poison them!" Ann put her hand on his and smiled reassuringly at him.

"Would her drink still be at the house, by chance?" asked Dr. Moser.

"No, she dropped it when she fell. It broke," said Ann.

"Well, we still might be able to get a sample from the broken glass," said Dr. Moser. "Although I'm almost certain of the kind of poison we're dealing with here, it never hurts to be one hundred percent sure."

"Do you want me to go back to the house to get it?" offered Joe.

Dr. Moser nodded. "I think that would be best."

"I'll have someone retrieve it," Officer Daschle said. "We're going to need the glass for evidence."

"Evidence!" cried Frances. "But you can't think that this was intentional. None of us had any reason to hurt Bonnie."

"But that is not true," said Julian from where he stood a few feet away from the rest of us. "You were all very angry at her for trying to invest your money!"

"Just because we wanted to stop her from making a foolish investment doesn't mean we tried to hurt her!" Frances retorted, glaring at Julian.

"You should also know that Bonnie had concerns over her late husband's death," Julian went on, ignoring Frances. "She felt that there was something odd about it . . ."

"The man died after a long battle with cancer," snapped Aunt Winnie. "The only thing odd about it was that Bonnie didn't see it coming."

"Still, she wondered if his death could be connected to the

discovery of that man's body," said Julian. "Your family seems to have had much death in it lately."

Dr. Moser now took a decided step away from us. I really couldn't blame him. "I think this is a matter for the police," he said, glancing first at Joe and then at Officer Daschle, who was furiously scribbling in his notebook. He'd need a new one pretty soon if Julian was allowed to keep talking.

Officer Daschle nodded. "I agree. I think it might be best if we get a statement from everyone. In the meantime, let me call the station about getting out to the house to obtain the glass. Why don't you all have a seat and I'll be right back."

Within an hour, Joe and Officer Daschle had retrieved not only Bonnie's broken glass but Julian's and Reggie's glasses as well. Both had been handed over to the hospital staff for analysis. Bonnie remained in serious but stable condition. We all sat in the waiting room, numb with shock, an object of curiosity for the other patients who stared at and whispered about us while waiting to be called by the triage nurse.

Another officer had joined our company. Officer Newell was a trim black woman who appeared to be in her early thirties. She and Officer Daschle took our statements. Thanks to Julian they seemed very interested in the discovery of Michael's body, the circumstances surrounding Uncle Marty's death, and the level of anger toward Bonnie over the investments. Thanks to Kit they also knew that Ann and I had done a little investigating into the murder of Michael and that we'd discovered that Bonnie had possibly been out at the house in St. Michaels when the murder took place.

"It could be that whoever killed Michael tried to poison Bonnie today to keep her quiet," Kit told the officers. "That's just one possibility, of course," she added knowingly. I wanted to smack her, but it didn't seem in my best interests to hit a pregnant woman in a hospital and in front of two cops.

Dr. Moser returned, his face tired and drawn. "We've received the lab report. Mrs. Reynolds was definitely poisoned with lily of the valley. However, we found no traces of it on the broken glass. We did, however, find it in the other martini glass on the table."

Julian leaped to his feet, his face pale with shock. "That was *my* glass! But how can that be? I am not sick!"

"You and Bonnie switched seats, remember?" said Aunt Winnie. "She said the sun was giving her a headache. She probably picked up your glass by mistake when she gave the toast."

Julian was unconvinced. "But how do you know that the drink was not intended for me? Whoever did this might have wanted to kill me! I might now be the one who is near death!" He moved farther away from us. "You people are crazy!" He pointed an accusatory (and manicured) finger at us. "I demand police protection! I refuse to be left near them! I want police protection—my life is in danger!"

It might have been my imagination, but the more upset Julian got, the more his accent faded. By the end, I detected a strong hint of a Jersey upbringing.

"Why do you think that you were the intended victim?" asked Officer Daschle.

"I don't know!" Julian said. "Maybe they think I know something about the other deaths! Maybe they want to keep me away from Bonnie!"

Officer Daschle eyed Julian dubiously. "I don't think you need police protection." He looked to Joe as if to confirm this. Joe shook his head to indicate that he thought it unnecessary as well. Officer Daschle continued, "I can't see any evidence that you were the intended victim."

"Oh, no?" Julian cried. "But I was threatened right before the party started!"

I groaned as Officer Daschle asked, "By whom?"

"That woman right there!" Julian said, pointing an angry finger at Aunt Winnie.

Officer Daschle glanced inquiringly at her. She rolled her eyes in derision. "I did no such thing," she scoffed. "I merely warned him not to take advantage of Bonnie. I reminded him that she was not without friends."

"Some friends you turned out to be—you poisoned her!" he shot back.

Several voices rose in angry reply to this, and it took several minutes before Officer Daschle could restore order. When he finally did, he turned back to Aunt Winnie and said, "I'd like to hear exactly what you said to this man to make him think his life was in danger."

Aunt Winnie affected an I'm-taking-this-seriously-even-though-it's-ridiculous expression. "I was worried that Mr. St. Claire's interest in Bonnie was financial. I told him that I was watching him and that if he tried to use Bonnie in any way, he would not be successful."

"She told me I'd end up dead like her brother!" Julian screamed.

Officer Daschle raised an eyebrow and glanced back at Aunt

Winnie. She shrugged. "Just a figure of speech, I assure you. To the Irish, exaggeration is as normal as breathing. I have no intention of harming Mr. St. Claire."

I spoke up. "My aunt talks a great deal, sir, and always with animation, but she is not a violent person." *Normally,* I added privately.

Officer Daschle looked as if he was about to get a large headache. Aunt Winnie has that effect on a lot of people, especially people in law enforcement. After a moment, he turned back to Julian. "The fact remains, Mr. St. Claire, that you do not seem to be the intended victim here, despite what may have been said to you earlier." Officer Daschle shot Aunt Winnie an accusatory look. She produced a guileless smile. The smile was not returned.

Julian sniffed indignantly. "Well, in any case, I refuse to stay in that house! I intend to check into a hotel. Immediately." He turned away from us and yanked out his cell phone. With a few agitated jabs, he dialed a number and then pressed the phone to his ear. He spoke rapidly into it, his free arm gesturing dramatically. Within minutes, he hung up. "I have given you my statement," he said. "Am I free to go now?"

Officer Daschle glanced at Officer Newell. She shrugged. He then looked at Joe. Joe shrugged as well.

"You can go, Mr. St. Claire," Officer Daschle said. "Just make sure you provide us with an address where we can reach you."

"You can reach me at the Ritz," he said, as he turned on the heel of his open-toe sandal and headed for the doors.

I wondered if the Ritz could use that as a marketing tool: You might not be able to get police protection, but you can always get a room at the Ritz.

CHAPTER 25

It was, perhaps, one of those cases in which advice is
good or bad only as the event decides.
—PERSUASION

A<small>FTER ALL OF OUR STATEMENTS</small> had been taken,
Joe and Ann talked privately for a while, then he
left for St. Michaels, where he lived. I don't know what Joe said,
but whatever it was it seemed to agree with Ann. Despite the
hellish evening we'd had, her face was oddly peaceful.

The rest of us returned to Uncle Marty's house. We were
tired, starved, and in shock. Laura was back at the house, having already returned from driving Nana back to St. Michaels.
Both were scheduled to give their statements to the police at a
later time.

Laura had thoughtfully set out a buffet of steak sandwiches,
salad, and iced coffee for us in the kitchen and we gratefully fell
upon it, spending the next several minutes eating in that quiet
hurried manner of people who are famished. Laura wisely refrained from asking us questions until we'd finished. Once done,
however, she lost no time.

"What happened?" she asked, posing the question that was
both the simplest and most complicated.

Miles shook his head. His face seemed to have aged ten years since this morning. "I wish I knew. Apparently, she was poisoned. Some toxic flower or something . . ."

"Lily of the valley," Kit provided authoritatively.

Miles nodded. "Right. Lily of the valley. The police think that it was in her drink."

"Is she okay?" asked Laura.

"She's in pretty bad shape," Miles said. "But the doctors seem cautiously hopeful that she'll pull through."

"But how could this have happened?"

Miles gave a rueful smile. "Well, that's the sixty-four-thousand-dollar question. The police seem to think that it was deliberate. Unfortunately, her friend Julian didn't help matters much. First he yammered on about the family's opposition to his handling the investments. Then he started in about Bonnie's suspicions about Marty's death and a possible connection between that and Michael's murder. For his final act, he completely flipped out and claimed that he was the intended victim."

"Wait," said Laura. "Why did he think he was the intended victim?"

"Because the glass that held the poison was in front of his seat," Kit again provided in a helpful manner. If you call a helpful manner one in which the person speaks slowly and condescendingly.

I don't, but *you* might.

"But," said Aunt Winnie, "as I pointed out to him, he'd just switched seats with Bonnie so it was *her* drink that was in front of him, not his."

"Not that that mattered, of course," continued Miles. "The

little twit carried on as if his life was in imminent danger. He went so far as to demand police protection."

"Police protection! From whom?"

"From us, apparently."

"Did he get it?" asked Laura, aghast.

Miles shook his head. "No," he said, with a ghost of a smile. "He got a room at the Ritz."

Laura fell silent as she absorbed all this information. "But honestly," she said after a moment, "why could anyone want to poison Bonnie? It doesn't make sense."

"It may not make sense," said Aunt Winnie, "but it appears to have been what happened. There *was* poison in her drink. And *only* in her drink. It's not the sort of poison that commonly finds its way into a martini."

"Not the way I make them, anyway," added Reggie. Although her words sounded flip, we could see she was genuinely upset at the potential implication of her having made Bonnie's drink.

Aunt Winnie reached out and patted Reggie's hand. "No one thinks for a minute that you had anything to do with this, Reggie."

"The police do," Reggie muttered.

"Then the police are wrong," Aunt Winnie said loyally.

"Don't forget, I'm the one who brought them out," said Miles. "I'm sure *that* didn't go unnoticed by the police."

"So that brings us back again to the question of how the poison *did* get in her drink," said Kit. "We need to think this through." I shot her a look. Could she be a bigger idiot? Obviously, someone who was at the cookout tried to poison Bonnie.

Correction—someone at the cookout *did* poison Bonnie. Try as we might, we couldn't ignore the fact that at the very least someone had tried to hurt Bonnie. At the very worst, kill her. And the chances were pretty high that that person was still here with us now.

And yet Kit kept on yapping away, oblivious.

"Do you think there could be anything to what Bonnie said about Uncle Marty?" Kit asked.

Several voices spoke at once. "Absolutely not!" "Kit, he was sick for years!" "Don't be ridiculous!" "Kit, for the love of God, use your head for once!" (Okay, this last one was me.)

"Okay, okay!" Kit said, holding her hands up in defense. "It was just a question. Wasn't it Poirot who said that you need to dismiss every option, and the one that remains, no matter how absurd, is the solution?"

"No, Kit, that was Sherlock Holmes. And I hate to point this out to you, but it was also fiction," I said.

Kit glared at me. "I am only trying to help. Poor Bonnie is lying in a hospital bed having had her stomach pumped after poison ended up in her drink!"

No one spoke. People shifted uneasily in their seats and glanced about furtively as if looking for a way to escape. Unfortunately, it was a common side effect of having Kit around.

"What about Julian?" I asked.

"What about Julian?" replied Frances.

"Well, do we know if Bonnie has given him the money for this investment yet?"

Around me everyone shook their heads.

"Does it matter?" asked Laura.

"It might," I said. "If Julian already has the money, he might be ready to move on."

"You mean Julian might have poisoned Bonnie because he'd already gotten the money?" asked Laura.

"It's a possibility," I said.

"So his whole freak-out at the hospital was just a show?" asked Reggie.

"I don't know," I said. "It's just a theory. But if it were the case, his freak-out gave him a nice reason for leaving the house and moving to a hotel."

"From where he might be able to leave unnoticed," added Frances.

I nodded. Frances looked thoughtful. "I wonder," was all she said.

Around me, people began to discuss this possibility. I did not participate. Mainly because I didn't really believe it was a viable option. I merely said it to defuse the tension that Kit had created. While Julian was clearly a con artist, he didn't strike me as a murderer. No doubt he'd made a lucrative career out of swindling daffy middle-aged women out of their money. That he was a criminal, I was sure, but I would bet he was of the wormy cowardly variety rather than the hardened violent type.

I thought about Bonnie's poisoning. Reggie had made the drinks and Miles had brought them out. Both freely admitted as much. Could either of them have really poisoned the drink? And, if so, why? So much depended on *why* someone tried to kill Bonnie. Was it because of Michael's murder, or because she was planning to give Julian the money?

Bonnie was at the house around the time that Michael was buried under the pool. Could she have seen something? Or was she involved? She couldn't have seen Miles, as he'd already left for his business trip to New York. However, Reggie could have come back to St. Michaels with Donny in tow and buried Michael, but why on earth would she? She'd just ended it with Michael and at that time had no idea about his attack on Ann or the embezzlement.

If, however, Bonnie had been poisoned because of her plan to give Julian the money, then Miles had no motive while Reggie did. Yet I had a hard time believing that this was because of the money.

Bonnie had seemed genuinely shocked when she realized that she had to have been at the house when Michael was placed in the pool's foundation, but something about her reaction didn't ring true. What had she said? I tried to remember. She'd gone on about how terrible it was that she'd been at the house and how she might have seen something. She'd seemed concerned that her lack of seeing something had resulted in the mess today. What had she said? I closed my eyes. *But that's just the problem. I didn't see anything. And I feel just terrible about it because I should have!*

Why did she feel she should have seen something? Was it simply because she was there? Or was it because she knew someone else was there as well? I remembered the wineglasses. Could Bonnie's visitor have been the killer? Is that why she felt she should have seen something? Could Reggie have distracted Bonnie with a few friendly glasses of wine while Donny buried Michael? I tried to envision that, but the idea of Reggie sharing a cozy evening with Bonnie seemed improbable at best.

But even if that was the case, why would she mention it to-day in front of Reggie? Why would she hint at her suspicions? As I pondered this, a horrible thought occurred to me. Had Bonnie actually been trying to blackmail Reggie? Was she sending a message to her that she knew or suspected? If so, and Reggie or Donny was indeed the killer, it was a dangerously stupid thing to do.

I sighed. Yes, if it was a dangerously stupid thing to do, chances were Bonnie would do it.

CHAPTER 26

Man is more robust than woman,
but he is not longer lived.

—PERSUASION

HE CONVERSATION DRIFTED to Julian and his obvious designs on Bonnie's money. Thankfully, no one revisited the matter of Michael's murder or Uncle Marty's death. After a while, Miles and Laura left, followed by Kit. Aunt Winnie reluctantly went home with her. I don't know if she was more reluctant to leave Ann and me to discuss the situation without her or to sleep in the dreaded Jungle Room. Both were pretty compelling reasons. Peter had an early meeting he still needed to prepare for, so he headed home. Both Frances and Reggie were getting ready to head out, too, when Ann remembered the items that Uncle Marty had willed each of them. She'd collected everything and had boxed them. She now gave each her box.

They sat down in the living room and quietly sorted through the items. In all the chaos of the past week, I doubted if either had really had a moment to mourn their father. Now, as they looked through the items that he'd put aside for them—ranging from family heirlooms to saved artwork from their youth—both Frances and Reggie seemed to sag under the realization that their father was gone forever. It hit Reggie particularly hard. As she held an elaborate drawing of the family tree bequeathed to her, she gently traced her name with her finger. "Look," she said, "there's a space next to my name. Father never filled in the line for spouse."

"It was supposed to be a wedding present, I believe," said Frances. "For you and Michael."

Reggie scoffed. "It never would have happened. Not with me, anyway."

"It's still a lovely drawing," said Ann.

"I'll make you a copy," said Reggie and then added, more to herself, "Or maybe it would be more appropriate to give you the original and for me to keep the copy."

It took me a moment to realize what Reggie was saying, but it was the second time I'd heard her use that word. When Michael had proclaimed his love to Ann, he called Reggie a "pale copy" of her. Ann had only told me that and yet Reggie seemed to know about it when she told Frances that she wasn't a lovesick "pale copy" of who she was eight years ago. Before I could think, I found myself saying in surprise, "You never broke up with him, did you?"

Two blank faces turned my way. The third knew exactly what I meant. "What are you talking about?" Ann asked, her arms around Reggie.

"I'm talking about Michael," I said. "You overheard Michael that night, didn't you? You heard him tell Ann that he loved her and not you."

Frances looked at me like I had three heads. "What the hell are you talking about?"

Reggie shifted uncomfortably on the couch, her gaze sliding away from mine. "Does it really make a difference now?" she asked sullenly.

"I think it matters a great deal," I said. "You didn't break up with Michael that night, did you? You overheard him with Ann. What happened next? Did you run back to the house? I can't believe that you sat by and let him attack her."

"Of course I didn't! What a horrible thing to suggest!" Reggie shot back. Turning to Ann, she said, "I had no idea of the attack, I swear!"

"But you overheard him?" Ann asked, pulling her arms back in surprise.

Reggie looked down at her lap. "I did. I saw you two by the dock talking and made my way over to you. Neither of you saw me, I guess, and I heard everything Michael said about me and about you. I don't remember much after that. I ran back to the house and went to my room. I had a pretty bad night, but it was nothing compared to what you had to endure," Reggie said to Ann. "Anyway, in the morning I planned on telling him to go to hell, but of course he was gone when I got up. Since I planned on ending things with him, I just sort of . . . sped things up a bit and said I'd already done the deed. I guess I didn't want to have to hear about what happened from Ann."

"So you had no idea of his feelings for Ann?" I asked.

"No. I mean, I . . . I don't know. I might have suspected some preference, but I tried to convince myself that his affection for Ann was of a brotherly nature. Clearly I was wrong." She stared at the floor for a moment before continuing. "Michael was always something of a ladies' man, but I really loved him," she said quietly. "I guess I always knew—on a certain level, anyway—that he wasn't faithful, but I didn't care. Not really. I convinced myself that that would change once we were married." Reggie looked at Ann and continued. "But when I saw him with you, I knew the whole thing was a complete sham. I knew he was drunk, but it wasn't the wine talking. You know what they say, 'in vino veritas' and all that. He didn't love me. He was just using me for the money and the position at Daddy's business."

Frances looked at Reggie in surprise. "So you lied all these years? You told us you broke up with him when you didn't? Why on earth would you do that?"

Reggie lowered her head. "Blame it on the Reynolds pride, I guess. Mine was in tatters after that night. I couldn't tell you. I couldn't tell anyone."

My head was spinning when I went to bed that night. The fact that Reggie had known about Michael's feelings for Ann and lied all these years about how things ended with him troubled me. Reggie was known for two things: her beauty and her temper. Had her temper finally pushed her too far? By lying about what she'd overheard and the breakup, she instantly provided a valid reason why Michael wasn't around anymore.

I remembered that I saw her with Donny after Michael's body was found. They appeared to be discussing something very serious—could they have been discussing Michael? Donny was on the crew that put in the pool. Reggie could have killed Michael and then called Donny to help her bury the body.

There were so many possibilities, so many reasons for killing Michael. He was that kind of guy. I needed to figure out *which* reason had gotten him killed. Was it because of Reggie? Was it because of Scott? It was no secret that Frances wanted Scott to take over her father's business. Could she have wanted it to the point that she was willing to murder the competition? Or was it because of the embezzlement? Had Michael been double-crossed? And if so, by whom? Had Bonnie been his partner, or had she witnessed something when she unexpectedly returned to the house? And why had Bonnie been poisoned? Was it because she had seen something, or was it completely unrelated to Michael? She was planning on giving Julian a large amount of money to invest. It was clear that Julian was nothing more than a scam artist. Had Bonnie known that when she agreed to give him the money? Was she using him to get back at the family? I'd dismissed the idea earlier, but now I considered it again. Could *Julian* have actually been the one who poisoned Bonnie? I tossed and turned, no closer to an answer and no closer to sleep.

I revised my earlier characterization of Julian as a cowardly larcenist. I decided he could have poisoned Bonnie. I decided it mainly because I didn't like Julian and that solution didn't involve family members. I decided that, at least for tonight, I'd lay the blame at his door. It was a much nicer solution and one that allowed me to get to sleep.

Of course, any real hope I had that it was Julian was dashed to hell when he was found murdered the next day.

CHAPTER 27

You have delighted us long enough.

—PRIDE AND PREJUDICE

IT WAS ANN who woke me with the news. Roughly shaking me, she simply said, "The police just called. Julian's dead. Murdered. Here's your coffee."

"Murdered? At the Ritz?" I asked sleepily, sitting up and taking the offered cup.

"Yes. He was poisoned."

I was now fully awake. I stared blankly at the steaming cup. Who needs coffee when you have murder? "Don't tell me," I began.

She nodded. "Yup. Lily of the valley. Again."

I rubbed my eyes in confusion. "But how?"

Ann sat down heavily on the bed next to me. "They don't know," she said, and then reconsidered. "Or if they do know, they're not telling me."

"How . . ."

"The hotel maid found him this morning."

I looked around for the clock. "Wait, what time is it?" I asked.

"Twelve thirty. I let you sleep in."

"God, I haven't slept this long in ages."

"Yeah, well, you've had a rough week," Ann said kindly.

"Me? You're the one who should be sleeping in." I shook my head. "So Julian is really . . . ?"

"Dead. Quite dead," Ann said, with a hint of a smile. "Oh, except it turns out his name isn't Julian St. Claire."

"Imagine my astonishment," I murmured. "What is . . . sorry, what *was* it?"

"Melvin Gibs and he was from Trenton, New Jersey, where he is wanted for six counts of larceny."

"Oh, this just gets better and better."

"I guess that depends on your definition of the word 'better,'" Ann said with a sigh.

Word spread quickly about Julian's (aka Melvin's) death. By unanimous consent, it was decided that Bonnie not be told right away. According to Dr. Moser, she was resting comfortably and probably could receive visitors later today. "That's only if," he added somberly, "it's okay with the police."

Officer Daschle came by the house around one thirty to take additional statements from both Ann and me. His attitude toward us had decidedly chilled since yesterday. Of course, he hadn't exactly been a fan before, but compared to how he glared at us as he took our statements, yesterday's interview seemed almost chummy. Of course, it probably didn't help Officer Daschle's mood that Julian had practically screamed for police protection, been dismissed as a crackpot, and then turned up dead. Some days you just can't catch a break, I guess.

"As you know," said Officer Daschle, "Mr. St. Claire, as you knew him, was found dead this morning. Preliminary reports indicate that he died from the same kind of poisoning adminis-tered to Mrs. Reynolds."

"Could he have drunk from her glass after all?" asked Ann.

Officer Daschle shook his head. "He would have already been ill by the time we arrived. No, it seems that Mr. St. Claire was poisoned later—*after* he left the hospital."

"But why?" I asked.

Officer Daschle fixed his gaze on mine. "Well, that's what we'd like to know as well, Miss Parker. I do remember Mr. St. Claire mentioning something about an investment?"

I turned to Ann. It was probably better if she explained it.

Ann took a deep breath. "Before my father died, he sold his property in St. Michaels. The proceeds were to be split among the three of us—Reggie, Frances, and me. For some reason, Bonnie thought it should be split four ways, with her being the fourth. Our father sold the property before he died, but he didn't have a chance to distribute the proceeds. The split is not mentioned in the will. Anyway, when Bonnie got back from her spa retreat"—Ann tried to keep the disgust out of her voice when she said this—"she brought Julian back with her. She told us that he was some kind of 'whiz investor' and would be invest-ing *all* the proceeds from the sale. There were some among us who objected to this arrangement."

"Some?" said Officer Daschle.

"Okay, all," Ann amended. "We were discussing it when she collapsed."

"What exactly was said?" asked Officer Daschle.

"Nothing really. We just told her that we didn't want her

investing our share of the money with him. We didn't think he was legit."

"Well, you were right on that count. He was most certainly *not* legit."

"But we didn't poison him! Just like we didn't poison Bonnie! None of this makes sense!" cried Ann, burying her face in her hands.

Officer Daschle was unmoved by Ann's distress. "Do you know if Mrs. Reynolds had given Mr. St. Claire the money to invest yet?"

"No. For some reason, I thought that she hadn't, but maybe that was just wishful thinking."

Officer Daschle did not answer right away. He appeared to be caught in some kind of internal debate. "We were able to access Mr. St. Claire's bank accounts," he finally said. "It appears that your stepmother had not given him the money."

"Oh," said Ann. "Well, that's good, I guess."

"You had no idea of this?"

Ann shook her head. "No. I only knew what she told us, which was that she was planning on it."

"Well, I suppose whoever killed Mr. St. Claire wanted to make sure that she didn't get the chance. After the failed attempt on your stepmother, it appeared that the plan was to prevent her from continuing with her original plan," said Officer Daschle. "I need to know your whereabouts last night."

"I was here," said Ann. "With Elizabeth," she added.

I nodded. "After we left the hospital, everyone came back here and had a late supper. Everyone left around nine thirty, I guess,"

258 /3 Tracy Kiely

I said. I didn't see the point in revealing the part where we'd learned that Reggie had been lying all these years about ending things with Michael. I didn't see how the two could be related.

"You said Julian was wanted for larceny. Could someone from his past have tracked him down and done this?" Ann asked hopefully.

"With the same poison that was used on your stepmother?" came the dubious reply. "That's quite a coincidence, don't you think?"

"I guess so," agreed Ann.

"Well, that's all I have for now." Officer Daschle got up to leave. "Obviously, we'll be in touch. I'd prefer it if neither of you went anywhere. I'm sure we'll have more questions as we learn more."

"Of course," said Ann. "We'd be happy to do anything we can to help."

From the cold expression in his dark eyes, it didn't look like Officer Daschle believed her. I rather thought it was time to call Joe.

Joe arrived an hour and a half later. As soon as he appeared, I discreetly left. I don't think either of them noticed.

I drove to the local Whole Foods, where I got an assortment of food and then brought it all back to Uncle Marty's house. Ann and Joe were out back, so I slipped in unheard and unloaded the groceries. I left a note for Ann on the counter and then, after packing a small bag of gourmet goodies for myself, headed to Peter's apartment. I let myself in with my key and, after putting the food and wine in the refrigerator, flopped on the couch and closed my eyes. Although I'd slept past noon, I was still exhausted.

Once again I tried to make sense of the events of the last few days. Bonnie had brought Julian back claiming that he was her soul mate and new investor. That had of course upset everyone, but apparently it had upset someone more than the rest of us and he or she had tried to poison Bonnie. Next Julian had been poisoned, this time successfully. Were both attacks because of the money? Had the poisoner hoped to prevent Bonnie from giving Julian the money? When it appeared that Bonnie was going to live, had the poisoner then killed Julian just so that Bonnie couldn't go through with her plan? I knew that Ann had nothing to do with the attacks. But if money was the motive, that meant it had to be Reggie, Frances, or Scott. Reggie admitted to preparing the fatal drink but claimed to have merely made it and then placed it on the counter. Frances was in the kitchen when Reggie put the drink on the counter. Could Frances have poisoned it then? Frances and Scott needed the money to replace what they put into the business. Frances clearly had no problem stretching the truth—if not lying outright—if she thought it would help Scott. But would she go so far as to commit murder? Was she really capable of that?

My eyes grew heavy and my thoughts became fuzzy and disjointed. Reggie floated by in a wedding gown trimmed with lilies. She stood under an enormous arbor upon which wild animals twisted and curved in gaudy relief. Laura and Miles stood behind her. Laura was smiling at Reggie. Miles was laughing at the arbor. Frances and Scott stood to Reggie's left. Upon further reflection, I saw that Frances was standing on Michael.

Scott didn't seem to notice. Bonnie walked past them, a glass of wine in her hands. She didn't notice Michael either. I tried to cry out, but Peter kissed me and I woke up.

I blinked several times as Peter kissed me again. "Hey, sleepy-head, this is a nice surprise. I like coming home to you," he said, nuzzling my neck.

I tried to sit up. "What time is it?" I asked upon waking for the second time that day.

Peter glanced at his watch. "Six thirty. I tried calling you on your cell, but it went to voice mail. I missed you." He nuzzled my neck again.

I closed my eyes and gave in to Peter's kisses. In a moment I'd have to ruin the mood by telling him about Julian, but for now it was a welcome escape. Sometime later (never mind how much later, thank you very much) I said, "I have some news."

Peter caught the somber tone in my voice and groaned. "What now?"

"Julian's dead. Murdered, actually. With the same poison that was used on Bonnie."

Peter sat up in astonishment. "Are you kidding me? No, I can see from your face you're not. Jesus Christ! And you're just telling me now?"

"I got distracted."

Peter smiled briefly. "When did it happen?"

"Last night, I guess. The hotel maid found him this morning."

"Do the police have any idea who did it?"

"Not that I know of. They took Ann's statement and mine this afternoon, but I haven't heard anything else since then."

"Well, you wouldn't have. Your cell phone is going straight to voice mail. Is it dead?"

A nervous apprehension settled over me. I jumped up from the couch and grabbed my purse. As Peter said, my phone was indeed dead. I quickly unearthed my charger and plugged it into the nearest outlet. As the phone chirped to life, I saw that I had missed several calls. Four were from Peter. Two were from Ann. The first was to thank me for the food. The second was to tell me that Scott had been arrested for the murder of Julian and the attempted murder of Bonnie.

CHAPTER 28

*Oh! dear; I was so miserable! I am sure I must have
been as white as my gown.*

—EMMA

Y THE TIME PETER AND I got to Uncle Marty's house,
everyone else was already there. Frances was hysterical, her usual poised tweedy façade in tatters. "He didn't do it!"
she kept crying to us all. "Scott wouldn't hurt a fly!" Thing One
and Thing Two hung on to their mother, their cries both loud
and pitiful.

"What exactly happened?" I asked Ann.

"Apparently Scott went to the Ritz last night to talk to Julian," she said. "They had a drink in the bar. The bartender
remembered Scott."

"But it was *my* idea!" protested Frances. "I was the one who
told him to go! I told him to meet with Julian and see if he
could get him to see reason about the money."

"And did he?" I asked.

Frances's face darkened in anger. "No. He basically told Scott
to go to hell, but in more colorful words. Scott left and came
home. That's *all* that happened!"

But apparently Officer Daschle had other ideas. He'd arrested Scott and charged him with murder. Lawyers had been summoned, but bail had been summarily denied. With one murder and one attempted murder on their hands, the courts weren't about to let the main suspect back on the streets.

"What am I going to do?" Frances cried. "They can't think Scott killed Julian! Oh, God, what if they try and pin Michael's murder on him, too?"

Miles put a fatherly arm around her shoulder. "Frances. Please, calm down. It's going to be fine. The police have made a mistake—they've done it before and sadly they'll do it again. But it doesn't mean that the mistake can't be rectified. We *will* get him out. There is no real evidence against him. Having a drink in a bar does not make him a murderer. No judge or jury would ever convict on such flimsy circumstantial evidence."

Frances said nothing. She turned her face into Miles's shoulder and quietly sobbed. "It's all my fault," she moaned after a minute. "I was the one who told him to go. He didn't even want to. I made him go and now he's in jail!"

At this, the boys began to cry louder. Hearing their cries jarred a memory from the night of the party. I'd already turned in for the night when I'd heard them crying—they'd been babies then. The crying kept up, and after a few minutes I got up and headed for their room. Scott was passed out on the bed and Frances wasn't around. I was just soothing the boys when Frances appeared, somewhat out of breath. She'd quickly thanked me and hustled me out of the room. I hadn't thought anything of it until now. The boys' cries were so loud that she would have heard them had she been in the house. So if she wasn't in the house, where had she been? And why had she lied about it? Was it just to cover for Scott, or was it to cover for her?

"Frances, you had no idea that it would end up like this!" said Miles. "You were just trying to get the family's money back. Don't beat yourself up. That's not what Scott needs right now. He needs you to be strong."

Frances gave a teary nod and made an attempt to pull herself together. "You're right," she said. "I can do this. We can clear all this up."

"Of course, we can," Miles said.

I knew I was probably going to regret this, but I had to ask. "Frances? The night of the party you said you were with Scott . . ." I paused, unsure how to continue.

Frances looked at me in teary confusion at first, but then a seed of comprehension took root in her brain. She knew I'd remembered her absence. "Yes," she said with deliberation, "I was with Scott all night. He and Michael fought, but he couldn't have killed Michael." Her eyes pleaded for understanding. In a sense Scott's fate was in my hands. I shut up.

I glanced at Peter. I saw the doubt I felt about this statement reflected in his eyes. I had to admit, it didn't look good.

We were allowed to visit Bonnie the next day. Ann, Aunt Winnie, and I arrived with flowers in hand. Bonnie lay quietly in her hospital bed, pale and dazed. Her eyes were bloodshot and swollen from crying. Seeing us, she merely said, "Who did it?"

Not sure what she knew yet in regard to Julian, Aunt Winnie said, "Who did what, honey?"

"Who poisoned me?"

"We don't know what happened," Aunt Winnie said gently. "We're trying to figure that out."

"Then get out," Bonnie said.

"What?" asked Aunt Winnie.

"You heard me. Get out. Until I know what happened, you can all just stay the hell away from me." Bonnie jabbed at the call button on her bed. Moments later a harried-looking nurse appeared. Bonnie said, "I want these people out."

The nurse turned to us, her face apologetic but firm. "I'm sorry, but I'm going to have to ask you to leave."

"It's all right. We understand," replied Aunt Winnie, setting the flowers on a table. "Bonnie, I'm really sorry. I hope you're feeling better soon."

Bonnie turned her face toward the wall.

Bonnie was released from the hospital the next day. Upon her return, she kicked Ann and me out of the house and hired a day nurse. Phone calls were not returned.

Ann returned to her house in Bethesda. I went back to the Jungle Room, which I now shared with Aunt Winnie. Having a giraffe with Graves' disease stare at you while you slept was bad enough, but having to deal with that along with someone who kicked and hogged the covers—I could not tolerate the prospect of being so miserably crowded.

"I don't know how Randy puts up with you in bed," I groused

as I attempted to pull back my half of the comforter over me the next night.

"I have had no complaints in that department," Aunt Winnie replied with a mischievous grin. "Ever."

"Okay, first of all eww, and second of all . . . eww. My point is, you are impossible to sleep with."

"Back at you, babe. You snore."

"I do not!"

"Then you speak to chain saws in your sleep. Call it what you like."

I rolled over and stared at the hippo. After a moment, I asked, "Do you think Scott did it?"

"No," Aunt Winnie said promptly. "Now if it was Frances who was sitting in jail charged with both murder and attempted murder and you asked me that, I might have a shadow of doubt. But not with Scott. Violence just isn't in that boy's blood."

"Who do you think did do it, then?"

"I don't know, honey. I really don't know. It's all so confusing. I'm not sure we know the real reason Bonnie was poisoned."

"Well, considering that Julian was poisoned, too, it would seem that it was because of the planned investment."

"But you don't buy that, do you?" she asked.

I thought about it. "No," I said finally, "I don't. I think it's a dodge of sorts. I think we're meant to think it's about the money, but I don't think that'll turn out to be the real reason."

"So what is the real reason?"

"I don't know. I think it all goes back to Michael, though. I just haven't figured out how yet."

Aunt Winnie sighed. "Well, let me know when you do. In

the meantime, I'm tired and I'm going to sleep." With a baleful glance at the ceiling, she added, "Besides, that damn giraffe is giving me the creeps."

Work the next day was a challenge, to say the least. Dickey returned, but rather than summon us all into the conference room, he just summoned me. Then he asked me to shut the door. I thought he was going to fire me. However, rather than experiencing a cold moment of fear at such a thought, my spirits actually soared. If that's not a sign that it's time to quit, then I don't know what is.

"Please have a seat, Ms. Parker," Dickey said, gesturing to the empty seats around the table.

I slid into the nearest chair to the door and adopted what I hoped was a politely interested expression.

Dickey did not speak but rather tapped his pen on the table. I couldn't be sure, but I think he was trying to play the percussion portion of "Wake Me Up Before You Go-Go" by Wham! My politely interested expression began to slip. Finally he said, "Well, Ms. Parker, I suppose you know why I've called this meeting."

"Not really, sir."

Dickey's eyebrows shot up in exaggerated surprise. "I find that hard to believe, Ms. Parker. Well, *you* may pretend, but I will not."

I stared at Dickey with unfeigned astonishment. I felt a bit like Elizabeth when she has it out with Lady Catherine in the side garden.

Dickey continued. "Well, I must say I would have thought

that you of all people would be sensitive to the position your family has put our little paper in."

"My family? What position?"

Dickey snorted at my question. I clearly wasn't scoring any points with him today. Which, when I really stopped to think about it, was actually a point in my favor. "I am referring to the revolting matter of the arrest of your cousin's husband. It's all over the news how he tried to kill his mother-in-law and then went on to kill that other man." Dickey glared at me as if I were somehow responsible.

"Scott never poisoned anybody," I replied evenly. "There's been a terrible mistake."

"Well, that may be so," Dickey said with a peevish expression. "But you can appreciate the delicate position it puts our paper in."

"Excuse me, but I don't see how it affects anyone but our family."

Dickey's mouth pulled into a frown and he slammed his pen onto the table. "If I may say so, that's a very selfish attitude. We are getting ready to publish the first of our Significant Humans in Town series tomorrow, featuring none other than your great-uncle, and every paper in town is filled with coverage of this scandalous murder investigation featuring your family! I am your boss. I have a right to know about everything that affects this paper!"

I stared at Dickey, dumbfounded. What the hell did he expect me to do about it? "Sir, I don't think I understand exactly what you want me to do. If it's a problem, pull the piece."

"I intend to. However, I will need something to run in its place." He paused. The shoe dropped. The light dawned. I got it.

"You want me to write a replacement piece?" I asked in astonishment.

"By the end of day, please."

Sitting there in the conference room, with Dickey in his cheap suit and the faces on his vanity wall smiling down at me, something snapped. I did a quick calculation in my head regarding the contents of my savings account and stood up. "I've got a better idea for you," I said, and then told him.

Dickey sputtered in shock at my rather vulgar suggestion. I, however, felt better than I had in weeks.

"You selfish, horrible girl! How dare you speak to me like that! How dare you quit on me like this! Have you no regard for me or this paper?"

I was so tempted to snap back with, "I am only resolved to act in that manner which will, in my own opinion, constitute my happiness, without reference to *you,* or to any person so wholly unconnected with me," but I didn't. Dickey wouldn't get the reference. Instead, I turned without a word and walked out. I quickly stuffed my few belongings from my desk into an empty cardboard box, told Sam I'd call him later, and waved a cheerful good-bye to my former coworkers. Truth be told, I was on top of the world. It was like that scene in *Bridget Jones's Diary* when she tells Daniel off and quits. With a cheeky grin, I picked up my box and headed for the elevators for the last time.

It wasn't until I got back to Kit's house that I realized when I calculated my savings account in my head, I carried a one that didn't exist.

Moron.

* * *

Kit was surprised to see me wander into the kitchen in the middle of the afternoon. "What are you doing here?" she asked. "Are you sick?" Pauly looked up from the table where he was eating a peanut butter and jelly and waved a sticky hello.

I slid into the seat opposite him and said, "No, I'm perfectly fine, actually. I guess you could say I'm no longer one of the working-class drones. I am now a woman of leisure. A lady who lunches—"

"You got fired!" Kit gasped. It would have been better if she hadn't sounded as if she'd foreseen this day coming for some time.

"No, I quit," I said with as much dignity as I could muster.

That got her attention. "Quit! In this economy? Are you crazy?"

"Probably. But you've no idea what I just went through." I quickly told her about Dickey and his stupid SHIT and all the rest of it. When I finished, she said, "What an . . ." Glancing at Pauly, she rethought her words. "Very bad man," she amended.

"That's kind of what I thought," I said.

"Well, don't you worry about a thing. You can stay here—rent free—until you find another job. And you will find another job, one you'll like better. I still can't believe that idiot took you to task for . . . oh, well, it's not worth discussing. My point is that you can and you will do better." She paused. "I know! We'll treat this like a celebration. I'll go to the store and get us something nice for dinner and then I'll rent some silly movie for us all to watch."

I smiled. "Thanks, Kit, but you don't have to do all that . . ."

"Don't be silly. It's my pleasure. That's what family is for. Now, you just go relax. Hit the hot tub or something. Aunt Winnie is out shopping. I'll take Pauly with me so you can have the house to yourself. How about I invite Peter?"

I got up from my chair and gave her a hug. "Thank you, Kit. This is really nice of you."

Kit shrugged off my thanks and headed out to the store with Pauly. As I went to my room, I wished she could always be so supportive of people, but Kit is one of those people who shine only when your world is messed up. She revels in playing the role of motherly helper. Mainly because it makes her feel better in comparison. It's when you're on top of the world that she gets all snarky.

I called Peter and told him what I'd done. After laughing at the various expressions and suggestions I used in my resignation to Dickey, he, too, offered to house me while I looked for a new job. While I knew that I could never live with Kit for more than two weeks, Peter was another story.

"Are you serious?" I asked. "You really want me to move in while I look for a new job?"

"No, I just want you to move in. Permanently."

My heart gave a flop. Then a flip.

"Really?"

"Really, really."

"Can I think about it?"

"Take all the time you want," Peter said. "Just don't think I'm doing this because you're out of a job and might be forced to live in the Jungle Room. Although those are compelling reasons. I'm doing this because I love you and want to be with you. Even if you do snore."

"I don't snore."

"You do. Like a jackhammer. But that's my point. I don't mind."

My next call obviously was to Aunt Winnie, not to talk about my new status as unemployed but about Peter's offer. "Peter asked me to move in with him," I said. "What should I do?"

"Why the hell are you asking me?" she replied, laughing. "That's for you to decide."

"I know, but I'm confused."

"Do you love him?" she asked.

"Yes."

"Well, that's a start. Only you know what's right for you, honey."

I sighed. "You're right. I need to figure this one out on my own."

"Damn skippy you do."

That night Kit outdid herself, making roast beef, scalloped potatoes, and carrots. For dessert she served apple pie with vanilla ice cream. It was times like these when the difference in our lifestyles became all the more apparent. Kit made domesticity look both glamorous and feasible. I thought about Peter's offer again and wondered if I was ready to settle down and create a home with him. Later, as I helped Kit clean up the kitchen, I told her about Peter wanting me to move in with him.

"What?" she cried, pausing with a dish in hand.

"He wants me to move in," I repeated.

"You aren't seriously considering it, are you?"

"Well, actually . . ."

"You know Mom will freak," she persisted.

"I doubt that. After all, she's living with George."

"But that's different! She's older. She's already been married and had kids."

I paused. "That doesn't make any sense."

"You know what they say, don't you? Why buy the cow if you're getting the milk for free?"

I stared at her. "You didn't just really say that, did you? You did! I can't believe you! Do you really see me as the cow in this scenario?"

Kit sighed. "No. You know what I mean. Well, you'll do what you want, of course. You always do anyway. But let me just say, you won't get this time back. I don't think you realize what you have. You're free to come and go as you please. You can *do* what you want. You have so much freedom! There are times when I'd give anything to get that freedom back again."

I stared at her in near shock. "Wait. You think my life is great? I thought you thought I was some colossal screwup."

Kit laughed. "Well, you *are* a screwup at times, but I don't think you're a *colossal* screwup. Don't get me wrong, I love my life. I love Paul and little Pauly. But sometimes I just wish I could run off and check into a hotel for the weekend." Kit paused and rubbed her belly. "I guess what I'm saying is, I know you love Peter and he's a great guy. But think about what you have before you go changing it."

I was stunned. Here was my perfect sister, the one who constantly tried to run my life, telling me that she envied what I had. Not every day or every minute, of course, but at times. It certainly put a new spin on how I viewed her and our relationship. "Thanks, Kit," I said finally. "For everything. I really appreciate it."

She smiled at me before turning back to finish loading the dishwasher. "No problem. Besides, you can't move in with Peter until you learn how to cook something besides spaghetti."

After the kitchen was cleaned, we all gathered in the living room where we settled in front of Paul's fifty-two-inch plasma flat-screen TV to watch *Meet the Parents*.

We'd just gotten to the scene where Ben Stiller's character inadvertently sets fire to the chuppah, when something clicked. Of course! The chuppah! I leaped from the couch.

"What's the matter?" Peter asked.

"I know who did it!" I cried. "I know who killed Michael and poisoned Bonnie and Julian."

CHAPTER 29

It isn't what we say or think that defines us,
but what we do.

—SENSE AND SENSIBILITY

*A*FTER EXPLAINING MY THEORY to everyone, I called
Ann and told her that I was coming over.

"What's wrong?" she asked, hearing the excitement in my voice.

"I think I've figured it out. I think I know who killed Michael!"

"Who?"

I paused. While telling her wouldn't be easy, I didn't want to do it over the phone—that wouldn't be right. "I'm coming over," I said. "I'll tell you when I get there."

Ann wasn't happy but agreed. I told her I'd be there as soon as I could. Peter, Aunt Winnie, and I drove over to her house, where she answered the door with a worried expression.

"Okay, tell me," she said once we were inside.

"Well, I think I know who killed Michael," I said, suddenly loath to tell her who it was.

"You mentioned that," she said in exasperation. "*Who is it?*"

"I'd be curious to hear your theory on that as well," said another voice. I turned. It was Joe. I glanced back at Ann. She gave me a quick smile. Well, at least there was some good news tonight. Having Joe here would definitely make it easier for Ann. And for me.

Taking a deep breath, I quickly explained everything. When I finished, Joe said, "Well, I'll be a son of a bitch."

Ann slumped against the wall, her face pale. "Are you sure?" she asked.

I nodded. I knew it was hard for her to hear. "It has to be the explanation. It's the only one that makes sense."

"But how do we prove it?" Joe asked.

"That's the tricky part," I acknowledged. "There's no proof. Only a few odd facts that could easily be explained away."

"So what do you propose?" Ann asked.

"We pay a visit to Bonnie," I said. "Maybe we can convince her to do the right thing."

"And if that doesn't work?" Joe asked.

I paused. "It has to. It's our only hope."

"What exactly is your plan?" he asked.

When I explained, the room erupted in various levels of outrage and opposition. Peter was especially adamant. "This is the stupidest idea I've ever heard of!" he cried. "You can't be serious."

"Peter, it's the only way. And you know it. Unless we do this, we'll never be able to prove how Michael was killed," I said.

"I don't care!" he yelled back at me.

"Peter, please. If I don't do this, then a murderer—a murderer who's killed twice—goes free. Can you really live with that? Because I can't." Peter did not answer. "I'll be fine," I promised. "Besides, Joe will be there the whole time. Right, Joe?"

Joe looked unconvinced. "I don't know, Elizabeth. It's dangerous."

"It's no more dangerous than to let a killer keep killing," I retorted. "And what about Scott? He's sitting in jail for something he didn't do! There's more proof against Scott than the actual murderer. If we don't do this, there's an excellent chance that he'll be convicted."

That seemed to win him over. "Okay," he said reluctantly. "We'll give it a try."

"If this is going to happen, then I want to be there, too," said Peter. Joe grudgingly nodded.

I smiled reassuringly at them. I'd won the argument. I just hoped I was right.

We drove over to Bonnie's in silence. To be on the safe side, we didn't call first. The house was dark and I hoped that Bonnie hadn't gone out. However, once we were at the door I could hear the faint murmuring of a television playing inside. Our first knock was ignored, but Joe knocked again and then finally yelled through the door.

"Mrs. Reynolds," he called. "Please, open up. It's Detective Muldoon. I have to talk to you."

After a moment, we heard movement from inside and finally the sound of the door's lock being slid back. The door then was slowly opened a crack. A blue eye peered out suspiciously from the other side. The door opened a few inches wider, revealing both Bonnie and Scarlett. Scarlett gave a happy bark at seeing Joe. From the faint scowl on Bonnie's face, it was clear that she did not share Scarlett's excitement. Upon opening the door even wider, Bonnie saw the rest of us huddled on her doorstep. Instantly, her expression changed from one of mild annoyance to outright fury and she moved to slam the door shut. Joe anticipated her and stuck his foot out to block the door from closing.

"I specifically told the police that I didn't want to see anyone! Especially *you* people!" Bonnie hissed, as Joe nudged the door open. Bonnie scurried back into the foyer still glaring at us. She was dressed in a silky pink robe and holding Scarlett, who now happily wagged her tail.

"Get out of my house," Bonnie said, backing farther away from us. "I don't want you here. You people tried to kill me. You killed Julian!"

"Bonnie, I swear to you that none of us had anything to do with Julian's death," said Ann.

Bonnie scoffed. "You're all a bunch of conceited, black-hearted varmints and I don't know why I should let you come in my house." Bonnie might still be suspicious of us, but she was apparently still happy to quote *Gone with the Wind*. Oh, well. I had Jane Austen. Bonnie had Margaret Mitchell.

Joe stepped forward. "I'm sorry, Mrs. Reynolds, but I need to talk to you about the murder of Michael Barrow."

Bonnie's eyes flew open in surprise and then shuttered, but not before I caught the sly, knowing look that crept into them. "I have nothing to say to you about that," she said, tipping her nose in the air.

"Oh, but I think you do," Joe replied calmly. "Why don't we talk in the living room where we can be more comfortable?"

Bonnie stared at Joe a moment before blowing an angry breath through her nose. Tilting her head in acquiescence, she turned on her heel and marched into the living room and set-

MURDER MOST PERSUASIVE ⌘ 279

tled onto the couch. Picking up the remote, she clicked off the television. We followed her and took seats on the chairs. Joe remained standing.

"What do you want from me?" she snapped.

"The truth," said Joe.

Bonnie turned to him, her face incredulous. "But I've told you the truth!"

Joe shook his head. "No, I'm afraid you haven't."

Bonnie's mouth pulled down into a stubborn frown. "I don't see what you expect of me. After all, I'm the victim here."

Joe explained what he expected. Bonnie's eyes widened in shock. "But how did you know . . . ?" she sputtered.

"That's not really the point, is it?" Joe said.

"Well, it's absurd in any case. I've done nothing wrong— nothing *criminally* wrong."

"That's not exactly true, Mrs. Reynolds," said Joe. "I think I could make a very good case for your being an accessory after the fact."

Bonnie's eyes widened and she looked at Joe with real fear. "Is that true? I mean, could you really charge me—?"

"Yes," Joe answered, cutting her off.

Bonnie dropped her head and focused on her hands. No one spoke. After a moment, she said in a low whisper, "Fine. I'll tell you what happened." As she recited her tale, Ann turned her head away in disgust. Bonnie saw the movement and threw her head back and glared defiantly at Ann. "Don't you dare judge me!" she spat out. "Don't you dare! You have no idea what a miserable man your father could be at times. He used me, plain and simple! He didn't love me! I was nothing to him! Nothing!"

Ann glared back at her with contempt. "You could have left. You didn't have to stay."

"And do what? Go back to being a secretary? I don't think so."

"Seems to me, then," Ann replied, "that he wasn't the only one doing the using."

Bonnie closed her eyes and said, "Fine. See what you want. Paint me as the bad guy. Why should any of that change now? Go ahead, what exactly do you want from me?"

Ann turned to Joe. Clearing his throat, he said, "We need you to do something for us, Mrs. Reynolds."

"What?" came Bonnie's wary reply.

When Joe told her, Bonnie blanched, then called him a son of a bitch and Ann far worse, but in the end she agreed to do what we asked. In silence, we watched her make the phone call.

Two hours later, I lay in the bed nervously readjusting the sleep mask on my face and the wig on my head. The room was unnaturally silent. I couldn't hear Joe or Peter, and I had to restrain myself from calling out to them. When I finally heard the bedroom door ease open, I pretended to be asleep and forced my breath into a calm and even rhythm. Everything depended on how the next couple of minutes went. I had to sell this. My heart began to pound furiously and I prayed that the figure I sensed slowly easing my way couldn't hear each terrified thump and beat.

The figure drew closer. I could hear the breathing; it was now practically next to me. My nerves were frayed and it took every ounce of my self-control not to fling myself out of the bed and run screaming for the door. Then I thought of everything that had happened, of the people killed and hurt, and I forced myself to remain still.

Suddenly a low voice hissed, "You stupid, greedy bitch!" and a pillow was roughly pushed down over my face. I flung my hands up to push the pillow off, but the hand that held it down wouldn't budge. Panic overtook me and I frantically tried to get out from under the crushing pressure. Where was Joe? Within seconds, the pillow was yanked away and the hands holding the pillow were secured, but those seconds felt like an eternity. I sat up and pushed off the sleep mask and wig, blinking at the bright lights that now flooded the room. Before me, the figure struggled in Joe's steely grip. Peter ran over to me. "Are you all right?" he asked, cradling my face in his hands. "I can't believe I let you do this. You're crazy, you know that, right?"

"I'm fine," I assured him, although it would have been more convincing if my voice hadn't come out in a scratchy croak. After taking a restorative breath of air, I glanced at the figure across the room from me, now being handcuffed. I studied the face; it was the same old face, but there was a ruthlessness in it that seemed new to me. Who knows? Maybe it had always been there and I'd just never noticed.

Seeing me in the bed and not Bonnie, the figure sputtered, "Elizabeth! What the hell is going on here?"

No remorse, just surprise. I was suddenly furious. "It's over," I said. "That's what's going on. It's done. You're done. You're not going to hurt anyone anymore, Miles."

CHAPTER 30

What is right to be done cannot be done too soon.

—EMMA

ILES GLARED AT ME and struggled against the handcuffs.

"How could you?" I asked. "How could you do this? You were a part of this family! And yet you stole, and killed an innocent man to cover your crime."

"I don't know what you're talking about," Miles said. "I didn't steal . . ."

"Shut up," I snapped, pushing myself up and out of the bed. "Just shut up." Standing in front of him, I continued to berate him, my voice shaking with anger. "Bonnie told us what happened between you two. You were at the house in St. Michaels the night after the party. You didn't expect anyone to be there, but someone was—Bonnie. You seduced Bonnie and convinced her never to reveal what happened between you two."

"What the hell are you talking about?" cried Miles. "What did Bonnie say? She's an idiot, for Christ's sake! You can't trust anything she says!"

I couldn't believe him. He was still trying to pretend he was innocent. "Miles, for God's sake! You just tried to kill me thinking I was Bonnie!" I yelled. "Don't you get it? It's over! We set you up! We were there when Bonnie called you earlier. We heard everything. You came here to kill her. You shoved a pillow over my face thinking it was her! It's over!"

Miles turned away from me. "Stupid bitch," he muttered. I didn't know if he was referring to me or Bonnie. I didn't care.

"Does Laura know?" I asked. That got his attention. His head whipped back to face me. "No!" he cried, finally showing some real emotion. "She has nothing to do with any of this. You have to believe me about that at least. She knows nothing. I did this for her. I did this alone."

"Do you really think that was what she wanted? For you to steal and kill for her?"

He looked at me, his eyes suddenly pleading. "I had to, don't you understand? I had to! She never would have married me unless I was a success."

I shook my head. "You're wrong. She loved you for *you*, not your business."

"I couldn't take the chance."

"That's your justification? Did you never stop to think how Laura is going to react to all this? You've destroyed several lives, including hers!"

Miles lowered his head and said nothing.

Joe read him his rights.

CHAPTER 31

She told the story, however, with great spirit among her friends; for she had a lively, playful disposition, which delighted in any thing ridiculous.

—PRIDE AND PREJUDICE

WE WERE IN ANN'S LIVING ROOM. I sat on the couch curled up next to Peter. Across from me sat Aunt Winnie and Ann. Miles had been taken into custody. Reggie and Frances arrived full of questions. Ann deferred them to me. "Elizabeth's the one who figured it out; she should really be the one to explain."

They all looked expectantly at me. I have to admit, I felt very much like an Agatha Christie detective, calmly explaining the solution while in an elegant drawing room full of people. All that was missing was a tea cozy and a plate of cucumber sandwiches. "Well, I guess it all started with Reggie's wedding arch," I said. "I remember Miles laughing about what it looked like." I paused, realizing my gaffe, and glanced at Reggie. "Sorry, Reggie."

Reggie waved away my apology. "It doesn't matter," she said impatiently. "Get on with it."

"Well, anyway, my point was that Miles knew what it looked like. But according to him, he left for New York City on July

284

fifth and didn't return until the twenty-ninth. However, Nana said the arch wasn't delivered until the sixth and was removed on the fifteenth. By Miles's own admission, he *couldn't* have seen it, and yet he *did*. He joked about how it looked to Laura, who had seen it. She came back from her trip just as he left. Then I remembered seeing the records for his trip to New York and it struck me again that there were no receipts for cabs. Every other possible receipt was in the file but not one for a cab. I wondered why. After all, people visiting New York usually use cabs. I wondered if he might have rented a car. If he did, he'd be able to drive back to St. Michaels."

"I don't understand," said Reggie. "Why would Miles kill Michael?"

"Because Miles was the real embezzler. Michael never had a thing to do with it. He was just the fall guy."

"But why would Miles embezzle from Dad?" Frances asked. "They were practically best friends!"

"Because he needed money to start up his own company and to impress Laura. He loved her, but he believed that he didn't have a chance with her unless he was successful. He saw her reaction to Joe and Ann's relationship. He wasn't going to let that happen to him."

Ann hung her head when I said this. I was relieved to see Joe grab her hand and murmur something to her. Ann raised her head and smiled at him.

"But how did he do it?" Reggie asked. Her face was pinched with emotions I couldn't read or begin to understand. For all these years, she'd thought that Michael had stolen from her father and run out on her. He'd done none of those things, but he had used her and tried to attack her sister. In some ways his chapter in Reggie's life had closed; in other ways it was a fresh hurt.

"I imagine that Miles killed Michael sometime after the party and hid both his body and his car," I said. "He then drove Michael's car to the airport on the morning of the fifth. He was scheduled to leave for New York anyway. He met Laura at the airport and proposed on his way out. In New York, he rented a car and drove back to St. Michaels, where he knew construction on the pool was to have begun. He buried the body in the newly dug hole, knowing that the foundation would be poured the next morning. Before he left, he went inside to shower. Unfortunately for him, Bonnie had arrived unexpectedly, having just had a fight with Uncle Marty. Miles couldn't let Bonnie suspect the real reason he was at the house, so he had to create a reason that he knew she'd never repeat." I paused.

Ann's mouth grimaced in disgust. "He seduced her."

I nodded. "He knew Bonnie's feelings for him and he used them to his advantage. I don't know what he said to her once it was over, probably something like 'this can never happen again.' Remember, Bonnie seemed to suddenly hate Laura and Miles after she learned of their engagement."

Around me heads nodded in agreement.

"Anyway," I said, "after that he drove back to New York and pretended that he'd been there the whole time."

"But why poison Bonnie?" Reggie asked.

"Because as daffy as she is, she figured it out. She realized that Miles was at the house around the time that Michael was killed. She not only realized it but was going to use it against him. Don't you remember at the party how she kept going on about how she should have known who it was because she was there? She was sending Miles a message. She needed money and she was banking on Miles giving it to her. Unfortunately, she didn't think he'd try and kill her."

"But how did he get the poison?" asked Frances.

"He pretended that he was pushed into the pool," I said. "The boys were right. They didn't push him."

"I knew it!" cried Frances. "Oh, and when I think of how Scott yelled at them—"

I interrupted her. I wasn't up for hearing about the twins' essential innocence. From the annoyed faces around me, I doubted if anyone else was either. "Miles fell in the pool so he'd have an excuse to go home, where he knew there were vases full of . . ."

"Lilies of the valley," finished Reggie. "That bastard."

I nodded. "As an owner of a landscaping business, I'm sure he knew the toxic aspects of the flower. I don't imagine that it was too hard to dump a few drops into Bonnie's drink and then bring it out to her."

"But why kill Julian?" Frances asked.

"To distract everyone from the real reason Bonnie was poisoned. If the police thought this was all about the investments, they'd look at a completely different circle of suspects—a circle that he wasn't in."

"But how . . . ?"

I shrugged. "I don't know for sure. He probably went to the Ritz sometime after Scott had left and went to Julian's room on some trumped-up reason, where he slipped the poison into his drink."

I paused to take a sip of water. Ann took up the tale. "Once

Elizabeth figured it out, though, we needed Bonnie to help us. Bonnie called Miles and told him that she wanted money or she was going to the police. Then Elizabeth pretended to be her by lying in her bed while we waited to see if Miles would strike."

"Which he did," I added.

"Joe jumped out from the closet where he was watching the whole thing and arrested him," said Ann proudly, giving his hand a squeeze.

"That was very brave of you, Elizabeth," Frances said after a moment. "Thank you. I know Scott will want to thank you as well."

I nodded.

Frances leaned over and squeezed my hand. "No, really. Thank you." She continued. "If you'd said what you knew about that night, I don't know what the police would have done to Scott. Now that it's all over, I guess I can tell you." Seeing everyone else's confused expressions, she clarified. "Scott did fight with Michael that night at the party. I heard them from my window. By the time I got downstairs to break it up, Scott had tried to hit Michael. He was so drunk, though, that all he did was lose his balance and fall, cutting his hand. I tried to defuse the situation, but Michael was particularly nasty about it. He threatened to ruin Scott. I got Scott upstairs and put him to bed. I went back down to talk to Michael, but he was gone. I looked for him, but I couldn't find him. I was afraid to tell anyone because I knew how it would look."

"It's okay," I said to Frances. "I understand. You were just trying to protect him."

"Dear God," said Reggie, shaking her head. "What a rat bastard Michael was. I really can pick them, can't I?"

"Speaking of picking them, are you really back together with Donny?" Ann asked.

Reggie shrugged. "I could do worse. Hell, who am I kidding? I *have* done worse."

"Amen to that," said Ann.

CHAPTER 32

Let me recommend Bath to you.

—EMMA

NN AND I VISITED LAURA at her house the next day. As expected, she was devastated. Her face was blotchy and her eyes were red and swollen from crying. "What am I going to do?" she asked when she saw us. "I can't believe this is true. Miles! Miles a killer? There has to be some mistake!"

"I'm sorry, Laura," said Ann quietly. "I really am. But I'm afraid there's no mistake. He tried to kill Elizabeth. He thought she was Bonnie."

At the mention of Bonnie's name, Laura's mouth twisted in hate. "That bitch. That stupid bitch."

"Laura!" cried Ann in surprise. "None of this is her fault!"

"She slept with him!" Laura shot back.

"No, Laura," Ann said firmly. "*He* seduced *her*! He took advantage of a lonely, stupid woman to hide a crime. He killed Michael and then used Bonnie!"

Laura buried her face in her hands and broke down. "I know. I'm sorry. You're right. I just don't know what to think anymore. Oh, what a horrible mess this is," she moaned.

"Have you seen Miles?" Ann asked gently. "Has he said any-thing?"

Laura shook her head. "No. He won't see me. He doesn't want me to see him in jail."

I stayed quiet. If Miles's act of restraint was supposed to im-press us, it fell short of the mark.

"I am sorry, Laura," said Ann. "I really am. If there's any-thing Joe and I can do . . ."

Laura's head shot up. "Joe? Are you and Joe . . ."

Ann nodded. "We're together. He's been wonderful. He's always been wonderful," she added pointedly.

Laura gave a small smile. "Good. I'm glad for you, then." She paused. "I'm sorry, Ann, for steering you wrong all those years ago. I was too focused on the things that don't matter. I screwed up your life and mine. Look where my ideals got me. Married to a murderer."

Fresh tears flowed down her face. Ann went to hug her. "It's going to be okay, Laura. You've got us. We're your family. We'll always be here for you."

I eased out of the room to give them their privacy and went to wait on the front steps. The day was gloriously clear, although there was now a distinct chill in the air that had been absent all week. The lingering warmth of the summer was gone. I rubbed my hands together and waited for Ann. A little while later, she came out. "Is she okay?" I asked.

"As well as can be expected," Ann said sadly. "This has been such a shock to her. On more than one level."

I nodded. "Are you okay?"

Ann smiled at me. "I am, actually. Better than I've been in years. I feel terrible for saying it, but it's true. I feel like I've been given a gift, a second chance with Joe."

"Good," I said, returning her smile.

"I don't know how to thank you," she said. "You were amazing. If this doesn't convince Kit that you have a real talent for solving crime, I don't know what will."

I laughed. "I wouldn't be too sure about that. Kit thinks she should get the credit because it was her idea to watch *Meet the Parents*."

"Well, *I* think you've got talent. And what about you?" she asked. "What are you going to do about Peter? Are you going to move in?"

I told her my decision.

She nodded. "I can see your point."

Who can be in doubt of what followed? When two people are in love, they are pretty sure by perseverance to carry their point. Joe and Ann picked up almost exactly where they had left off eight years earlier, and I anticipated that I would be eating cake at their wedding in the very near future.

As for me, I told Peter that I needed more time to decide about moving in. I loved him and was pretty sure I wanted to spend the rest of my life with him, but was this really the way to start that life? I didn't want my current situation of not having a job or decent place to live to be the impetus of our moving in together. Although I wasn't, to quote Jane Austen (oh, please, don't act surprised), pursuing a man merely for the sake of a situation, I still was bothered by the circumstances surrounding his pro-

posal. So much had happened over the past two weeks that I guess I just needed time to sort it out. Peter took it well, saying that he understood. And although he swore that he wanted me to move in regardless of my employment status, I remained unsure.

A few days later, Aunt Winnie called. She was back on Nantucket. I had barely answered the phone when she shouted out to me, "Elizabeth! You've got to pack. I just scored us tickets to the Jane Austen Festival in Bath!"

"Are you kidding me? How'd you get tickets? I thought those were nearly impossible to get!"

"Friend of a friend. I'll tell you when I see you. I've booked us a flight, but you have to get your skinny ass up here by tomorrow. We leave in two days!"

I stared in disbelief at the phone. Bath. I was going to Bath for the Jane Austen Festival!

For once in my life, words failed me.